FIONA RINTOUL

Fiona Rintoul is a writer, journalist and translator who won the Virginia Prize for Fiction for her debut novel *The Leipzig Affair*.

Fiona's writing has previously appeared in anthologies and magazines, and she is a past winner of the Gillian Purvis New Writing Award and the Sceptre Prize.

Outside Verdun, her new translation of Arnold Zweig's first world war classic, *Erziehung vor Verdun,* was published in May 2014 by Freight Books.

Fiona's journalism concentrates on financial topics. As a journalist, she has received a State Street institutional press award and an IJP George Weidenfeld bursary for British and German journalists.

Fiona lives in Glasgow. For more information about the author: **www.weepress.co.uk**

THE
LEIPZIG
AFFAIR

For Agnes

Published in the UK by Aurora Metro Books in 2014.
67 Grove Avenue, Twickenham TW1 4HX
www.aurorametro.com   info@aurorametro.com

The Virginia Prize for Fiction is sponsored by ea Change Group:
www.eacg.co.uk

The Leipzig Affair © copyright 2014 Fiona Rintoul
Cover Design: Paul Scott Mulvey
Editor: Cheryl Robson

Aurora Metro Books would like to thank Neil Gregory, Richard Turk,
Suzanne Mooney, Emma Lee Fitzgerald, Hinesh Pravin, Chantelle
Jagannath and Russell Manning.

Printed in the UK by Berforts Information Press, Hertfordshire.
ISBN 978-1-906582-97-5

THE LEIPZIG AFFAIR

BY

FIONA RINTOUL

AURORA METRO BOOKS

ACKNOWLEDGEMENTS

I am grateful to the Gillian Purvis Trust for a new writing award, which enabled me to travel to Germany to complete research for this book. Grateful thanks are also due to Sigrid Grünewald for talking to me about her imprisonment at Bautzen II and to the Gedenkstätte Bautzen for facilitating our meeting. Frau Grünewald and Jacqueline Braid were also kind enough to share extracts from their Stasi files with me.

I am also grateful to Freight Books for permission to reprint chapters one, three and twenty-one, versions of which have appeared in *Gutter* magazine.

I am indebted to my editor, Cheryl Robson, and to Felicity Parsons, Susan Kemp, Tamara Evans, Marianne Taylor and Mark Stanton for reading and commenting on previous drafts of this book. Last but not least, I would like to thank my husband, Peter Edwards, who has lived with this project for far longer than it was reasonable to expect and who is my constant inspiration.

Oh the shark has pretty teeth dear,
And he shows them pearly white
Just a jack-knife has Macheath dear
And he keeps it out of sight.

The Ballad of Mack the Knife
**Bertolt Brecht, The Threepenny Opera, 1928/
English translation, Marc Blitzstein, 1954**

She lied to me with her body you see
I lied to myself 'bout the chances I'd wasted.

The Saturday Boy, **Billy Bragg**

PROLOGUE

The version of Marek's death that Bob has played back to himself most frequently down the years is the one where Marek gets shot in the back. It goes like this:

Marek is walking across the raked sand of the death strip. His stride is loose. His head is held high. He looks confident, like a man who knows where he's going and what he's going to do when he gets there. He's wearing what he was wearing the night Bob first met him at the club in Leipzig: Levi's and a white cotton shirt. It's night time. The strip is floodlit. The sky is clear. A half moon casts an eerie glow over the dim-lit buildings of Berlin, Capital of the German Democratic Republic to the east and the lime trees of the Tiergarten to the west.

A guard's sudden cry cuts the air: "Halt!"

Marek stops, but casually, almost as if he didn't hear the shout. The beam from an overhead searchlight sweeps across the strip and finds him. He stands in a pool of ultra-bright light.

"Hands up!" the guard screams.

Slowly, Marek raises his arms. Then he leans his head back. His shoulder-length black hair shifts in the night breeze. He looks like Jesus Christ. For a moment, everything is still on the strip. Only the distant rumble of traffic disturbs the calm. Then Marek lets his arms drop and turns his head to look behind him.

Gunfire cracks. A bullet rips towards him. The impact punches the air from his lungs. His legs buckle, and he falls down on to the sand with a thud. His head is turned to one side, and he is looking straight at Bob, his sightless eyes wide in surprise. A trickle of blood forms at his parted lips. A red stain seeps across the white cotton of his shirt. It is strangely beautiful, like an exotic flower.

Bob knows, of course, that these imaginings are preposterous.

– Who would attempt to sneak across the world's most heavily fortified border in a white shirt?

– Why does he see Marek in Berlin when he knows he was planning to cross the border in the Harz Mountains?

– And how could Marek be looking at him when he wasn't there?

But that's his vision of it. Marek in a crisp white cotton shirt. Marek walking across no man's land with the easy grace of an athlete. Marek – beautiful, clever, bitchy Marek – mowed down by a single bullet fired into his back.

It's not hard to understand why this scenario provides him

with the most exquisite torment. He never knew exactly how Marek died. But he did know that he was shot in the back. And he knew who pulled the trigger: it was him.

He did it to save her. Or that's what he told himself. But she ended up hating him. Or at least rejecting him.

So ist ja eben das Leben. That's Life.

PART ONE

CHAPTER ONE

Magda –

You're sitting in a booth in the language laboratory with headphones on and Frau Aner's voice in your ear.

"Übung macht den Meister," she says.

Practice makes perfect. She thinks this is funny, and you see her smile to herself. Jana, the class snoop, laughs out loud and is rewarded with an approving look.

"State your names, comrades," Frau Aner says. You hate the way her voice rasps, very close, like she's in your head.

"Magda Maria Reinsch," you say.

The laboratory for interpreters and translators studying languages from non-socialist countries is on the twenty-third floor of the university tower, a 1970s' skyscraper that is meant to look like an open book but doesn't. The tower's one advantage is its view. From up here you can see all of Leipzig seeping out into the surrounding plain: the mediaeval city centre, the prefabricated apartment blocks, the flat spaces of the exhibition site that come alive every spring and autumn when foreign guests arrive for the Leipzig trade fairs. To the west lie the sumptuous villas that were once home to the bourgeoisie, crumbling now and interlaced with new buildings. The ugliest of these is a pebble-dash guest house for visitors from 'the socialist abroad'.

But today the blinds are drawn and your only possible view is of Frau Aner, the language-lab leader, sitting up at the control console, sliding the black buttons back and forward. Frau Aner is a red-faced, cardigan-wearing woman in her mid-forties, who bounds about sniffing out ideological impurities like a dog on the scent of a rabbit. Her grasp of political ideology is loose to say the least, but that doesn't stop her. She has the kind of nose for dissent that would make her a useful foot soldier in any regime. This, presumably, is why she has been put in charge of language-lab activities for the most dangerous language of all: English. It's certainly not because of her language skills. She speaks English with a comedy German accent and machine-guns it with errors. They like that: the powers that be. They like to give people responsibilities they're not quite competent to discharge.

A whirring in your ear tells you the tape is being rewound.

"We are going to run through this scenario one more time," says Frau Aner, "and this time I believe our efforts will be repaid."

You wish you were out of here. You wish you were sitting at a window table in Café Grossmann smoking a cigarette and drinking a bitter black coffee. But you also don't. Part of you is glad to be tucked away in the language-lab booth. You might meet someone you know in the café, someone from your old life, and that would be bad, because today you're wearing their clothes and you don't like to be seen like that.

Dressing for the new role you've adopted as a politically

reliable and diligent student at the Karl Marx University Leipzig is the hardest part for you, the part you struggle with the most. It's one thing to act like you want to conform, quite another to dress like it. Clothes are special to you. They've always been your escape, your rebellion. Everyone in the Workers' and Farmers' state has to have somewhere private to go, and this is where you go. It's your very own version of internal emigration: you do not wear their clothes.

Correction: it's where you went. You did not wear their clothes.

Unfortunately, your internal emigration was external. People could see it. That was dangerous, and so it had to stop. If people are to believe in the new you, to accept that your rebellious past is behind you, then every detail has to be right. Your rehabilitation, your resumed university career, your acceptance back into the Party and the Free German Youth: these things were only possible because your father pulled strings. Even then, it was touch and go. And so, to make it all work, you have to dress like them. (That's how you see it: *you* and *them*; dressing like *them*.) It's an essential part of your disguise. If you wear your own clothes it's a risk, and you can't afford risks. Marek has told you that a thousand times: it seems like a small thing, but it's not.

"This isn't just about you," he said when you told him you didn't think you could do it. And then you had to agree. Because he's waited for you when he didn't have to. He's waited for you because of the special bond between you, which goes back such a long way, and because he knows better than anyone how bad things were for you after your brother's accident.

But it's a struggle. Last week, in the Konsum department store, you tried. You tried very hard. But in the end you could not bring yourself even to try on the *Golden Fox* jeans from the People's Own Clothing Works in Zwickau or the badly cut blouses and tops made from Grisuten and other miracle fabrics.

Today, you're wearing a pair of stiff trousers the colour of sick and a striped sweater that irritates your skin. You hate these clothes. You long for the moment when you'll return to the hideaway you share with Kerstin on Shakespeare Street and rip them off. Worse still are the shoes. You drew the line this morning at the grey plastic loafers from Konsum. No one can see your feet in the language lab, and so, as a present to yourself, you're wearing your favourite boots: knee-high brown lace-ups you bought two years ago in Prenzlauer Berg from a girl over on a day visa from Berlin (West).

You couldn't take your eyes off the girl's boots. Marek's Uncle Ivan had been over the previous week on one of his periodic visits from New York and had given you a hundred Deutschmarks. The girl looked to have about the same size feet as you and so you offered her ten Marks for her boots.

She hesitated. "How about fifteen?" you said.

She smiled, this breezy, blonde-haired West German girl, and you thought she was going to say she didn't want to sell them at any price. Instead she shrugged and said, "Ten is okay."

She was doing you a favour. You didn't like that but you took it anyway. "It's a deal," you said.

You tried the boots on in a back alley. They fitted perfectly. The girl put them back on, and you went into town on the tram together so she could buy some cheap shoes to wear on the train back to West Berlin.

"It's good to have something to spend the money on," she said as you headed towards the Centrum department store on Alexanderplatz. "It's always hard to get rid of the compulsory exchange."

But the canvas shoes she chose were cheap and didn't use up much of her twenty-five East Marks.

"Shall we take a look on some of the other floors?" you asked.

She glanced around her. You knew how old-fashioned the wood and glass display counters must look to her, how rude the stony-faced assistants must seem.

"Let's just go," she said.

You took possession of the boots in the Centrum toilets and headed back out on the Alexanderplatz with her.

"Do you want the rest of the money?" the girl asked when you were standing by the Friendship Between Peoples fountain, saying your goodbyes. You gave her a hard look. You imagined her telling her friends in West Berlin how kind she'd been to a poor East German girl.

"I didn't mean – "

"Thank you," you interrupted, taking the money and shoving it in your pocket.

The boots are beautiful. You love them. You've polished and nurtured them, and they look as good today as when you bought them. The boots were the beginning. You got them shortly after your brother Jürgen's accident – difficult days. Soon, you stopped buying clothes from the shops altogether. It was your way of refusing, of showing you didn't accept what had happened to your brother. It wasn't easy, but you managed. You had your sources: hand-me-downs from Aunt Vladka, things you ran up yourself on your grandma's old sewing machine, the odd skirt or blouse picked up in Prague or Budapest.

A hissing in your ear indicates that the tape is back at the beginning. Frau Aner fixes the class with one of her build-the-revolution looks.

"Commence!" she says, pressing the 'play' button with a dramatic flourish.

Frau Aner is wasted on university students. She'd be much better leading a troupe of Pioneers, sweet little baby communists in white shirts and red neckerchiefs. You can just see her standing in front of them, swinging her arms about like a human windmill, teaching them to love Honecker and sing *Youth Awaken!*

The voices start again. The scenario is this: Mr Green, a representative from the Greater London Council, is visiting Berlin where he is being shown around by Comrade Schwarz, a member of the Municipal Assembly of Berlin, Capital of the GDR. You are to interpret for them.

"My Goodness," says Mr Green, "considering that Berlin, Capital of the GDR is such a big city, the air is very clean. How did you achieve this result?"

Frau Aner rarely listens in on your work. It upsets her because your English is so much better than hers. You take a chance.

"Scheisse," you say, "wenn man –"

But you've miscalculated. There is a buzz in your ear. "No!" barks Frau Aner. "This is incorrect. Begin again."

"Himmel," you say, "wenn man –"

There is a long pause before Comrade Schwarz speaks again. "The answer is simple, Herr Green. In our Republic, state and society attach major importance to the rational use and protection of nature, mineral resources and raw materials. Measures to keep the water and the air clean, to protect the soil –"

It's as bad as the 'news' in *Neues Deutschland*, the Party newspaper: *The USSR and the Czechoslovak Socialist Republic sign an agreement to deepen friendly co-operation. Comrade Erich Honecker,*

General Secretary of the Central Committee of the Socialist Unity Party of Germany and Chairman of the GDR Council of State, is greeted by cheering crowds in the model new town of Hoyerswerda. You buy *Neues Deutschland* every day now and hold it in front of your eyes on the tram but you never read it. You don't believe anyone does. It's unreadable.

"In keeping with the Environmental Policy Act of 1970," Comrade Schwarz continues on the tape playing in your ears, "many elected deputies of local people's assemblies are making broad efforts in the area of air quality and –"

It's hard to concentrate on this rubbish. You know what the air is like in Berlin, Capital of the GDR – a mix of brown coal dust and two-stroke fumes that leaves a bleak ferrous after-taste. It was always the first thing you noticed when you returned to the city from your parents' dacha as a child. And right now it's harder than usual, because yesterday, Marek received a telegram from John Bull-Halifax in Edinburgh. It said (in code) that the Scottish research student who is arriving after the summer break will bring you four pairs of Levi 501s: one to keep and three to sell. Marek is to collect them from him. It's safer that way.

Naturally, you can't breathe a word of this to your fellow students of interpreting. The only person you can tell is Kerstin, and you're burning to see her.

"Comrade Reinsch!" Frau Aner barks in your ear. "You have not translated the last sentence. Please apply yourself at once."

"Yes, Frau Aner," you reply, though you have no idea what Comrade Schwarz just said.

Soon you'll be out of here. You'll be at Shakespeare Street with Kerstin, pulling on your own clothes. Then you'll drive off in her father's much-repaired Trabant to spend the weekend at the hut that her parents rent by the lake to the south of the city. For now, you must concentrate. Everything, all your future plans, depends on your getting a place on the Study in the Non-Socialist Abroad Programme and travelling to Great Britain. And only the best students and the most politically reliable – the ones like Jana who don't ask awkward questions about the air in Berlin or even think awkward thoughts about it – get places on that.

CHAPTER TWO

It was my counsellor, Sally, who got me thinking about Leipzig again. We did an exercise one day. She got me to write things down. It was hard at first, but after a while I got into the swing of it.

"Start with your name," she said. "Just write it down. My name is Robert. I know it sounds silly, but it'll get you going."

She always insisted on calling me Robert. *My name is Bob,* I wrote.

After my name I was to write down some basic facts about myself. "By facts we mean things that are indisputably true," Sally said.

I gave it a go. *I am Scottish. I have green eyes. I used to work in financial services. Now I am a consultant (=unemployed). I have thinning, gingerish hair. I am not tall.*

I could have written: *I am an alcoholic.* But I never say those words. And Sally wouldn't have liked it. They don't believe in alcoholism at the South Islington Alcohol Advisory Centre. They believe that some people need help to manage their alcohol consumption, and that there are various ways of doing this. That was one of the things Sally and I talked about during our sessions: how to manage my alcohol consumption. According to Sal, that could mean total abstinence or it could mean a return to normal drinking. A return to normal drinking. What a joke! Sally has no idea what it's like. She doesn't know how reduced my life is. She doesn't understand that when you drink everything gets chipped away until there's almost nothing left. She doesn't realise that I'm only a tiny fragment of a person.

Next Sally asked me to write about what happened. She meant *What Happened to Me in Leipzig*. She said that was how I saw it: in italics with capitals, like the title of a book or film. I didn't want to write about that. Or talk about it. I'd only told her that I'd spent time behind the Iron Curtain to counter any idea she might have that I was some kind of Tory City boy because I worked at Liebermann Brothers for fourteen years and went out with a girl who worked as a PA for a hedge fund manager in Mayfair. I wanted her to understand that I was as much of a fish out of water at Liebermann Brothers as she would have been. That I was a Labour voter just like her. A woolly liberal with a bleeding heart. But she latched on to it – with a hint of desperation, I thought – and so I played along.

The trouble with counsellors is they're just people. They have their problems, their issues. Take Sal. I'd been seeing her for nearly six months by then and I reckon I'd got to know her pretty well. I knew that when she crossed her legs and leant forward clutching her clipboard to her chest, she was about to make an important point. We'd reached a crossroads and she wanted to make sure we went the right way. And I knew that when she turned up in trousers and flats she was having her period. Normally, she wore smart above-the-knee skirts with glossy tights and high heels that showed off her slender ankles and shapely calves. But once a month, regular as clockwork – trousers and flats. And a couple of times when we had morning appointments, her eyes were red-tinged and she was distracted and found it hard to get the session going, and I knew she'd had a fight with her boyfriend. Maybe even had a few too many the night before. And why not? There's no law against alcohol counsellors having a drink.

The thing was Sally was new to the job. She was still on day-release training. She wasn't getting anywhere with me, and she thought it was her fault. It wasn't. It was me. I'm a cagey bastard. But she thought it was. She was worried. I could see it in her eyes. She was starting to think maybe she wasn't going to be any good at this counselling lark. The writing was her brilliant idea to draw me out. She thought she was on to something with my Leipzig story and maybe she was. But that's not why I agreed to write about it. Or why I carried on talking to her about it when the exercise was over. I carried on because Sally was interested in a way that she wasn't interested in Liebermann Brothers and Annabel, my ex.

"That must have been fascinating," she said when I first told her I'd studied in Leipzig back in 1985.

"Well, yeah," I said, feeling for the first time that she wasn't listening to me because she was paid to but because she wanted to, that she was just a girl and I was just a guy. Maybe I was a little bit in love with her.

The big problem with writing about what happened to me in Leipzig was: where to start?

"Start at the beginning," Sally said in her brisk, that's-enough-now voice.

But where was the beginning?

I was born in a caravan at Uig on the Isle of Lewis

that my Uncle Norman had lent to us. My mum went into labour unexpectedly, and my big sister Shona, who was only four at the time, had to go and get the farmer to drive us to Stornoway because my dad was out fishing. By the time the farmer got there, it was too late and he had to deliver me himself. It made the *Stornoway Gazette*: 'Ardroil Man in Caravan Birth Drama'.

No. That wasn't it. Neither was the beginning in Calderhill, the Lanarkshire village in the shadow of the Ravenscraig steel works where I grew up. The story began in St Andrews where I began my DPhil on Heinrich Heine. If I hadn't gone there – and hadn't hated it so much I was willing to do anything to get out – I wouldn't have met John Bull-Halifax and he wouldn't have organised a study place for me in Leipzig.

I went to St Andrews because Eugene Bramsden, the head of the German Department, was the leading Heine scholar in the UK – or so I told myself. Unfortunately, Bramsden was also a right-wing prick. He regretted the presence of students from state schools at 'Scotland's premier university', and rumour had it he'd once dismantled a wheelchair ramp with his bare hands to prevent a disabled student from entering the modern languages building.

Bramsden and I never got on. He was a relic of a bygone age: a time when the likes of me would've been down the mines and students wore cream-coloured cricket jumpers and drank Pimms. The grubby reality of university life in the 1980s, when, even at as august an institution as St Andrews, one could be confronted by a postgraduate student who'd clawed his way out of a Lanarkshire comprehensive and somehow wangled a first-class degree (even if it was only from Glasgow) was not really to Bramsden's taste.

Our first meeting of the term set the tone for our future

dealings. Bramsden was in convivial mood. He had on one of his spotty bow ties, and there was a decanter of port on his desk from which, it was clear, he had already liberally imbibed. In the manner of a bachelor uncle conferring a substantial inheritance on a much-loved nephew, he informed me that I might call him 'Prof Bram'. I told him I'd stick to Professor Bramsden if he didn't mind.

"Ah-ha!" he sniffed. "I see."

He slid the decanter across his desk for another salvo. "Fancy a tipple?" He smiled, revealing a mouthful of crumbling teeth.

"No, thank you, Professor Bramsden."

His eyes hardened and he sat back in his chair. I could see the cogs turning beneath the wisps of grey hair that dotted his cranium. A mistake had been made. I wasn't at all the kind of chap one could do business with. After that, his nose twitched whenever I entered his office as if he expected me to stink of manure or chip fat or both. He winced at my accent, rubbished my ideas, and when I tried to explain my thinking, he stared out of the window, a pained smile etched on his thin lips.

It was a sorry state of affairs. A good working relationship with your supervisor is essential for a DPhil. I should have transferred back to Glasgow. But I didn't. I persevered because, whatever I'd told my friends and the Arts & Humanities Research Council – and myself – I hadn't really chosen St Andrews because of Bramsden. I'd chosen it because Chris, my best pal in the whole world, was already there doing his PhD. I'd known Chris since I was five. At twelve we were separated when he was sent to a fee-paying school in Glasgow. Since then we'd never been in the same place at the same time. This was a chance to put that right.

It was a stupid reason to choose a university. Childish. Ridiculous. The stage was set for me to do something daft. And what could be more daft than completing my DPhil at the Karl Marx University in Leipzig?

CHAPTER THREE

You're lying on your back on Hencke's bed counting the polystyrene squares on his bedroom ceiling, wondering if he'll notice if you pick your nose. Hencke's bald freckled head is between your legs and he is licking you, jabbing at you with his tongue. It's your own fault. You told him you liked it.

"Oh, Heinzi," you said. "I like that."

You've been coming here for more than six months now. It's always the same. Two bottles of beer on the coffee table when you arrive and a glass for you. You have a drink together. You sit on the beige plastic armchair and he sits on the beige plastic sofa. It's part of his thing. It's a social call. You like him.

The first time you came you thought maybe it was a social call. He talked for a long time. About the difficulties of learning English with its irregular spelling and pronunciation. "Tja," he said, shaking his head, "very tricky." He talked about the telephone that had recently been installed in his apartment. "If you ever wish to receive or make a telephone call, you are very welcome to do so here in my little apartment." And about your family.

"State Secretary Comrade Reinsch," he said, according your father the title he never achieved, rolling the words round in his mouth like boiled sweets. "Hmm. Yes. How is he?"

"Fine," you muttered, keeping your tone even.

"And Frau Reinsch?"

He knows all about your parents. Your mother's affair and your father's revenge. The cello that was once your mother's saviour and now languishes in a dusty cupboard in her tiny apartment in Pankow.

You squeezed out the word: "Better."

"Ah," he said. "I'm so glad. Such a lovely woman. I mean, she was so lovely." A sly gleam came into his eye when he said that. "Of course, she suffered so much when Jürgen – " He spread his hands in a gesture of hopelessness.

You turned away and swallowed hard. Impossible to talk to Hencke about what happened to your brother Jürgen.

"Have you ever been to West Berlin?" you asked, knowing how much Hencke loves to talk about the legendary time a few years back when he visited the capitalist enclave. (It's a lie. He told you before that he'd never been to the West. Or maybe that was the lie.)

"I did visit West Berlin once, yes. Of course, it seems very bright and colourful when you arrive at Berlin Zoo, but one quickly notices certain problems."

He rattled on like this for a while, then he said, "A schnapps perhaps, little mouse?" and you knew what was coming next.

It takes all your self-control to remain supine on his brown nylon sheets and not knee him in the face. It'll be worth it, you tell yourself, it'll be worth it in the end. This is your insurance policy, your way of making sure that your plan works. Later, you'll laugh about Hencke with Kerstin.

She'll poke fun at his jam-jar spectacles, his little pot belly and the West jeans he wears low on his hips. Then it won't seem so terrible.

Hencke pulls himself up the bed. His eyes are bleary with lust as he fumbles for his cock.

The first time it happened you were almost pleased. That's it, you thought. I'm home and dry. I'll definitely get a place now. But it gets harder each time. And recently it's stopped just being sex. He wants to hold your hand when you sit beside him on the sofa. "You do love your Heinzi a little bit, don't you?" he says, chucking you under the chin.

Now he's heaving up and down on top of you. His face is beetroot, and his bald head is covered in fat beads of sweat. You have a terrible thought: what if he has a heart attack and dies before he can sign the form that will allow you to travel to Leeds University in England and never come back?

You must have made a sound because Hencke is saying, "What's the matter?"

Before you can answer, he rams his tongue into your mouth. You think of the words on a flyer you have tacked to the wall at Shakespeare Street. It's for a nightclub in Munich, a city you've never visited. Marek gave it to you. He knew you'd like it because it's from over there. He got it from an American called Vincent he met in a club in Berlin. On the flyer is a photo of a crazy guy with wild staring eyes and below the photo are the words:

Mittwoch, 22H – 4H

Lindwurmstraße 18, 80337 München

DJs G.R.O.S.S & PHONETIC

PRETTY FUCKING FAR FROM OKAY!

The 'C' in fucking is a hammer and sickle. The 'K' is a star.

That's what screwing Hencke is like. It's pretty fucking far from okay. But not as far from okay as spending the rest of your life in a country that has already destroyed so much that was dear to you.

CHAPTER FOUR

Chris. My old pal. I hadn't thought about him in years. Hadn't let myself. Now it all came out. I suppose Sally knew that would happen. That was the idea behind her writing ploy.

"Chris was a good friend of mine," I told her at our next session. "Yup," I added, filling the silence as she presumably knew I would, "Known him since I was five."

"Was a good friend?" Sally asked, clasping the clipboard to her chest.

"Yeah," I said. "Haven't seen him in a while." Then, knowing that I was playing right into her hands but unable to stop myself: "I don't believe all this crap about everything being rooted in your childhood. That's just … crap." God, I was Mr Articulate today. "He was a pal. That's all there is to say."

I scowled at her then looked away. When was the last time I'd seen Chris? When I first moved to London to take up the job at Liebermann Brothers he used to visit me every couple of months. Then he got married and he came down less. Then he had kids. And then … Well, I suppose he got a bit fed up with me after the hospital incident.

Sally sat back in her chair and smiled her counsellor smile. She'd touched a nerve and she knew it. *Good session,* she was probably thinking. *Well done me.*

*

I met Chris on my first day at primary school, and we became instant firm friends. He sought me out. I never knew why. We were chalk and cheese. He was Mr Popularity; I was your archetypal ginger-no-friends. He was tall and good-looking with curly black hair; I was wee and specky with thick glasses to correct a lazy eye. I was embarrassingly clever and painfully shy. Chris was clever too, but his smarts fell off him like rain off a cagoule, whereas mine stuck to me like dog shit.

Chris was exotic; I wasn't. His family lived in a bought house on the outskirts of town. We lived in a rabbit hutch rented off the council. Their house had a room lined with books called 'the study' and a spare bedroom for guests. There were fruit trees in the garden and a patio where the family had their tea in good weather. His mother was off Italian. She wore her glossy black hair piled high on her head and had full, red-painted lips. In the summer, Chris's family went to the Amalfi coast and Capri, returning copper-coloured. His three wee sisters were precocious and bonny, destined to break many a heart.

My mum was from the windswept Isle of Harris. Her hair was permed in tight curls, and she wore tweed skirts and sensible shoes. I loved the holidays we took at my grandparents' house in Geocrab, but they didn't have the glamour of Capri – especially in the retelling. My big sister, Shona, was lumpen, ugly and dull.

But none of it mattered, because I was Chris's best pal.

That protected me from the slagging and name calling that would otherwise have been my due. Then, when we were twelve, a terrible thing happened. Mr O'Driscoll sent Chris to St Ignatius' College, an independent Catholic secondary school in Glasgow. I knew, of course, that the O'Driscolls were Catholics. My dad, a dyed-in-the-wool Rangers man, had sniffed that out straight away. But I hadn't expected this. Mr O'Driscoll had always been against separate schools. "Once a Catholic, always a Catholic," said my dad. "The old man says I'll get better marks there," said Chris.

And so I had to face the secondary school in Motherwell alone. The first year was a nightmare. With my ally out of the picture, I got picked on. My glasses got smashed. My school blazer got dunked in a vat of Copydex. I had my head kicked in more than once. All the wee neds from Calderhill Primary School had been dying to have a go at me for years. Now there was no more "Hands off the wee man, sparko" from Chris, they could do me over and make themselves look big. If Chris had been there it wouldn't have happened. But he wasn't. He was at St Ignatius' College, where they wrote 'AMDG' on every piece of school work, short for *Ad Maiorem Dei Gloriam*: 'To the Greater Glory of God'. As I trudged the two miles to school every morning, I thought of Chris being driven into Glasgow in his dad's sleek maroon Jaguar with cream leather seats. Mr O'Driscoll had once let me sit in the driver's seat and play with the controls. The engine made a thrilling, throaty roar when I pushed down on the accelerator.

My mum said I'd lose touch with Chris when he went to St Ignatius': "It's a different world." She was trying to soften the blow, but I hated her for it. And she was wrong. We still met up at weekends and in the holidays and did the same things we'd always done. Mucked about by Legbrannock Burn. Built fires on the waste ground across from the chippy. Pissed up the walls in the underpass and ran away.

Often we hung out with boys from my school who ordinarily wouldn't have given me the time of day. They were all impressed by Chris. If any other boy had been sent to a school where they wrote 'To the Greater Glory of God' on their jotters it would've been social death. But it made no difference to Chris. He wore his new situation lightly, like he did everything. When he was around, my life was transformed. I stopped being the wee freaky guy with specs and a hideous flesh-coloured eye patch and became Big Chris's Pal. Not only did nobody dare touch me when Chris was there, his charisma rubbed off on me, floating down on to my shoulders like angel dust. Suddenly, my jokes were funny. The fact that I was clever and knew things wasn't pathetic. It was actually quite cool.

"Hey, listen to this," Chris would say. "Listen to the wee man." He'd nudge me. "Go on. Tell them."

I'd tell them whatever it was I'd found out about whatever it was – the Roman legions, Rommel's North Africa Campaign, dinosaurs, the sex life of plants – and they'd listen. When I was done, Chris would say, "Amazing, eh? That's dead cool, man." They'd all nod.

Later, things changed for me at school. We got streamed and I had a wee quiet pal called Donald Black whom I sat beside in maths and English. He understood about my eye patch because his sister had one. I no longer spent intervals and lunchtimes alone. I hung out with Blackie and a couple of other loser, swotty types. Later still, my eye was fixed and I got normal glasses, then contact lenses. I grew taller, started to do sport and filled out. One day when Ian Bagley called me a poof and put his foot out to trip me up in the corridor, I turned round and stuck one on him. There was a satisfying crack as my fist connected with his nose. It started to bleed and he ran away squealing.

No one ever came after me again. The dark days were over. I didn't need Chris in quite the way I had before. But I needed him in other ways. His house was a sanctuary for me, an escape from home. The happiest days of my childhood were spent at the O'Driscolls' house. I saw things there I'd never seen before. Whole coffee beans, which Mrs O'Driscoll turned into a bitter, intoxicating liquid that bore no resemblance to the instant coffee at home. Real oil paintings where you could see the brush strokes in the paint. A married couple who liked each other. I watched mesmerised as Mr O'Driscoll came up behind his wife in the kitchen, ran his hands over her hips, kissed her on the neck and called her pet names like 'honey' and 'sweetheart'. He said things to her – "You're looking lovely today, Isabella" or "What's for tea, gorgeous woman?" – that thrilled and embarrassed me in equal measure.

It seemed to me that Mr and Mrs O'Driscoll almost certainly had sex. If my parents had ever had sex it must have been a grim affair. My father was a sour man who bullied his wife, ignored his daughter and despised his son for being clever. He worked at the steelworks and thought that any man who didn't wear a boiler suit to work was a pansy. The men he worked with all wanted their sons to do well and get out of Calderhill. Not my dad. The better I did at school, the less he liked it. I grew to hate him, and although my mum was an altogether gentler soul, a soft-spoken book lover who doted on her only son, she didn't stand up to him, and so I came to despise her too.

I went to the O'Driscolls' to forget, but as I got older and spent more time there, something else happened. Chris started to need me as much as I needed him. He was clever but not as clever as me and he didn't have the application. I helped him with his homework, and my visits became important. Mrs O'Driscoll brought us coffee and cakes and shooed her girls away from Chris's room. Mr O'Driscoll made sure to pop his head round the door and say, "How's it going, Bobbie? How's the old brainbox today." The O'Driscolls became my second family. When I was made Dux of my school, it was Chris's parents who made a fuss, not my own. Mr O'Driscoll shook my hand and said, "You'll go far, Bobbie," then produced two tickets for the first game of the season at Celtic Park. Mrs O'Driscoll hugged me and gave me a card containing a £10 book token. At home very little was said, though my mum slipped me a five pound note when my dad was out and said, "I'm very proud of you, son."

When it came time to go to university, I was worried rather than excited because I knew my time with the O'Driscolls was coming to an end. The private school and Mr O'Driscoll's money made a difference now. Chris did English 'A' levels at St Ignatius', sat the Oxbridge exams and got a place to read chemistry at Magdalen College, Oxford. Mrs O'Driscoll threw a party for him, and it wasn't long before I realised how out of place I was in Chris's new world. I pronounced 'Magdalen' as it's spelt and Gerard Kelly, Chris's friend from St Ignatius' College, roared with laughter.

"Bloody stupid way to say it if you ask me," said Mr O'Driscoll, slinging a comradely arm round my shoulders. But I minded that I'd got it wrong.

That summer, Chris and I went on a road trip to France, bankrolled by Mr O'Driscoll. It was my first trip abroad – the best thing ever. We slept in the open, smoked *Gauloises*, tried dope for the first time and eventually got laid. But the whole time I was aware that it wasn't just a holiday; it was the end of something.

I needed a replacement for Chris. I found it with Aloïse, a thin, nut-brown girl who hung out with us for a few days in Antibes and relieved me of my virginity. I came inside her in seconds. I was in a frenzy, clawing at her small breasts till she slapped my hand away. It was blissful but perhaps not quite as blissful as the feeling of control I'd had earlier the same evening when I'd got properly drunk for the first time. Now that was special. I cracked jokes and people laughed. I smiled at girls, and they smiled back. All my cares fell away, and I didn't need Chris for angel dust to fall on my shoulders. I'd found a new best friend.

CHAPTER FIVE

Lanky Jana is there when you arrive at the University Tower to find out if you've been awarded a place on the Study in the Non-Socialist Abroad programme. Everyone knows she is Frau Aner's right-hand woman.

The results are posted on a board outside Hencke's office. Students have travelled back to Leipzig from other cities to see them before the letters go out, not because they want to know what mark they got in prose composition, but because they want to know if they got a place on the Study in the Non-Socialist Abroad programme. It's a golden chance to travel to the West. There might never be another.

Jana doesn't pretend there is any reason for her to be there. She just stands in the middle of the corridor like a block of wood, while the others look at the board. Looking at it now is Dieter, who dresses like a Texan ranch hand and speaks English with an American drawl picked up from Armed Forces Radio. His unhealthy interest in things American means he has no chance of a place, but unlike Jana he has a reason to be there.

Jana has already been to the West. The previous year, she spent three months at Leeds University. She didn't like it. She said everyone had green hair in England, and there were no cows.

People gasped. "No cows? That's incredible!"

"It certainly is," said Dieter, and you and he exchanged a look.

You nod to Jana and the others as they move aside to let you pass and try to read their expressions. You're the best student in the year. Everyone knows that. If the places were handed out on merit alone you wouldn't need to be here; you'd know your place was secure. You have no relatives in the West. There are no impediments apart from your rebellious past. And you have a secret weapon to counter that. You have Hencke and his promise to you.

You approach the board. It's very still in the corridor. Everyone is waiting for you to the look at the board. They're all waiting for Magda Reinsch, the daughter of a former high-ranking official from the Ministry for Foreign Affairs who rebelled and disgraced her father then came back to the Party, to learn if she has been granted a place to study in England.

You scan the list of names. Your name is not there. You look again. An absence is so much harder to be sure of than a presence. It's not there. You knew it wouldn't be as soon as you saw Jana in the corridor. You close your eyes and take a deep breath.

"What a pity!" says Jana, appearing at your shoulder. "You tried very hard for this place."

You swing round. Your English is ten times better than hers. For a moment, you consider punching her in the face, smashing her beaky red nose to smithereens. Then you look into her pale blue eyes. Her gaze is steady and cool. Is there something new there? Does she know about Hencke?

At the lift, Dieter comes up to you and claps you on the shoulder. "I'm sorry," he says.

You force a smile, suppressing the urge to cry. "I'm not the only one who didn't get a place."

"You're the only one who deserved a place who didn't get one."

"Did you – ?" You didn't look for his name.

He shakes his head. "No, but then … maybe I'm too crazy," he says in English.

You laugh, and he touches your cheek. "You should laugh more often, Magda. It suits you."

In the lift, he invites you for a coffee. You hesitate. "C'mon. Let me buy you coffee and cake," he says. "Let's cheer ourselves up."

Your first impulse is to refuse, but what will you do if you don't go? Marek is in Berlin, and Kerstin is attending a lecture by a visiting academic from Afghanistan in Halle and won't be home until later. You'd pinned all your hopes on the study place. If you have coffee with Dieter you won't have to think about it for an hour or so.

You expect him to take you to the Mensa, but he says he doesn't want to go to the student canteen. You don't want to either: too many familiar faces. Instead, he suggests *Café Riquard*.

"But *Riquard* is expensive."

He shrugs. "Who cares?"

The café is half empty, but you have to wait a long time for a table. "Comrade," Dieter says to the waitress, "why are we waiting?"

She scowls, looks round and points to a table at the back near the stairs that lead to the toilets. "You can sit there."

"Couldn't we sit in the window?"

"Reserved."

"But there's no one there. Please, I'm treating my friend."

"It's reserved, Comrade!" she screams, and the few patrons look over. At the table, she slams the menus down. "Order with me," she says and stalks off.

Dieter sighs. "Why can't she just be civil?"

The waitress makes you wait a good ten minutes before she sidles back over. "Yes?" she says.

You order chocolate cake.

"We don't have that."

"Apple strudel?" Dieter asks, and she shakes her head. "What do you have?" he asks.

"We have what's on the menu, young man."

"How about apricot cheesecake?" you ask.

"We're out of apricot cheesecake."

"Plain cheesecake?" The waitress nods sullenly. "I'll have that," you say.

"The same for me," says Dieter, "and a pot of coffee for two. It's crazy that you didn't get a place, Magda," he says when the waitress has gone. "You were the best in the class."

You shrug. "Well – "

"What will you do now?"

You give an involuntary start. The question is unusually direct. In theory, there is no such question. You must finish your training and become an English-German interpreter without ever having been in a country where English is spoken. To ask such a question is to imply that you had ulterior motives for wanting the place. You eye him carefully. He's very short, barely one metre sixty, with dark curly hair. He is a little ridiculous in his ersatz cowboy outfits, like a teddy bear with spurs. He looks entirely harmless, but aren't they always the worst? You know Kerstin doesn't trust him. She thinks his love of America is too obvious. She prefers the quieter refuge of the dead languages she's learning in Cuneiform Studies. But Dieter sometimes does little jobs for Marek in return for certain treats. That should mean he's on the right side. You hope he is. In case not, you change the subject.

"If you could go anywhere in the world where would you go?" you ask.

"Moscow," he says, and you snort with laughter. "Yes. Why not? I've always wanted to see Red Square." He bursts out laughing. People look over, and the waitress frowns. "No, I'd go to New York City," he says when you've both regained your composure. "I'd like to visit the Empire State Building and the Cotton Club in Harlem. And you?"

You think of all the places you'd like to go. Kerstin would say Mesopotamia or Assyria. That's why she's so stable. No one can go to the places that capture her imagination, not even West Germans.

"Paris," you say. "Or maybe London."

"Who would you go with?"

Do you detect an edge in his voice? You'd go with Marek. Always with him.

"I like to travel alone," you say.

*

When you leave the café you storm across Karl-Marx-Platz to the post office and phone Hencke.

"Little mouse," he squeaks. "Goodness."

You have never phoned him before. He didn't give you the number when the phone was installed. But it's printed on the rotary dial, and you memorised it.

"To what do I owe – ?" he begins.

"I need to see you," you interrupt.

44

"I'm afraid it's not very convenient right – "

"It's important."

"My dear girl, I really don't have time now."

You fight the anger rising inside you and put on a little-girl sexy voice. "But I have something to show you, Heinzi. You remember the present you gave me? I spent it. I went to the Exquisit shop in Berlin at the weekend and bought some new underwear. I want to show it to you. It's your favourite colour."

"Ah," he breathes, "how you tempt your poor old Heinzi. But what colour can you mean? I don't believe we ever talked about this."

"Red, Heinzi. Isn't it red? I thought it would be red. I bought red panties, a red bra – "

"Now, little mouse," he interrupts, perhaps thinking of the censor, who listens in on every phone call. "I think you should be running along."

"I need to see you."

"Little mouse – "

"It's important."

He sighs. "Very well. But I won't be able to spare much time."

Stay calm, you tell yourself as you jump on the tram. *Don't let him see how upset you are.* You change lines at the train station, and the tram rattles out along the ring road, then over the Zeppelin Bridge past the Central Stadium where you watched your brother compete in the Gymnastics and Sports Festival three years ago. Hencke lives in a modern development near the end of the line. All the streets are named after flowers. You march down Carnation Way, which houses the nicer, more spacious apartments. It's hard to get one of these apartments – very hard for a single man. You need connections. Hencke has connections. You press his buzzer, thinking you wouldn't live in one of these centrally heated boxes for anything in the world. The regime's corn and compass emblem is stamped on every stone.

"This is a pleasant surprise," Hencke says as you pass through his front door. He rubs his hands together, then reaches up and pecks you on the cheek. "But in future you must give your Heinzi more notice. And please be careful what you say on the telephone. We don't want any misunderstandings. I didn't realise you had the number. It's really best not to telephone. Shall we go through?"

He sits down on the sofa, and you say, "I went to the University Tower today. I didn't get a place on the study programme."

"Ah, yes." He clasps his hands together as if in prayer. "Such a pity."

On the shelving unit behind the sofa sits a wooden gong inlaid with a bronze medallion of Lenin's profile and inscribed with the words: '30 YEARS OF THE GDR!' You briefly consider grabbing it and caving Hencke's skull in.

"You promised me you'd see to it," you say.

"And I tried, little mouse. I spoke up for you at every opportunity, but in the end there was simply nothing I could do. The others were determined to make a different choice."

"We had an agreement," you hiss.

"It's just a small trip abroad. There's really no need to get upset."

"That's easy for you to say."

"It's never been my privilege to travel to the West either," he says, forgetting all the stories he's told you about West Berlin.

His left arm is stretched along the back of the beige plastic sofa. He smiles, and his eyes glitter behind his thick spectacles. "Let's not fight,." He pats the cushion next to him. "Come and sit with your Heinzi. Let's have a little cuddle and then you can show me your exciting new things. Exquisit indeed! We have been good to ourselves."

"You told me you'd see to it."

"Little mouse, I'm afraid you overestimate my powers."

He smirks, and you think of all the ghastly afternoons you've spent in this sterile little apartment. Tears prick your eyes, and you fight back a sob.

"Are you quite all right, my dear?"

You take a deep breath and pull a packet of cigarettes from your bag.

"Now, you know I don't like smoking in the apartment." You give him a hard look. "Well, all right then. Just this once. I'll get an ashtray, but please catch any ash that falls before I get back in your hand."

He scurries off like the neurotic little housewife he is. Your hand shakes as you light a cigarette. You drift over to the glass doors that open on to the balcony and look out at the park. It's a warm June day. Children are playing in the sun. People are walking their dogs. Hencke clomps back into the room and deposits the ashtray on the window ledge. He slides his hands up your back and starts to knead your shoulders.

You shrug him off.

"Now, now, whatever is the matter?"

You swing round to face him. "You lied to me. You told me you'd fix it and you didn't. I mean, why did you think I was fucking you, Heinz? Surely you didn't think I liked you?"

He moves back, a thin smile on his lips. His small, pointy teeth make him look like a vicious little animal: a weasel or a wild cat. "I do think you're rather over-reacting, don't you? I don't blame you. It's the showman in you. You get it from your mother. I remember seeing her in concert many years ago. It would be many years ago, wouldn't it? I don't believe she plays now, does she? All those wild flourishes. Very dramatic. But in the end not all that convincing. If you examine the facts – the facts – I'm sure you'll see that there's no question whatsoever of anyone having lied. I didn't promise you anything. Perhaps you thought our special understanding would help you in some way, that our delightful little times together would give you certain advantages. It's quite understandable that you might have thought that. But if you consider the matter carefully I'm sure you'll realise what a foolish idea that was. And not just foolish, little mouse. Illegal. Against all the ideals and principles of our Republic. In the Workers' and Farmers' State, we do not get a place on an important study programme through friendships and connections. We get a place through hard work and application. Remember the words of Comrade Ernst Thälmann: *No success without pain and work.* I suggest you study those words. Didn't you pledge to follow Comrade Ernst Thälmann's example when you were a Pioneer? *Ernst Thälmann is my model. I promise to learn to work and struggle as Ernst Thälmann teaches.* How sweet you must have looked in your little white shirt and red neckerchief. What I wouldn't give to have known you then."

You walk towards him, lift your hand and slap him full in the face. The sting feels good. "You're an arsehole, Heinz," you say. "That's what I came here to tell you. And all the pretty speeches in the world won't make you any less of an arsehole."

You pick up your bag and turn to go. He grabs your arm and yanks you back round to face him.

"You are making a big mistake, Comrade Reinsch," he spits, switching from the informal *Du* to the formal *Sie*. A vein twitches in his neck. He grabs you by the collar. His face is very close. His spit speckles your cheeks. "So you didn't get your little trip to England, hmm? You won't get to see the Golden West. What a pity. My heart bleeds. Do you know what that makes you, Comrade Reinsch? That makes you the same as ninety-five per cent of the citizens of our Republic. Are you ashamed to count yourself among their number? You should be proud to be one of them. But no. You think you're different. You think you deserve special treatment. And when you don't get it, what do you do? You barge in on a respected citizen such as myself who has laboured all his life to fulfil the goals of the Party in the interests of the working class and make obnoxious insinuations. Well, it won't do, Comrade Reinsch. You will pay dearly for this. This little disappointment regarding England will shortly seem like a very small matter. When you lose your university place. When your old friends in Berlin are detained. Oh yes, I know all about them. When your special friend, Comrade Marek Dembowksi, is picked up by our People's Police after one of his nights out."

He releases you with a shove. "He sleeps with men, you know. Rather disgusting, wouldn't you say? But then what can you expect from a Jew boy."

His mouth is a little round hole, and he spits the insult out. How thin the veneer is. How many times have you heard Hencke's Holocaust speech? And his Spiel about Israel? How painful it was for a German state to have to break off diplomatic relations.

His face softens. "Little mouse," he says, switching back to *Du,* "don't be foolish. You're upset. That's understandable. But do you know what I think? I think we can resolve this situation to our mutual satisfaction. Why don't you sit down?"

"There's nothing you can offer me."

"What if I were to say that it might be possible to organise an additional place on the Study in the Non-Socialist Abroad programme even at this late date?"

He sits down on the sofa and pats the cushion next to him. "Sit down, my dear."

You sit down and wait to hear what special favour will buy you a trip to England. Nothing would surprise you. He opens his briefcase and takes out a piece of paper, places it on the coffee table and slides it towards you.

"Don't look so worried. All you have to do is copy out this statement in long hand and sign it."

You read the paper:

Leipzig,
28.09.1985

COMMITMENT

I, Magdalena Maria Reinsch of 2034 Leipzig, Tarostraße 14, freely commit myself to work for the Ministry for State Security (MfS) of the GDR. I have taken this decision of my own free will and as a result of my political-ideological convictions.

My work will have an unofficial character and will therefore require the utmost discretion with respect to all third parties, institutions and other organs, which I declare myself ready to maintain.

I will support the MfS to the best of my ability and will deliver honest, objective and thorough information regarding the designated object, DEMBOWSKI, Marek, to the MfS colleague who has been made known to me.

In order to protect the secrecy of the operation, I will adopt the following code name, chosen by me: **"CORALIE STREIBERT"**

"Coralie," Hencke says, "it's a lovely name, isn't it? I chose it myself. It suits you. And do you know what name I've chosen for Comrade Dembowski? Lech. Perfect, isn't it, for a little Polack?"

He places a blank sheet of paper from his briefcase on the coffee table and hands you a pen. "Just copy the statement out in long hand and sign at the bottom. Think! This time next year you'll have been to England. You'll have seen the Golden West with your own eyes."

You stare at the sheet of paper. It's your ticket out. You might never get another one. If you refuse him, he'll cause you all sorts of problems. You don't know how far his connections reach.

"Why do you want me to copy it out? Couldn't I just sign it?"

He waves an admonitory finger. "Tsk, tsk, tsk, little mouse. We mustn't be lazy. Commitments from unofficial collaborators must always be written out. That way no one can wriggle out of it later, hmm?"

You sit on Hencke's plastic sofa holding the pen. Would it really be so bad to do this? You could tell them things that weren't important – things that perhaps weren't even true. You could be clever.

Hencke is watching you. "You are right to consider carefully." His tone is flat, his eyes cold. "This is a very serious matter. Our State Security Service is the sword and shield of the Party. It protects our socialist way of life. A commitment to work for the MfS should not be undertaken lightly." He sits back. "But I know you. I am fully convinced you are up to the task."

For a moment, you're tempted. Betray a friend in exchange for freedom. It must happen all the time. Marek need never know. No one need know. And soon you'll be gone anyway, both of you, and then none of it will matter. You turn the pen in your hand and suddenly you see: there was never going to be any deal without this. You pull the sheet of paper towards you.

Sometimes it is necessary to be hard and selfish to get what we want in life. We can't always think of others and be kind.

"Good," says Hencke. "It will also be better for your family if you follow this course."

Your family. The paper swims before you, and it all comes back to you – what it was like in the days after your brother's accident. Marek was the one who helped you then, the only one who stood up to your father. You're in this together, you and he. Always have been, always will be.

You put the pen down and turn to Hencke. "Fuck off," you spit. Then you grab your bag and run.

CHAPTER SIX

I decided to leave St Andrews in the summer term of my first year. I had to get out of that wee, grey town and fast. Relations with Bramsden had deteriorated. I'd heard he was telling people I didn't have the wherewithal to complete my DPhil. "This is what happens – " I imagined him saying, leaving the sentence for others to complete. This is what happens when you let scumbags from dying Lanarkshire steel towns into Scotland's premier university. Still, if it had just been Bramsden, I could have coped. But it wasn't. It was the whole place. It did my head in. I was a fish out of water: an East End boy in a West End bar. It was great sharing with Chris, but he wasn't there that much. Slowly, I came to realise that the kind of friendship we'd had in the past was just that – in the past.

I didn't choose Leipzig as a destination. I was all set to spend a year in Düsseldorf, a pleasant West German town on the banks of the Rhine. Why would I go to Leipzig? I wasn't particularly political. I hated Thatcher and voted Labour, but where I came from that was par for the course. I had only the vaguest of notions as to what lay behind the Iron Curtain. When Dr Bull-Halifax first mentioned Leipzig to me, I wasn't even sure where it was. I had to look it up in an atlas. All I knew about East Germany was that it won a lot of Olympic medals – and of course that there was a wall in Berlin, dividing the city.

And if I didn't choose Leipzig, I most certainly did not choose John Bull-Halifax, the junior Soviet Studies lecturer who organised my study place. I didn't know him, but I'd seen him about and I didn't like what I saw. Self-consciously political, he made sure everyone knew he was a card-carrying member of the Communist Party. The door to his small office in the modern languages building was always open, revealing walls decorated with posters in the socialist-realist style. He walked about town with a copy of *Marxism Today* tucked under his arm, dressed in old-fashioned suits from second hand shops, always with a CPGB pin in the lapel. Given that he'd gone to some minor public school and then to Cambridge and was now teaching at St Andrews rather than, say, Bradford, I assumed that, like his fake streets-of-London accent, it was all a pose. He carried it off, I believed, because he was good-looking, with strong regular features, a mop of red-gold curls and a big film star smile. He even wore black National Health specs because paying for glasses was private health care, which was wrong. Having endured National Health glasses all through primary school, I had no time for this. But other people didn't see it for the affectation I thought it was.

One afternoon, Bull-Halifax buttonholed me on the stairs in the Modern Languages building. I'd never spoken to him, but he clearly knew who I was. I tried not to be flattered. I might feign to despise him, but he did know his stuff and he was something of a legend in the department. Rumours, most of them contradictory, flocked to him like seagulls to a discarded chip poke: He was ultra-fit and didn't drink or smoke because he modelled himself on the Bolsheviks. He was a secret alcoholic now on the wagon. He slept with a different girl every night. He never touched a woman because sex would distract him from his work.

Girls loved him, especially the glossy, upper-class Yah girls with whom St Andrews was stuffed. I often saw them fluttering their eyelashes at him in the corridors: *Dr Bull-Halifax, have you got a moment? Oh really? Oh yah. Oh, that's so interesting.*

He told me he was in the process of setting up a number of student exchanges between the UK and the Eastern Bloc countries. He had already arranged for three Russian under-graduates from St Andrews to spend a term in Vladivostok. He also had connections in East Germany and he could almost certainly organise a research place for me at the Karl Marx University Leipzig if I was interested.

"I know you want out of here," he said in a confidential tone. "Can't say I blame you. I've got a flat in Edinburgh and I spend as much time there as I can. A place at Leipzig could be just the ticket. Very well regarded in East Germany, Heinrich Heine. And it would fit well with your topic. You're looking into the political side of his work, aren't you?"

"Uh-huh," I mumbled. So he knew about my research. "But I've already got something sorted out."

"Oh, yes? What's that?" He probably knew all about that too but he acted like he didn't.

"I'm going to Düsseldorf."

"*Düsseldorf?*" He made it sound like Ulan Bator.

"The archive's there. Professor Bramsden suggested it."

"Of course. He was a visiting lecturer there once, wasn't he? Well, I wish you the best of luck." He fished a card out of his pocket. "But if it doesn't work out for any reason, give me a call. They really do respect solid intellectual endeavour over there, you know."

"Why would it not work out?" I asked, suddenly suspicious.

"Oh, I'm sure it will." He gave me one of his film star smiles and clapped me on the shoulder.

I smiled back, feeling grim. He knew it wasn't going to work out, I realised. This wasn't a chance encounter on the stairs. He'd planned it. There had been rumours in the department about Bramsden's health. He was drinking too much, going gaga. My application was in his hands. I was funded from home, so it should have been a formality, but what if he'd forgotten about it?

I went to see Bramsden that very afternoon. He was a little drunk, his eyes bleary. He scratched his head as he rifled through the papers on his desk.

"Well," he said at last. "I'm afraid I can't find it, Robert. Awfully sorry."

He smiled gamely, but there was desperation in his eyes. I'd found him out, and he knew it. I had a choice: I could lodge a complaint about him with the university authorities – I knew it wouldn't be the first – or I could phone John Bull-Halifax. I despised Bramsden but seeing him sat slumped behind his desk with all the drive gone out of him, I found myself unable to finish him off.

I hurried back to the beautiful flat overlooking the sea that I shared with Chris and phoned John Bull-Halifax.

CHAPTER SEVEN

You scramble down the stairs of Hencke's building and burst out on to the street. Hencke is shouting your name. Is he following you? You glance back. He is! You sprint down Carnation Way, your bag banging against your hip. He's running behind you, screaming abuse. People are staring. He must have lost his mind. You swing on to Daisy Way. There's a tram at the stop. One last push. Your lungs are bursting as you jump aboard. For agonising moments the doors remain open. Hencke appears on Daisy Way, panting. He sees you and ups his pace. Then the doors bang shut and the tram shudders into motion. You stumble to the back and collapse into a seat. Out of the window, you see Hencke slumped against the tram stop, glaring after you. You're shaking, you suddenly realise, as pent-up tears prick your eyes.

At the train station, you change to the tram that goes to Shakespeare Street. That's where you need to be right now. Impossible to go to the room at the student residence that you share with three fellow students from the English interpreting and translation course, including Jana. She's hardly ever there because she has a nice room at her parents' house in the suburbs. But she'll be there today. They all will.

When you get off the tram, you head to Körner Street where old Frau Dannewitz lives. It's your habit to enter the rear house at Shakespeare Street through the Körner Street back courts. That way you don't have to go through the main house at the front. No one at the university knows about your hideaway at Shakespeare Street, and that's how you want to keep it. The building is dilapidated and no one ever comes here, but you can't be too careful.

As you run upstairs, you hear the Kempners bawling at each other in their second-floor apartment. Most of the apartments in the rear house are empty, but the Kempners cling on, along with mad Herr Hempelmann and his cats on the ground floor. You sprint past the communal toilet on the third floor, which as usual is leaking water to the steps, and up to the top floor. As you stick your key in the door, you hear voices; Kerstin is home from Halle, and Frau Dannewitz is in the apartment with her.

"Hello," Kerstin calls and comes out to meet you in the hall. "Well?" she mouths. "When are you off to England?"

"I'm not. I didn't get a place."

"No!" She clutches at your arm. "What do you mean? I thought Hencke told you he'd fix it."

You shrug. "He did."

"Is that you, Magda?" Frau Dannewitz calls from the main room.

"Yes, it's me," you reply. "We'll talk about it later," you say to Kerstin.

She follows you into the room, shaking her head. "I can't believe it. That dirty, lying old bastard."

"Frau Dannewitz!" You stretch out your hand to the old lady and tell her not to get up. She's sitting at the table with a cup of coffee and a slice of Kerstin's home-made cheesecake. "How are you, Frau Dannewitz?"

"Exceedingly well, my dear." Despite her arthritis, Frau Dannewitz is always exceedingly well. That's why she can climb the five flights of stairs to your apartment. "That girl can bake," she says, patting her lips with a napkin.

"I know." You drop down on the divan.

"So that's it, then," Frau Dannewitz says. "You're going to England. Well, I shall miss you."

You shake your head. "I'm not going. I didn't get a place."

Frau Dannewitz's mouth drops open. "What? But you're the best student in your year. Everyone says so. Even that friend of yours, the sarcastic one."

She means Marek. She doesn't like him.

Kerstin brings you a cup of coffee, sits down beside you on the divan and slings her arm round your shoulders. "Unfortunately, it's not just about being the best, Frau Dannewitz," she says. "There are other considerations – if you know what I mean."

"Ach." Frau Dannewitz shakes her head. "This is all wrong. This is not what we fought for, you know. This is not what we wanted."

Frau Dannewitz is an old Communist who was in the Anti-Fascist resistance during the war. It's because of this that you got to know her. When you rejoined the Free German Youth, you made a pledge to help elderly comrades who live alone. As a much decorated 'Fighter Against Fascism', Frau Dannewitz was the ideal candidate. It suits you to help Frau Dannewitz because it gives you a ready alibi should anyone ever ask about all the time you spend in this run-down area of town. But over time you've come to admire the old lady. She stayed put and fought for what she believed in. She didn't scuttle off into exile in the Soviet Union like your father. And she paid the price. She spent nine months in Buchenwald concentration camp. The stories she can tell about that and the day the Americans liberated the camp. *We prisoners had already taken control,* she always says.

"I should leave you young people," Frau Dannewitz says, grabbing her stick and pulling herself to her feet. "Perhaps you'll come over tomorrow and help me to clear out my tiled stove, Magda."

"Of course." Like this hideaway you share with Kerstin, Frau Dannewitz's apartment is heated by an old tiled stove. In winter, you haul the brown coal briquettes that feed it up to her third-floor apartment for her. It's been out all summer, but soon the weather will change and it will be time to light it again.

"You should move, Frau Dannewitz," says Kerstin. "You'd be much more comfortable in a modern apartment. We'd help you move, wouldn't we, Magda?"

You nod. "Absolutely. And we'd come to see you often. Think: you could have central heating and a private bathroom and perhaps a little balcony. Mimsie could sit out on the balcony and watch the birds."

Mimsie is Frau Dannewitz' cat. The old lady shakes her head, as you knew she would. You've had this conversation a thousand times. As a Fighter Against Fascism, she could easily get a place in a new development, but she doesn't want one. "Mimsie might run away," she says. "And anyway, I like it here. I'm used to this place. I've lived here for forty years. I have my freedom here."

You know exactly what she means. You have your freedom

too in this crumbling and forgotten attic apartment, still registered to Kerstin's grandmother. You and Kerstin have made a cosy den for yourselves here with some old bits of furniture and a few colourful rugs and cushions. The shelves are stacked with precious, hard-to-obtain books and copies of the underground magazines you used to contribute to before you started playing your part. It's your only home.

You help Frau Dannewitz into her cardigan, and she gathers up her bag. On her way to the door, she says, "I like this photograph." It's one you took when you were visiting your mother in Berlin during the summer holidays. The previous week you developed it in the small dark room you've created in the hall cupboard here. It shows tourists watching the changing of the guard at the Neue Wache memorial to the victims of war and captures a rare moment of inattention from one of the goose-stepping soldiers, a hint of a smile.

"Thank you. I'm pleased with it."

Frau Dannewitz takes your hand in hers and pats it. "Is it because of your photographs that you didn't get a place to go to England, Magda?"

The walls here are pinned with subversive photographs taken with the Zenit EM camera your brother brought back from the Moscow Olympics for you in 1980: soot-coated buildings, down-and-outs, funny moments like the one at the Neue Wache. But now you no longer publish them in underground magazines, you reckon it's a harmless occupation.

You smile at her. "No. It was just one of those things. There were other good candidates."

You want Frau Dannewitz to believe this. You don't want the last shreds of her belief in a system she helped to create in good faith to be ripped from her.

But she's tut-tutting and shaking her head. "It's not right," she says. "You were the best."

When she's gone, refusing any help with the stairs, Kerstin comes and hugs you.

"Magda, I'm so sorry," she says. "I just can't believe it. Without Hencke, I might not have been surprised. But after everything you did – "

She breaks off. You press her to you. She has the strong, firm body of a gymnast. She used to compete at gymnastics for her local town when she was at school, but as she got older her parents dissuaded her from training. They didn't want their daughter to be too good at sport. There was a time when you would have thought that was mad, but after what happened to your brother you know they did the right thing.

"I picked up a telegram for you at the hall of residence," Kerstin says. "It looks like it's from Marek. That's another reason I was sure you'd got the place. I thought you'd telegraphed him, and he was sending you his congratulations."

You rip the telegram open. He's in Leipzig the following week and wants to meet you. He says he'll be in Café Grossmann at 20.00.

CHAPTER EIGHT

It was early evening when I first crossed the border into East Germany at Wolfsburg/Oebisfelde, and the light was starting to fade. Perhaps that's why, when I think of it now, I see it in black and white – a monochrome blur of concrete, metal tracks and glaring searchlights. Or perhaps the many black and white photographs I've seen since have distorted my recollection of that first crossing.

The train was quiet when I went over, but a few miles from the crossing at Braunschweig an elderly couple boarded and took the seats opposite me. They moved close together when the West German border guards got on at Wolfsburg, and the old man patted his wife's knee reassuringly.

"Couldn't you find anywhere better to go?" the guard joked when he saw my entry visa with 'permission to remain for one year'.

"I wanted to go somewhere different," I said.

"Well, it's certainly different over there," he chuckled. "Isn't that so?" he said to the old couple. They smiled but didn't reply.

The guards jumped out of the train, banging the doors behind them, and I saw them standing on the platform smoking and cracking jokes. As the train creaked back into life and edged forwards, the carriage fell still. The elderly man took his wife's hand. The woman in the seat opposite put aside her knitting. A middle-aged man at the far end of the carriage, slid his copy of *Der Spiegel* inside his jerkin. We all peered out of the window for a moment, but when the border fortifications came into view the others stared into their laps. I alone kept watch, hoping for my first glimpse of a guard tower, a sniffer dog or a tumble of barbed wire.

We juddered to a stop again at Oebisfelde, and East German border guards exploded on to the train. "Passport control!" they yelled as they pounded along the corridors, wedging open the carriage doors. A stony-faced guard checked our passports while another combed the carriage, training his torch behind light fittings and under ceiling panels. There was a long delay while a third guard made a meticulous search of the man in the jerkin's suitcase and confiscated my copy of the *Guardian*. Then they were gone, slamming the doors in unison as they jumped on to the platform, and the train once again creaked into life.

"They took your newspaper," the old lady ventured once we were trundling through the fields of Saxony-Anhalt. "What a shame."

"It doesn't matter," I smiled. "I'd finished with it anyway." They were welcome to my newspaper. I was just relieved the guards had searched the man in the jerkin's suitcase rather than mine. My bag had four brand new pairs of Levi's in it that John Bull-Halifax had asked me to transport.

"Make sure you have a plausible story ready for the border

guards in case they search your luggage," he'd told me when I collected them from him. "You're allowed to import gifts up to the value of 200 East Marks, but people aren't allowed to sell goods on." But of course I didn't have a story ready.

"Are you British?" the old lady asked. I nodded, and she nudged her husband. "See, Vati. I told you. I took a peek at your passport when the guards were checking it," she confided. "Are you on holiday here?" Her tone suggested this was a fantastical possibility. I told her my business in Leipzig, and her eyes widened. "I didn't know such a thing was possible, did you, Vati?"

The old man shook his head. "Nope. Never heard of such a thing."

"What about you?" I asked. "Where are you going?"

"We're going home," the old lady said. "We've been visiting my sister in Braunschweig. I retired last month so now I can go where I like. Once you're past sixty they don't care what you do. You're no longer economically useful."

"Shh, Mutti," the old man said.

"Ach, Gerhardt, what does it matter? At our age, nobody cares what you say. I hadn't seen my sister for five years," she said to me. "Imagine that."

"Sometimes it's better to be quiet, Mutti," Gerhardt said, patting her hand.

"Five years?" I said. "That's a long time."

"It's not so very long. After sixty-one we didn't see my sister for twelve years, did we, Gerhardt?"

"That's when the border was fortified," her husband said in an undertone.

"Goodness. That must have been hard."

"It was," said the old woman. "Very hard." She told me how her older sister had moved to Braunschweig in 1956, seeking a better life. Initially, they visited each other often, but after 1961 that became impossible.

"When she got married, we applied for permission to travel to the wedding, but it was refused, even though we were leaving our two children behind. What better guarantee could there be that we'd return?"

Eventually, she told me, her sister's family had been able to visit them in East Germany every second year. But her sister's health had deteriorated in recent years and after her husband died she couldn't face the journey alone. "We spoke on the phone, but it's not the same. And we got a shock, didn't we, Gerhardt, when we saw her? She's aged so much. She's an old woman now."

Her husband nodded. "I could have visited her two years ago when I retired, but I decided to wait for my wife. But when I saw her I thought that I should have taken the opportunity to visit her earlier."

"And how did you like Braunschweig?" I asked.

"It was very nice," the old lady said. "We had a lovely time. But there's far too much of everything over there. Why do you need thirty different kinds of shampoo? Two or three is fine. And what – "

"Mutti, this is our stop." Her husband got up and started to wrestle their bags down from the luggage rack.

"Getting out so soon?" I asked. We'd only travelled a couple of kilometres.

"It's not far," the old lady said.

"Mutti, give me a hand here." I jumped up to help the old man, and as I was heaving their plastic holdalls to the train door, the old lady asked my name.

"Robert," she repeated. "Well, good luck, Robert." She patted my arm as her husband helped her down from the train.

I handed the holdalls down to the old man. "Presents from my sister in there," the old lady said. "Things we can't get here."

"Come on, Mutti." Her husband shook my hand and guided his wife away from the platform edge.

I stared out of the window, as the train trundled on towards Leipzig. The landscape was alien. The huge fields of the collective farms. The tiny Toy Town cars with their dim headlights. The poster on a siding that read: 1ST MAY – THE FIGHTING HOLIDAY OF THE WORKING CLASS! It was another world – a world where you could wait more than twenty years for permission to travel a couple of kilometres.

For a moment, I wished I hadn't come. I wished I'd shopped Bramsden or stuck it out at St Andrews with the posh Yah girls who looked through me like water. What had I said to the West German Border guard? *I wanted to go somewhere different*. But that wasn't true. I'd wanted to go to Düsseldorf.

However, as the train creaked into Leipzig, my mood changed to one of anticipation. What would life be like behind the Iron Curtain? Would I like this city? Leipzig was a musical city, I'd read. A city of books and fashion. A spirited place.

The station was crowded, but I spotted the man who was to be my minder straight away. Heinz Hencke was holding up a sign with the words WELCOME TO THE GDR, HERR ROBERT MCPHERSON! written on it. When he saw me, he set it down and started to wave like a maniac.

"Welcome to Leipzisch!" he gushed in his lisping Saxon dialect as I approached.

He was short with a little paunch nestling above his trouser belt. He wore beige cords – Levi's – a patterned shirt and a grey jerkin. He looked exactly as I would have imagined an East German minder might, had I ever imagined such a thing – right down to his eyes, which receded alarmingly behind his thick glasses, and were flat and cold despite his smile.

He grasped my hand and pumped it. "Pleased to meet you. How was your journey? Good, I hope. Yes, yes. Wonderful! Well, this is our GDR." He gestured around him at the vast and dusty station concourse. "This is our little Republic. Tja, we hope you will like it here. We hope – "

"How did you know it was me?" I interrupted, only half joking.

CHAPTER NINE

Marek is sitting at a window table in a white vest top, drinking a beer. At the next table is a noisy group of students from the new intake, who keep looking over at him. His shoulder-length black hair and the gold stud in his right ear mean he stands out wherever he goes.

"So boring," he mouths, nodding in their direction. Then he stands to kiss you and says, "*Goldener Krug?*"

Something in his manner tells you he already knows your news. You nod. *The Goldener Krug* is a dingy bar run by a suicide blonde called Ute with a weakness for black velvet hair bows. It's two streets away and never full.

Out on the street, Marek says, "I met Dieter on the tram. He told me you didn't get a place."

"That's right. I didn't."

He sighs. "That's terrible. I can't believe it. But let's not talk about it now. We'll talk about it at *The Goldener Krug.*"

"Well, well, I haven't seen this young lady in a long while," says Ute when you appear in her cavernous dive. She stubs her cigarette out and comes round the bar to give you a hug. This is Marek's haunt really. You only ever come here with him. He can spend whole evenings propping up the bar and chewing the fat with Ute as her deadbeat customers drink themselves into oblivion.

"This calls for a celebration," Ute says. "I only have the *Blue Strangler*, but it's on the house."

Marek lights a cigarette as she measures out three shots of cheap vodka from the familiar bottle with the blue snowflake label. You slide on to the bar stool next to him and take one of his cigarettes.

"Cheers!" He knocks the harsh spirit back and slams his glass on the bar. "Two more, Ute, and a couple of beers as well. Let's find a quiet table," he says to you.

The back room is empty, apart from two middle-aged men absorbed in a game of draughts. You sit down at a table in the corner, and Ute brings your drinks.

"Such a handsome couple," she says, ruffling your hair. "It's so nice to see you again."

You haven't been here in a long while. Marek was in Berlin all summer. Even during term time he wasn't in Leipzig that much. In theory, he's researching a doctoral thesis on religious motifs in post-war Polish literature at Leipzig University. But since the emergence of Solidarity and the closure of the border with Poland in 1981, there isn't much he can write that will get past the censor. And so he writes nothing and hangs out at his place in Berlin and the huge apartment overlooking Clara Zetkin Park in Leipzig registered to him and his mother lies empty most of the time.

"So what the hell happened?" Marek asks, when Ute has gone back to the bar.

"I didn't get a place is what happened."

"But how can that be?" He's angry. You were afraid he'd be angry, and he is.

"I don't know. Hencke lied, I guess."

"Have you been careful? Did you do everything the way we agreed you should?"

"Of course."

He slams his fist on the table, and the draughts players glance over. "Shit! This ruins everything. Look, Magda, are you absolutely sure that you didn't give them any reason to doubt you? They're not actually stupid, you know, the morons who run this country."

"I know," you snap. "That's why I was fucking Hencke, remember?"

"Did you speak to him?"

"I went round to his place when I found out."

"And?"

"It didn't go well: *We don't get places on important study programmes through friendship and connections. We get them through hard work and application.* I lost my temper and ran out. I was naïve to trust him. I can see that now. There's no point in talking to him again. He was never going to deliver."

You could tell him about Hencke's offer to you. But you don't. You don't want to make him angrier than he already is. And you don't want to curry favour: look what I did for you. He did enough for you in the time after your brother's accident. That's why you refused Hencke's offer. He doesn't have to do more.

"Come here," he says at last. You slide round to his side of the table and he slings his arm round your shoulders. He squeezes you and says, "I'm sorry."

For a long time you sit in silence, embracing, then he says, "We'll find another way."

It's what you want to hear. He could go without you. You've always known that. If he applied to leave the authorities would grant him permission immediately. A troublemaker. A half-Polish Jew. They'd be glad to be rid of him. He makes them uncomfortable. Maybe he'd take his elderly mother with him. She has a tell-tale tattoo on her forearm. That makes them uncomfortable too. His sister is already in West Berlin. For you it's different. Your father's star may have fallen in recent years, but he still has enough influence to block an exit visa for his only daughter.

Marek lifts your face to him and kisses you on the lips. "We'll find another way," he repeats. "Let's go back to my place. We haven't been there in a long time."

It's a warm summer evening. You make love on a mat on the balcony overlooking Clara Zetkin Park. The sky above the park is inky black and speckled with stars. You can hear the shouted laughter of late-night strollers in the park on their way home as he teases you with his tongue. You come over and over again, clinging to him as he moves inside you. It's best with him. It's always been best with him.

CHAPTER TEN

Leizpig train station was built at the beginning of the nineteenth century by the Saxon and Prussian rail companies. It has twenty-six tracks, thirteen for the Prussians and thirteen for the Saxons. It was forbidden to bring Prussian trains into the Saxon part of the station and vice versa. Everything was duplicated: two reception halls, two staircases, two waiting rooms. The result is a façade 270 metres long and a station much too big for the city.

I looked these details up to tell Sally. She'd never been to Germany and knew nothing about it. I had to draw her a map showing where the border had been and another map showing the Wall that had encircled West Berlin and the corridor road out.

The writing exercise was long over, but we were still dwelling on *My Story*. Sometimes Sally twitched, remembered she was meant to be talking to me about my alcohol consumption and changed the subject. But we always came back to it, and I was happy with that, because Sally was listening to me with genuine interest.

She was shocked when I told her about crossing the border. She wanted to know how come the old couple hadn't been able to visit the woman's sister before. I explained about the travel ban, which meant no one who was economically active could travel to the West without special permission.

"But that's terrible!" she shrieked. People who've grown up with central heating, easy credit and aubergines in every supermarket don't understand that there was once a time when there were power cuts across Britain, plane tickets were beyond most people's reach and Prague wasn't a stag-party destination.

"Well, I suppose that was the whole reason behind the Wall," I said. "People were leaving the East in their droves. The state was at risk of collapse."

"Well, it should have collapsed then."

"But they were losing all their young people. Skilled workers were being lured away by capitalist bribes. Or that's how the authorities saw it."

"They were imprisoning their own people," Sally said. "That's just wrong."

"They could still travel to other socialist countries. There probably wasn't much difference between the average Brit going to Spain for a fortnight in the summer and the average East German going to, say, Bulgaria."

"Well, I think it's just ridiculous," she said, shutting the subject down. She was agitated, her cheeks flushed. "Did you have a drink last week?" she asked brightly.

"No."

"Good! Excellent!" She nodded encouragingly but she wasn't listening.

*

I first met Magda at the train station. I wasn't meant to meet her at all. I had four pairs of jeans for her but I was supposed to deliver them to Marek.

"Too dangerous," John Bull-Halifax said. "She's training to be an interpreter, so she's not allowed to have contact with westerners."

"That's fucked up."

"Maybe. But that's the way it is. I'm warning you: stay away."

"You're warning me?"

"She's had problems. Her brother had an accident. She went off the rails a bit after that, chucked in her studies. Her father's a big noise in the government. He got her back into university, but she really has to toe the line now. It might seem weird to you, but it's standard practice for interpreters to be forbidden contact with westerners."

"Is that right?" I said. "Sure you're not just trying to keep her to yourself ?"

We were at Bull-Halifax's flat in Edinburgh. He'd invited me round for a kind of pre-trip briefing. I had in my hand a framed black and white photograph of Magda that I'd picked up from the mantelpiece in his living room. It was a professional shot taken in three-quarters profile, unsmiling in the Komsomol style. High cheekbones. Shapely mouth. Wide slanting eyes gazing into the middle distance. A beauty.

"Quite sure. We're just friends. She speaks good Russian. That's how I know her. I met her on a cultural exchange in Moscow. That was before her brother's accident. We've always kept in touch."

"But she's not allowed contact with westerners."

He gave me one of his film star smiles. "Fellow traveller,

mate. And I understand the boundaries."

"So, how come you have her photo?"

I'd been out with John a few times since the research place was agreed, and if I'd learnt one thing about him it was this: people who said he had nothing to do with women were talking crap. Girls were drawn to him like flies to shit, and he lapped up the attention.

"She gave it to me. Memento of the trip."

"Why would she give you a photo of herself as a memento of a trip to Moscow? Wouldn't a postcard of Red Square have been more like it?"

"Look, Bob, do you want to do this or not? If you'd rather not take the jeans I can find another way. It's no problem."

"It's fine. I'll take them."

I put the photo back on the mantelpiece next to a portrait of Bull-Halifax's mother when she was young. She was beautiful too. This was his world. Everyone was glamorous. Nothing was ever a problem. He didn't need you. There was always another way. It was a far cry from the faded Polaroids of grimacing relatives that constituted the McPherson family album.

"Great," he said. "But remember what I said: no contact with westerners. It's really important."

I left his flat with the jeans, feeling, as I often did with Bull-Halifax, that I'd somehow been tricked. Then, the day before I was due to leave for Leipzig, he phoned me at my parents' house. Change of plan. Please could I wait for Magda in the Mitropa canteen in the train station at 22:00 on the second Saturday after I arrived?

"Will you recognise her?" he said.

"Eh, yeah," I said, thinking: *how could I forget?* "But what about the whole 'no contact with westerners' business?"

"I know. It's a bit weird. Not sure what's going on, to be honest."

*

I arrived at the station early and passed the time staring at the exotic destinations on the departure boards: Prague, Bucharest, Warsaw, Sofia. There had been no time to look around the night I arrived in Leipzig. Hencke had bustled me straight out of the station and into the back of his waiting orange Wartburg.

I saw at once why Magda had chosen the Mitropa for the handover. It was chaotic and noisy and stank of fags, fried food and spilt beer. Most of the customers looked like they'd been there all night drinking beer and had no intention of ever taking a train. It was the perfect place to feel anonymous. I found a table near the back and ordered a coffee, which tasted like mud.

I recognised Magda as soon as she pushed through the swing doors. She was wearing a long black velvet coat and a little purple hat and she had a large canvas bag slung over her shoulder. I wasn't the only person who turned to look. She was even more beautiful than in her photograph (and her photograph had been quite beautiful enough). She scanned the room, caught my eye and weaved through the tables towards me. "Bob?" she asked.

I jumped up and extended my hand. "Yes."

She reached up and kissed me on the cheek. Being a Lanarkshire boy, I was a little taken aback by this public display of affection. It was all I could do to stop myself from touching my cheek in awe.

"Thank you very much for coming," she said. "I'm glad

I spotted you straight away."

She sat down and shrugged off her coat. It was the middle of October and the weather had abruptly turned cold, but she was wearing a sleeveless green dress – a lovely sleeveless green dress that showed off her shapely arms. She took her hat off and ran a hand through her dark, springy hair.

"Would you like a beer?" I asked.

She nodded. "Yes please."

I signalled to the waiter, who grunted in reply. "I have the parcel," I mouthed.

"Wonderful," she beamed. "Thank you very much. I hope it wasn't any trouble. You need Deutschmarks to buy Levi's here and for that you need relatives in the West and unfortunately I don't have any."

"It was no trouble," I said, thinking *I'd go to quite a bit of trouble for you.*

The waiter arrived and thumped our beers down. "One Mark twenty," he growled, and I searched for the right change.

Magda rolled her eyes after him. "So, how do you like our GDR?" she asked.

"I haven't really been here long enough to say. So far, it's been … interesting."

She laughed. "You're a diplomat." She raised her glass." Here's to diplomacy." We clinked glasses. "Have you met Hencke?" she asked. "He usually takes charge of students from capitalist countries."

"He collected me from the station," I said, trying and failing to recognise my homeland of Scotland in the term 'capitalist country'.

"Isn't he a creep?"

She was easy to talk to. She asked a lot of questions and listened to my replies, her head cocked to one side. Were there really three million unemployed in Great Britain? Had I ever been to Karl Marx's grave in Highgate Cemetery? What did I think of Mikhail Gorbachev? Then she said, "Would you like to come to a party?"

"I'd love to, but –"

"But what?"

"Well, John Bull-Halifax said – "

"No western contacts?" She laughed, and there was something thrillingly dismissive in her tone.

"Well, yes," I said. Could it be that she thought John Bull-Halifax was a bit of plonker?

"This is a private party. Just some old friends of mine. I think everything will be fine." She stood up and put her coat on. I handed her the parcel, and she slipped it in her bag. "Shall we go?" she said.

CHAPTER ELEVEN

You take the tram from the train station to the Südvorstadt area of town where the party is. It's raining, and the westerner suggests taking a taxi.

"I'll pay," he says.

"Taxis here go where they want, not where you want," you laugh, guiding him over to the tram stop. The only way a taxi driver will take you to the Südvorstadt is if the westerner bribes him with Deutschmarks, and you don't want to suggest that.

You jump into the last car of the tram and steer the westerner to the back window. Standing side-by-side, you watch the train station recede into the wet night.

"Leipzig train station is the largest train terminus in Europe," you tell him.

"Really?"

"Yes." Despite it all, you want him to like it here, to be a little bit impressed. You know what westerners are like. How they laugh at the World Clock on the Alexanderplatz in Berlin that spins round showing the time in all the places of the world that GDR citizens cannot visit. How they mock the so-called workers' palaces built in the 1950s on the great boulevards in Friedrichshain. It pains you, because you know how much effort and commitment went into clearing the rubble after the war to make room for those homes. Your father gave over one hundred hours to the National Rebuilding Campaign and has a pin and gold certificate to prove it. The workers' palaces may be stuffed full of apparatchiks now but they were built with hope.

The tram rounds the corner on to the ring road, and water sprays up from the tracks, tinged red from the tram's tail lights.

"It's going to be cold again tomorrow," you say, and your breath condenses on the air. "My aunt said so."

"Brr," he says with an ostentatious shiver. "I can't believe how cold it is here. You'll be all right in that coat though." He reaches over and strokes your sleeve – the first time he's touched you.

You pull the collar up round your throat. "It's fur-lined." You bend the sleeve back to show him. "From Russia. It was my mother's. My father brought it back from Moscow for her as an engagement present."

"Did he live there?"

"Not at that time. He lived there during the war." You smile at him. "Then he came back to build a new and better Germany. He's older than my mother. By the time they got together in the 60s he was travelling regularly to Moscow on government business. Hence the coat."

"Does he still go to Moscow a lot?"

"No. He has a different position these days."

"I'd love to go there," he says. "How did you find it when you were there on the cultural exchange?"

You stare at him, startled for a moment that he knows

81

this. Then you remember: John Bull-Halifax. Westerners have no sense of discretion. Should you tell him the truth about Moscow or lie? You decide on the truth. "I hated it."

"Oh." His face falls. "Why?"

"It was so run-down, and the food was terrible. The standard of living was much worse than here."

The tram pulls up the incline to Karl Marx Platz, which older people still call by its former name of Augustusplatz, and judders to a halt. Concert goers are streaming out of the concert hall, programmes in hand.

"Look at them," you giggle. "Don't they look bourgeois?"

He smiles. "I suppose so."

"There was once a beautiful church on this square. Over there." You point to the floodlit bronze relief of Marx that takes up an entire wall of the university building on the far side of the square. "It was called the University Church. The authorities blew it up. It was damaged in the war, but it could have been repaired. There was a big protest, but it was no use. "They still blew it up. Bang!" You raise your voice, suddenly wanting people to hear. The westerner is causing the frustrations of the past weeks to well up inside you.

People at the front of the car turn to stare, and the westerner looks embarrassed. "Sorry," you smile, fumbling in your bag for cigarettes. "Want one? It'll warm you up."

You light it for him, and he takes a deep drag, spluttering on the smoke.

"How do you like our shitty cigarettes?"

"They're okay," he croaks.

"No, they're not." You look down the tram at the sea of expressionless faces, and they infuriate you. Why do these people allow themselves to be terrorised? Why do they keep turning out for May Day demonstrations and sham elections?

Why do they tolerate sub-standard cigarettes? Why don't they rise up?

"They're shit!" you yell, and you're no longer talking about the cigarettes.

The westerner pulls you towards him. "Hey, take it easy," he says.

You look into his eyes. Green with hazel flecks. Kind. Concerned. "I tried Camel cigarettes once," you say, leaning into him. "I liked those."

He touches your cheek with the index finger of one hand. "Did you? I'll remember that."

You pull away from him. "This is our stop."

"So, what's the party in aid of?" the westerner asks as you walk towards an underground club called *The Sharp Corner* where they play banned music.

"It's my friend Torsten's thirtieth birthday."

It's over a year since you last saw Torsten. You had to cut yourself off from that crowd when you started playing your part. Some people may be surprised to see you. They may even be angry with you. They might think your role was real. But Torsten invited you to the party. That shows something.

At *The Sharp Corner*, you mutter the password through a grille in the door.

"Sweet Magdalena!" a man's voice cries. The doorman is Gert, one of Marek's neighbours in Berlin. He yanks open the door, and his big mangled face breaks into a grin as he envelops you in a bear hug.

"It's been ages," he says when he releases you. "It's good to see you."

"It's good to see you too."

And it is. This posse of dissident writers, artists and environmental activists became your family after your brother's accident. With them you found a sense of belonging and common purpose you thought you'd lost forever when you left the Party.

You follow Gert into the vestibule, which is warmed by a gas heater, and introduce the westerner.

"Pleased to meet you," Gert says. "Marek is inside. He's waiting for you."

"Is he? I'll look out for him." Gert raises a questioning eyebrow in the direction of the westerner. "We'll chat later," you say. But this is a lie. You don't want to talk to Gert about the westerner. The new plan you and Marek have devised and the role the westerner will play in it must remain under wraps.

"Let's find Torsten." You take the westerner's hand and lead him through a green velvet curtain into the dark club room, which is thumping to the strains of a new punk band from Dresden called *Decadence*.

Torsten is standing by the back wall, smoking and chatting to Kerstin, whose black hair is freshly cut in a fashionable bob.

"This is Bob," you tell her. "He's from Great Britain."

"Is he now?" she says and curtsies. *"Enchantée."*

You watch the westerner take in her low-cut top, trademark Kohl-ringed eyes and full lips, painted Soviet red. Is this how he expected things to be in the East?

You give Torsten his birthday present. It's a framed print of the photograph Frau Dannewitz admired at Shakespeare Street.

"Thank you," he says. "You've got such a good eye, Magda. When are you going to take some more photographs for the magazine? We miss your contributions."

Torsten is the editor of an underground magazine called *Not Only But Also*. "Soon," you say. "Very soon."

"You know I'm opening a new gallery, don't you? I'd love to

put on an exhibition of your work."

"I didn't know that."

"Yes, it got to be too much having exhibitions at home." Torsten has been running an underground art gallery from his apartment for the past three years. "We found an old disused warehouse over by the cemetery on Lippendorfer Street. Bit like this place. Maybe they'll move in and stop us. I don't know. But we're going to give it a go."

"That's great," you say but you're no longer concentrating, because behind you Marek is shouting at the westerner over the music.

"Well, well, well," he booms, "what have we here?" And you feel the westerner bridle.

"I'd better rescue my friend," you tell Torsten, who gives your arm an understanding squeeze.

"Don't forget to send in some photographs," he says. "The next issue is out in January."

"I won't." You turn away. "I see you've already met," you say to Marek.

"Oh yes," he smirks.

You grab the westerner's hand. "Let's dance."

"Just a moment." Marek pulls you to one side. "He'll do just fine," he whispers in your ear.

Later, when the music slows down, the westerner pulls you into his arms on the dance floor. You feel his hands on your back, pressing you close.

"I know somewhere we can go," you say, slipping your hand in his.

It's a risk taking him to Shakespeare Street, but you reckon it's worth it. If your plan is to work he has to trust you. In the back courts at Körner Street he stumbles and falls against you. He's had too much to drink. You steady him, and he pulls you close and bends to kiss you. "Not here," you say.

He nuzzles your neck. "But I want you." His breath is hot. He's hard against you. Everything is going to plan. You feel relief. And an unexpected stab of desire.

You take his hand and lead him up the stairs to your hideaway.

"This is a cool place," he says.

"There's something I have to tell you about it."

"Fire away."

"Nobody knows about this place," you say, going round the room lighting candles. "You mustn't ever tell anyone you've been here.

"Wow," he says. "Okay."

"It's important."

"I understand."

"Do you?"

"Of course." He fixes you with his green eyes. "But why is it such a secret?"

"We just don't want anyone to come here. We don't want people to know we use this place. Above all, you must never tell Hencke that you've been here."

"I won't," he says. "You can trust me."

Trust. It's an easy word for westerners to say. To you it means something more.

You sit down beside him on the divan. He reaches across and touches your face.

"Magda," he says, and you feel his hand caressing your thigh under your skirt. When you don't push it away, his fingers creep up your leg and hook round your pants. You look into his green eyes as he pushes you on to the divan and kisses you. His tongue is in your mouth and his hands are on your back, pulling at the zip of your dress. You squeeze his thickening cock and think: *our plan is working.*

A moment later, you're naked beneath him on the divan. He kneads your breasts and sucks each of your nipples in turn, breathing hard.

"Fuck, you're beautiful," he says, sitting back and running his fingers over your stomach. He begins to massage your clitoris. And you feel it again. That pulse of desire that is more than mechanical. He presses down on top of you and holds you tight. Then he's inside you. You move with him, digging your fingers into his strong, pale back. You gasp, and it's not pretend.

What did you think? Did you think it would be like fucking Hencke? Well, it's not. You remember then what Marek whispered to you before you left *The Sharp Corner: Don't fall in love with him now, will you?*

CHAPTER TWELVE

My therapist, Sally, was fascinated by Magda. Women aren't really interested in men. What they're really interested in is other women.

"Magda sounds amazing," she gushed. "Was she really so beautiful?"

"Incredibly beautiful," I said, warming to my subject. "She had this ... special quality. I don't know. It was like she shone or something. And in Leipzig at that time, surrounded by brown coal pits and chemical plants, I suppose she seemed quite exceptional."

Sally nodded dreamily. "I don't think she just seemed exceptional. I think she was exceptional."

I shifted on my orange plastic bucket chair, basking in Magda's reflected glory.

"Have you got any photos of her?" Sally asked.

This was strictly out of bounds, and she knew it. However, I'd anticipated it. I whipped out the photos.

"Oh, I don't want to see them," she said. "I just, you know, wondered."

"Go on. Have a look. I don't mind."

She grabbed them from me. "Wow!" she gasped, impressed as I'd hoped she would be.

"Who's the guy?" Sally asked, looking at a photo with Marek in it. He'd come up behind us one afternoon when I was taking some snaps of Magda near the Thomas Church. He said exactly what he'd said to me the first time I met him at *The Sharp Corner*: "Well, well, well, what have we here?"

"That's Marek," I said.

"They make a handsome couple."

"Yes," I replied stiffly. "Except of course they weren't a couple."

"Of course not," Sally said. We'd already excavated my past enough for her to know that she'd blundered. "I just mean … well, I think they both look very nice."

She handed the photos back, all brisk and professional. I expected her to change the subject, but she didn't.

"Do you want to talk about it?" she asked.

"About what?"

"Marek. He's the key, isn't he?"

She smiled. *She's a sharp one,* I thought.

∗

I never liked Marek: let me be clear about that. That only made it worse, of course, when the end came. If you like someone and they die, it's easy. They're alive; you like them. They're dead; you're sorry. If you don't like them, it's more complicated.

There were many reasons for my antipathy. Marek was smug, conceited, snide, bitchy and deceitful. He was also charming, good-looking, insightful and far cleverer than I would ever be. But mainly I didn't like him because he was always there, lurking in the background – and sometimes, it seemed, cavorting in the foreground.

I wasn't the only person who disliked him. He had many enemies. I've never known someone to have quite so many enemies and to care so little. In that paranoid little state, he had one rare quality that inspired both admiration and envy: he appeared to be free. He didn't kowtow to anyone; he didn't care what anybody thought. It was a dangerous way to be, but he somehow got away with it.

I was warned about him countless times. Watch out for that one. He's a slippery fish. Everyone had an opinion on him, an incredible story, a damning titbit.

When I first met him, I asked Dieter, a student on the 'Aspects of political and social life in Britain' discussion class I taught on Friday afternoons, about him. I often went drinking with Dieter after class in the Moritzbastei, a student club in an historic cellar near the University Tower. We were the same age, Dieter being older than the earnest girls in the class because of his four years' military service, and we shared a love of beer. He had taken it upon himself to guide me through the idiosyncrasies of life in East Germany.

"Trust me, in this shithole you need an insider to show you the ropes."

He hated the GDR and loved all things American. It was a miracle he kept his university place. Regime critics like him often found themselves inexplicably unable to continue their studies. After a couple of beers, he'd always ask me the same question: "What the fuck are you doing here, man? You could live in England and be free."

"Scotland," I'd say.

"Scotland, England, whatever. Give me a train ticket out of here, man? I'd grab it like a shot. Choo-choo!"

He rolled his eyes when I mentioned Marek. "Oh, this one.

No one knows how he manages it. Look at the clothes he wears: all things from the West. Where does he get the money? Trust me, one day we'll see him driving round the Ring in a Porsche, and no one will be surprised. You wanna hear my advice regarding Dembowksi? I'll tell ya: there's something about that guy that doesn't add up. I'd stay away from him."

But I couldn't stay away from him. He was part of Magda's life.

The whole time I was in Leipzig, I only spent any time alone with him once. He came round one morning to the apartment on 18th October Street that I shared with an English teacher called Kevin.

I was still in bed when the doorbell rang. Kevin was in, but I knew he wouldn't get it. I'd come home the night before to find him shagging Gaby, another student from my 'Aspects of political and social life in Britain' discussion class, on the sofa. Kevin's main motivation for being in Leipzig was to get laid. Being from the West afforded a person a certain cachet, even a person as unprepossessing as Kevin, a podgy Londoner with an obsessive love of Tottenham Hotspur FC and a fondness for phrases such as 'bloody Nora'. Kevin was working his way through his female students – and mine too, it seemed. I grabbed a towel, wrapped it round me and headed for the door.

Marek was on the landing, smoking a Kent cigarette, his signature brand. He was wearing a light leather coat and a pair of Rayban sunglasses although it was the middle of December and bitterly cold.

"Hi," he said, barging past me into the flat.

We hadn't made an arrangement for him to come round – I hadn't even told him where I lived – but he acted like we had. He marched into the living room, humming 'Addicted to Love' by Robert Palmer, and I trailed after him, uncertain what to do.

"So?" he said, settling on the sofa and flicking his ash into the ashtray.

"Eh…?" I said.

"We should probably go into town to complete our little piece of business. Change money," he mouthed.

I stared at him. I'd told Magda I was running short of cash, but I hadn't said anything about wanting to change money.

"Ah, I didn't actually – "

"It's better if we talk about it in town," he interrupted, putting a finger to his lips. "Can't be too careful."

"I'm, eh, not dressed."

"I can wait a few minutes."

"That's magnanimous."

If he detected any sarcasm, he didn't show it. Instead, he picked up the latest chapter of my thesis entitled 'Heine and the Impetus towards Socialism' from the coffee table and started to flick through it. Seeing no alternative, I went to my room and got dressed. When I came back, he was smiling.

"Now, listen to this," he said and read me the lines about the Prussian border guards I'd quoted from *Germany, A Winter's Tale:*

And still they strut about as stiff,
As straight and thin as a candle,
As if they'd swallowed the corporal's stick
Old Fritz knew how to handle.

The stick has never quite been lost,
Although its use has been banned.
Inside the glove of newer ways
There's still the old iron hand.

"But isn't it a little fanciful to suggest that those words somehow tie Heine to a socialist agenda? I mean, if he went to the border today he might very well think the 'old iron hand' was still there."

"Yes," I said, "I'm covering that. That's kind of my point actually."

"But you don't say anything about it here."

"I haven't got to that bit yet."

"I see." He put the chapter down on the coffee table. Then he caught sight of the title page and picked it up. *'Tripping the Light Fantastic: Political Virtuosity in the Works of Heinrich Heine.* Is that your title?"

Bramsden had said the same thing in exactly the same incredulous tone of voice.

"Yes," I snarled.

"Interesting." He let the page drop on to the coffee table. "Shall we go?"

The heating in the building on 18th October Street was controlled centrally, and my apartment was suffocatingly warm. The freezing air hit me like a punch. I pulled my sheepskin hat down and huddled inside my coat, but Marek didn't seem to feel the cold. He had no gloves or hat. We went to an expensive little bar in the Mädler Arcade, which also sold ice cream and disappointing cakes made with synthetic cream. Without asking me what I wanted, and although it was just after ten, Marek ordered a beer and schnapps for us both.

"Your very good health," he said, knocking his shot back. Wearily, I did the same.

He picked up his beer and led me to a booth at the back. "So," he said, lowering his voice, "I can change money for you. It's not a problem. I know some Polish people here who want Deutschmarks. How much do you want to change?"

The deal – a deal that I hadn't asked for but that was certainly going to help to tide me over – was done in a matter of seconds. He offered me an excellent rate. There was no reason to say no.

"You should come up to Berlin sometime," he said as we finished our beers. "You know I have a place there? It's bang in the middle of Prenzlauer Berg, where all the action is. I know how you westerners like to romanticise our little underground scene. We'll show you round. Berlin is a great city, even today."

We'll show you round. I knew what that meant and I didn't like it. That meant him and Magda. Magda and him.

Five days later, I met him on a park bench by the lake in Clara Zetkin Park. I gave him my Deutschmarks, and he handed me an envelope stuffed with East Marks.

"Count them," he said, and I did.

Everything was in order. It was a good deal. I should have been pleased.

CHAPTER THIRTEEN

One Friday shortly after New Year, you take the train to Berlin with Kerstin. She has an interview at the Pergamon Museum for a temporary position as a researcher. You tell everyone you're going to the launch party for the latest issue of *Not Only But Also*, which features some photographs you took in November of the area around Shakespeare Street. You are going to the party, but that's not all.

It's cold on the train. You and Kerstin sit in the dining car wrapped up in your coats, drinking endless cups of coffee and smoking cigarettes.

"I can't believe Marek invited your British friend to the party," Kerstin says.

"I can't believe he accepted the invitation."

She smiles and stubs out her cigarette. "He probably wants to keep an eye on you."

"Maybe. I think he would've suggested coming up tonight, which wouldn't have been great given the other business, but he has that class he teaches."

The other business is meeting Uncle Ivan, who is going to help you with your new plan.

"Ah yes. Gaby says you should hear the questions Jana asks. Apparently, your British friend's not used to discussing dialectical materialism. So, when is he coming up?"

"Saturday evening. Marek has given him keys to the apartment so he can drop off his bag there and join us at the party."

"Really? That's a first."

"I know. Perhaps Marek thinks it doesn't matter because he's from the West." Few people make it over the threshold of Marek's apartment on Pflaster Street. It's stuffed full of appliances and furniture from West Germany, procured by Uncle Ivan, and Marek keeps all his personal things there, including books and pictures, which reveal personal tastes not exactly forbidden in the Workers' and Farmers' State but not encouraged either. Just as Shakespeare Street is your sanctuary, Pflaster Street is his. It says things about him.

"Or perhaps he thinks a visit to Pflaster Street will throw him off the scent. About you two, I mean."

"I don't think he suspects anything. He's too, you know, straightforward."

"He doesn't like Marek."

"I know. But lots of people don't like him. I don't think he dislikes him for any particular reason."

"How long are you going to keep this up?" she asks, and there's an unfamiliar edge in her voice.

You take a cigarette from the packet on the table and light it. "As long as it takes. We need some cover. He can give us that."

"It's a dangerous game."

"Do you think it's wrong?"

She sighs. "I can see that you need a decoy. But you know,

Magda, you don't have to leave. You could stay. Plenty of people manage to make a life for themselves here."

You glance over at her. You understand what she means. You've thought about it too. Couldn't you take the well-trodden German path of internal emigration? Get a hut in the country like the one her parents have. Spend weekends there with a few trusted friends. Grill sausages and drink beer. Live only in the private sphere and find a simple kind of happiness.

"I can't," you say. "After Jürgen's accident, I lost the ability to think like that. I can't do it. "

She nods. "Okay. Fair enough. I'll miss you, that's all."

"I'll miss you too, but – "

"I know." She waves a dismissive hand. It's too painful to talk about. The train is pulling into the station in Berlin. "Do you want me to come with you to your mother's?" she asks.

"If you don't mind."

"I have time. My interview's not until 15:00."

Your mother takes a long time to answer the buzzer for the two-room apartment she's lived in since your father divorced her. It's not one of her better days.

"Ach, Magda," she says. "I thought you would be here sooner."

"How could we have been here sooner? I told you we were getting the 09:30 train."

"Did you? I don't remember. Would you like some coffee, Kerstin?"

Kerstin smiles. "Yes, please, Frau Reinsch."

Your mother shuffles through to the kitchen. "Don't get angry," Kerstin says to you in an undertone.

You sit down on the sofa. On the bookshelf is a photograph

of your mother playing the cello, taken at a concert to mark German-Soviet Friendship Day in 1976. It's like looking at a photograph of a completely different woman. You remember the woman in the photograph with the glossy blonde page boy from your childhood. She used to come into your bedroom smelling of hairspray and *Queen of the Night* perfume to leave a *Bambino* chocolate on your pillow after she'd played a concert. You liked her.

Your mother returns from the kitchen with coffee and slightly stale poppy seed cake. "So, how have you been, Frau Reinsch?" Kerstin asks.

Your mother likes Kerstin and so she makes an effort. "Oh, not too bad, dear. You know, the usual."

If you were here on your own, she'd say: *I have terrible pains in my leg.* Or: *I've been so dizzy lately. I don't know what's wrong with me.*

If it had been Jürgen's accident that made her like this, you could understand it. But it wasn't. It happened before that. Your father had her kicked out of the Berlin Symphony Orchestra after he found out about her affair with the second violinist, and that's what broke her. It's not fair to think she loved playing the cello more than she loved her children, but sometimes you do think that. But you know too that the cello wasn't just her profession and her purpose. It was where she went when the frustrations of living in this country got to be too much. Your father took that away from her. For that you'll never forgive him. There are no unemployed in the German Democratic Republic. Instead, there are people like your mother who have nowhere left to go.

You drink your coffee, while Kerstin chats to your mother about her studies. After three quarters of an hour, you can stand it no longer. "We have to go, Mama. Kerstin has an appointment."

"So soon?"

"I don't need – " Kerstin begins.

"We have to go," you interrupt, slamming down your cup on the coffee table.

*

The following morning, you and Marek meet Uncle Ivan by the Soviet War Memorial in Treptow Park. Uncle Ivan beams and hugs you, but briefly – he doesn't want to attract attention. You run through the details as quickly as possible, walking while you talk.

"Hungary is the best route," says Uncle Ivan. "It's not so tightly controlled."

"The idea is that we travel together to Budapest in the normal way," says Marek. "It's going to take a bit of time to organise everything, but we should be able to leave by the summer holidays."

"We often go to Hungary then anyway."

"Exactly. So the trip shouldn't arouse any suspicion."

"The Austrian couple will be in Budapest too, staying at a hotel," says Uncle Ivan. "My contact will collect the passports from them and leave them in a luggage locker at the train station along with some western clothes and your tickets to Vienna."

"We basically then meet up with Ivan's contact, get the key off him, collect the passports and so on, get changed and get on the train," says Marek.

"Once you're safely in the West, the couple will report their passports stolen," says Uncle Ivan.

"Won't the border guards know the passports aren't ours?" you ask. "It'll be hard to find a couple that looks just like us."

"I know someone who can fix that," says Uncle Ivan. "Which is why I need you to bring passport-sized photographs of yourselves to Budapest. Get a haircut beforehand so you look a little different than normal."

"Goodness," you say.

"Don't look so worried," says Uncle Ivan. "My contact in Budapest has done this many times. With him on board, our plan is foolproof."

"Thank you," you say. You know this must be costing Uncle Ivan a fortune. And it's because of you that it has to be this way, not because of Marek.

"You're welcome," he says. "And guess what? I have some exciting news. Even Marek doesn't know this yet. I've already found a couple in Vienna who are interested in helping."

After the meeting, you and Marek head to *Café North* to celebrate. You order a bottle of sparkling wine and laugh as you clink glasses. It's finally happening. You're getting out. When people ask what you're celebrating, you say it's a secret and laugh harder.

"Uncle Ivan has been good to me," says Marek. "He's not even my uncle. He's my mother's cousin. Or second cousin. I'm not even sure."

"He wants to help," you say. And it's true. He does. He's driven by an ideological zeal you don't entirely share. But beggars can't be choosers.

Soon Torsten and the others arrive for the launch party of *Not Only But Also*. The lights are dimmed and the music starts. After a time, a jazz singer in a long blue dress comes on and starts to sing *Mack the Knife*, one of your favourite songs. You grab Marek's hand and pull him on to the dance floor.

Just a jack-knife has Macheath, dear, she sings as Marek bends to kiss you. *And he keeps it out of sight.*

And just then you spot the westerner standing at the bar watching you.

CHAPTER FOURTEEN

Sally and I came to an abrupt end the week after the session when I showed her the photos of Magda. There was an incident. I'd rather not talk about it. It's embarrassing, painful. Well, you can probably guess. I made a pass at her. It was a stupid, stupid, stupid thing to do. But I do get lonely. I know everyone does, but I really have no one now. My friends have disappeared. Chris stuck it out the longest, but I haven't heard from him in ages. My ex, Annabel, used to text from time to time, but that all stopped when she met a new man. How am I supposed to meet a new woman? Believe me: chatting up women stone-cold sober is not easy.

My main social contact these days is the occasional phone lecture from my sister. Have you done this? Have you done that? Why not? And my mum still rings every week. We don't talk about my situation.

"How are you, son?" she says, and before I can reply she's on to the weather. "Oh, it's been terrible. The rain has been torrential. What's it like down there?"

Now that I'm officially in recovery, I'm supposed to pick up because not picking up is a kind of lying; it's pretending you're not there when you are, in fact, there. But I hardly ever do. There's a note of brave disappointment in my mum's voice that I can't stand.

I do think Sally over-reacted. There was no need to stop the sessions. I apologised straight away. But she got all take-no-prisoners with me. *You've broken the bond of trust, Mr McPherson,* she said. In the space of a nanosecond, I'd stopped being Robert and started being Mr McPherson. I'll never forget the look on her face. All the kindness was gone. Her counsellor mask had slipped. She actually looked quite hard. She got up, pulled her blouse down and marched out of the room without another word.

I didn't know what to do. Whether to stay or go home. In the end, I sat down on the orange plastic bucket chair and just waited, though I didn't know what I was waiting for. Sally had left everything in the room: her coat, handbag, case notes. Maybe that's why I waited. Part of me thought she'd come back, and we'd laugh it off. After a minute or two, I couldn't resist. I bent down, opened her handbag and looked inside. It was a mess: sweet wrappers, loose make-up, coins, scrunched-up tissues. But the smell of it was wonderful. It smelt of a woman, of all the mysterious, intimate things that women do. I was about to take her make-up bag out to inhale the scent when Phil, the other counsellor, came in.

"Put that down at once!" he yelled.

He's gay. I have no problem with that, but he does tend towards the melodramatic.

"All right," I said. "Keep your hair on." Then I had a brilliant idea. "I thought I heard Sally's pager."

"Hmm," he minced.

He took me to another room, and we had a 'chat'. He didn't pull his punches. Strange how they understand about your having a drink problem at places like the South Islington Alcohol Advisory Service. They don't judge. You're a person too. But any sign of a sex drive and they're down on you like a ton of bricks.

"Ms Cormack is quite upset at the moment," he said. Just as I was now Mr McPherson, Sally was now Ms Cormack. "I'm sure you'll understand that we can't at this moment in time make any decision as to how your treatment might proceed.

"For now you should go home. Phone us in a week or so. We should be in a position by then to advise you if your sessions here can continue, and if so, under what conditions." He brought his hands into prayer position. "Please allow me to assure you that we'll make every effort to accommodate you despite today's unfortunate incident."

Unfortunate incident. I wondered what Phil did for kicks.

On my way home, I came within a millimetre of buying a bottle. In the local shop I stared at the whisky shelf for so long that Murat, the shopkeeper, started chatting to me about the different brands.

"My father-in-law likes *Glenfiddich*," he said. "Buy him a bottle and you'll be in his good books for weeks. But me, I prefer *The Macallan*. It's smoother."

They had a good selection: a couple of island malts and a few Speysides, the usual blends and then the rubbish stuff. When I was drinking regularly I used to take the Low Flyer. No point in buying single malts when you're knocking it back the way I was.

The words "A bottle of *Grouse*, please" were forming in my mouth when I caught myself on. "A bottle of sparkling mineral, please," I said to Murat.

"Water's in the fridge, mate," he said, looking confused.

When I got home, I made a decision: no more Leipzig. It was delving into all that old stuff that had got me into trouble. In future, I was going to look forward, and if I were allowed back to the South Islington Alcohol Advisory Service, I was going to talk about my addiction to alcohol and nothing else. Christ, I'd a good mind to file a complaint against Sally. She was the one who'd broken the rules and taken us off-piste.

But, of course, it was too late. I'd opened my Pandora's box, and there was no shutting it again.

CHAPTER FIFTEEN

You sip your second glass of sweet Russian Champagne and stare out of the concert hall's tinted windows at the Neptune Fountain, which has been turned off to save water. Snowflakes drift down on to the people trudging across Karl Marx Platz. Where are they going? What are they thinking? What will they do when they get home? Do they sometimes scream with frustration, as you do, or is everything okay for them? Or are they happy simply to eat sausages, drink beer and watch West TV? Millions are Party members if official statistics are to be believed, one in four a Stasi informer if the rumours are true. Ninety-eight per cent voted 'Yes!' to the Socialist Unity Party candidates at the last elections, according to the newspapers.

The foyer of the famous Gewandhaus concert hall is filling up for this special concert to mark the anniversary of the February revolution. A new work is to be played by a composer from Jena: three pieces for viola entitled *February*. But you're not here for the music; you're here to be seen.

You wander over to the buffet and take a meat paste canapé.

You know that Jana is behind you, dressed in a floor-length skirt and a frilly yellow blouse that emphasise her plainness, talking earnestly to a female friend: a dialectical discussion of great import, judging by what you caught of it earlier.

Jana thinks she's very clever. Her surprise when she bumped into you in the foyer earlier was quite convincing. "Magda, how nice to see you! And what a surprise! I thought you were away."

You watched her take in your clothes: the miniskirt made from Aunt Vladka's old velvet curtains, the boots you bought from the West German girl, the black chiffon blouse purchased last year in a department store in Budapest.

"I was away."

"Berlin?" she asks. You shake your head and smile. You were in Brandenburg at the rehabilitation centre, visiting Jürgen. Is Jana obvious enough to say: "Where were you then?" Not quite. But you're pretty sure she's here because you're here. She's no longer simply the class snoop. Someone, you don't know who, Frau Aner maybe, or Hencke, has given her the special task of watching you. There's been a change since your showdown with Hencke. Well, that's fine by you.

As you turn away from her, you catch sight of the westerner striding across Karl Marx Platz towards the concert hall, dressed in the Russian army greatcoat and sheepskin hat with ear flaps he bought in Konsum. He blends in better now, but you can still tell he's a westerner at a hundred paces. He glances up at the vast ceiling fresco that dominates the concert hall's interior, then spots you and waves. You run over and fling your arms round him. "Hello!" you pipe.

He flushes with pleasure, squeezes you to him and kisses you on the mouth. "Hello there you," he says.

He's pleased to see you. Well, you're pleased to see him too. You slip your arm through his and guide him over to the buffet, where he chooses some canapés and accepts a glass of Russian fizz. You can feel Jana's eyes on you. You imagine her writing it all down later. *Unauthorised contact with capitalist elements.*

After the concert, a cacophony that is booed by some members of the audience, there is the problem of how to get to Shakespeare Street. You want Jana to know about the westerner, but you don't want her to know about Shakespeare Street.

"I'm going to take you back a different way tonight," you tell the westerner.

"Why?"

"I think Jana's watching us," you whisper.

He glances round with the supreme nonchalance of someone who doesn't know what it is to be watched.

"She was staring right at us," he says. "If she is watching us, she's got all the finesse of a rhinoceros."

"Let's just go," you say. "If she follows us, you get off at 18th October Street. I'll get off at Taro Street and meet you on the path by the railway tracks half an hour later."

Sure enough, Jana and her friend are on the tram, and so the westerner gets off at 18th October Street. You travel on with them to Taro Street, where you and Jana get off. Her friend lives near the end of the line in Lößnig and stays on.

"You should be careful," Jana says, as you walk together towards the hall of residence. "Western contacts are not desired for interpreters."

"I just bumped into him. I didn't want to be rude." You reckon this obvious lie will give her more ammunition than the truth ever could.

"Hmm." She purses her lips. "All the same."

On the second floor, where your shared room is, you wish her good night. "I'm going to have a night cap in the bar upstairs. Would you like to join me?"

"No, thank you. I need to get to bed."

You take the stairs to the top floor, where the late-night student bar is, but don't go in. You wait on the landing and watch the street. Sure enough, Jana appears a couple of minutes later. There's still time to take a tram to the station and catch a train back to her parents' house in the suburbs.

The westerner is waiting for you by the railway tracks. You take his hand and lead him into a little-used tunnel, half concealed by bushes. It's dark and stinks of piss, but it takes you through to Shakespeare Street.

"How did you find this?" he asks.

"I use it all the time. It connects my two worlds."

"Does it now?" he says, and there's an edge in his voice. He's never said anything about what he saw at *Café North*, and later, back at Marek's apartment, you did things for him that made him forget all about it. But every now and then, he makes a cryptic remark that lets you know he's not stupid.

Perhaps because what you said about the tunnel reminded him of *Café North*, the westerner is fierce that night. His pale, freckled face is a mask as he steers you from the cold hallway at Shakespeare Street into the main room, which is warmed by the tiled stove. He tips you on to the divan and pushes up your skirt. His hands are all over you, pressing, pinching, probing, and his mouth bruises your lips.

"You're beautiful," he mumbles, turning you over on to your stomach. He parts your legs with his knee and grabs your waist. He's on fire. And so are you. You lift your hips towards him, pushing back against him as he moves inside you. Losing yourself. Melting into him.

Afterwards, you pull away from him and light a cigarette. He strokes your arm and lights one too. You want to push him away. You're frightened now. When did you last feel this way? When you were first with Marek? That was so special. But lately, it's been different. Sometimes you have the kinds of boring arguments any couple might have. And sometimes, you look at the boys he hangs out with and feel something close to disgust.

The westerner stubs out his cigarette and strokes your face. "What's the matter?" he says. "You seem preoccupied."

"I'm fine."

"Tell me. Are you worried about Jana?"

"No. It's not that," you say too quickly. And then because you can't tell him what's on your mind, you say, "I visited my brother earlier this week. He's not very well."

"I'm sorry. What's wrong with him?"

There's something about the simple concern in his voice that breaks you're heart.

"He had … an accident. He – " Suddenly, tears well up in your eyes, and you can't continue.

"Hey." He reaches over and brushes them away.

"I'm sorry."

"Don't be sorry. Tell me about it. John Bull-Halifax told me your brother had an accident, but I didn't realise he was still unwell."

"Did he? He shouldn't have."

"Why not?"

Why not? Everything is so simple for the westerner. The tears come again. You don't want to cry. Crying is weak. But you can't stop.

He pulls you to him and hugs you, stroking your hair. You don't want this either. You don't want love. But he's strong and kind, and it feels good to be close to him. He runs a finger down your cheek, kisses you softly on the lips and tips you over on to your back. You grip on to his shoulders as he moves inside you once more. And it's there again. That melting feeling.

CHAPTER SIXTEEN

Spring came quickly to Leipzig that year, almost overnight. One day a freezing wind was whistling down the streets; the next, the sun was high in the sky and temperatures were hitting 25 degrees.

The sunshine changed things. Not only did the city look shabbier in the bright spring light, suddenly there was nowhere to hide. Roaming Leipzig's dark streets muffled in winter coats and hats, it had been possible to feel anonymous. In winter time, John Bull-Halifax's warning about no western contacts had made my relationship with Magda seem thrillingly subversive. Now his words rang in my head like a threat.

Spring also brought a flurry of political activity that made it harder for us to forget where we were. Magda had to travel to Berlin for a cousin's Youth Initiation ceremony, a secular coming-of-age ritual with 19th-century roots that had been adopted by the regime to replace confirmation.

"She got her copy of *Socialism – Your World*," Magda told me afterwards. "And she pledged to deepen friendship with the Soviet Union and fight in the spirit of proletarian internationalism. It's such rubbish. But she believes every word of it – just as I did at her age."

Then preparations began for the May Day demonstrations – "We're obliged to 'freely' demonstrate," Dieter said with a shrug – and for the elections that were due shortly afterwards. The city was festooned with placards: APPROVE THE SOCIALIST UNITY PARTY CANDIDATES!

But on 26th April something happened that took people's minds off all of that. A nuclear reactor exploded at Chernobyl.

In the East, the incident was played down. *Neues Deutschland* published a small story on an inside page saying that two people had died, and the situation had quickly been brought under control. But people had West TV, and the place was buzzing with rumours. In West Germany, they were closing children's playgrounds, handing out iodine tablets and withdrawing fruit and vegetables from the shops. My mum wrote to ask me if I was coming home. The BBC had said 2,000 people were dead and no one knew how far the radioactive cloud would spread.

The more the international outcry grew, the shriller the denials in the East German press became. *Western Panic-Mongering Designed to Deflect Attention from Peace Initiative,* ran one headline in *Neues Deutschland.*

"It's sickening," said Magda. "They're lying to people with no thought as to the consequences."

She had friends in the environmental movement. They believed the accident was a catastrophe and that their government's attempt to play it down was endangering people's health. Some of them had been detained to shut them up.

May Day came, and the demonstrations went ahead as if Chernobyl hadn't happened. The following day, we went to a satirical cabaret at *The Sharp Corner*. "Everything's so wonderful!" the comedienne exclaimed. "Isn't it wonderful that's it's all so wonderful?" Magda gave a hollow laugh that I didn't entirely like.

Later, we went for a meal in a pub in a suburb near the end of the tram line, a depressing place decorated with greasy plastic plants. The landlord, a sullen man in his late fifties, slammed our drinks down on the counter, while the straggle of patrons at the bar stared into their glasses as if looking for salvation.

"Let's go away," Magda said when we'd finished our meal of fatty chicken and soggy cabbage. "You have a reading week coming up, don't you?"

"Yes, but you're not off, are you?"

She shrugged. "No, but I don't care. Let's go away."

"But won't it look bad if you miss class?"

"Oh for God's sake," she snapped. "I need to get away. I've had enough of this place. If you don't want to come with me, I'll go on my own."

She stared at her plate, her face hard and closed. She'd been tetchy all evening. She hadn't wanted to come to this place. She'd wanted to go to a Cuban restaurant near the Clara Zetkin Park, where decent food could be had for a higher price. It was me who had insisted on going somewhere out-of-the-way. I had John Bull-Halifax in my head: *no western contacts*. But she didn't seem to care. I put it down to her disgust at the patently false denials from the East German authorities about the accident at Chernobyl.

When she looked up, her expression had softened. "I thought maybe we could go to Prague."

"Prague?"

She nodded. "Have you ever been there?" She knew I hadn't.

"Oh, well, it's wonderful. You'll love it. It's so beautiful. Let's go to Prague where it's beautiful. I'm sick of this place."

I should have said no. I'd promised my mum that I'd come home for the reading week. I hadn't gone home at Christmas and I knew she'd been disappointed. My dad hadn't been too well. I couldn't remember a time when he had been well, but this time my mum's reassurances that it was nothing serious, just a bit of heart trouble, didn't ring true. I knew I ought to see for myself. Everything was arranged. I'd cleared it with Hencke and been to the police to get my visas.

But I said yes. Of course I did. Prague was an exotic destination to me then, but that was only a small part of the attraction. I had grasped that there was something going on between Magda and Marek that went beyond friendship, even if I didn't fully understand what it was. Back then I dismissed most of what I picked up on the basis that Marek was gay. All the same, I was jealous of him. This was my moment of triumph. She wanted to go away with me, not with him. He was the past; I was the future.

Later that evening, I phoned my mum from the central post office. As usual I got a line out much more quickly than all the other people in the queue, who were waiting to call relatives in West Germany. They glared at me as I went into the booth. They might wait three hours for a connection, longer if they were calling West Berlin.

I swallowed hard and told my mum I wasn't going to be able to come home for the holidays after all. I said I had too much work.

"Oh well, these things can't be helped," she said, concealing her disappointment, as I'd known she would. "Your studies come first. Your dad will understand."

"Should I have a word with him?"

"He's upstairs having a wee snooze. It's probably best to leave it. I'll tell him you rang."

"How is he? Has he been feeling any better?"

"Oh, he's fine."

"And how are you?" I continued, benevolent now in my relief that I wasn't going to have to speak to my dad, wanting to keep her on the phone a little longer to salve my conscience. "How are you managing?"

"Me? I'm fine. We're managing fine."

"I'm sorry about the holiday. It's just that – "

"This must be costing you a fortune," she interrupted. "I'd better let you go. Shona's well, by the way. She passed all her exams with flying colours."

"Good," I muttered. My sister was training to be an accountant, an occupation perfectly suited to her dull personality. "I'm sorry," I said again, but she wasn't listening.

"I'll let you go, dear. I'll tell your dad you were asking for him. We'll hear from you soon."

CHAPTER SEVENTEEN

You go to Prague on the night train. The westerner pays for a couchette, and you have it to yourselves. As the train leaves the station you say, "Now's our chance." You know they'll check the tickets after Dresden. Then there will be the border guards.

He makes love to you slowly and tenderly on the bottom bunk. When he comes, he buries his head against your shoulder. Afterwards, you curl up together, and he falls asleep. You lie awake and think about the last time you made this journey. You were with Kerstin, and you told her about Hencke for the first time. Her face clouded, then she shrugged and said, "You have to do what you have to do."

At Dresden, the train screeches to a halt. You hear doors bang, and people shouting compartment numbers to one another. As the train is pulling back out of the station, the ticket collector yanks your compartment door open. The westerner wakes up and gives him the tickets. "Please," the guard says, handing them back to him as you pull aside the curtain and watch Dresden's palaces slide past.

As the train moves beyond the city, you let the curtain fall back. "Have you been to Dresden?" you ask.

"Yeah. Kevin and I tagged along on one of those excursions Hencke organises for foreign students. He took us to the Memorial to the Victims of the Fascist-Imperialist Anglo-American Bomb Attacks – or something like that. He gave a long talk, pure propaganda, and at the end he said, 'Are there any questions?' Guess what Kevin said? 'Yes, have you ever been to Coventry?'"

"You can't compare Dresden with Coventry," you say, unable to stop yourself, though you resolved months ago never to argue with the westerner about the Second World War. "Thirty-five thousand people died in the Dresden fire-bombing."

He frowns. "I don't think it was as many as that, was it? Not that it matters. It was terrible. I'm not trying to say it wasn't. But you have to remember that – "

"It was completely unnecessary," you interrupt. "The war was nearly over. It was a war crime."

"Well," he says carefully, "I don't know about a war crime. It was obviously a terrible thing for the people on the ground. But then it was total war. And we didn't know that the war would be over in a few weeks. It didn't look like Hitler would surrender. We had to find a way to bring the war to an end."

We. Twenty million Russians died fighting the Nazis, but the westerner thinks the British won the war. "Let's try to get some more sleep," you say, though you know that won't be possible.

A little later, the train grinds to a halt again. A German border guard raps on the compartment door then throws it open. When he sees you both in the bottom bunk, he tells the westerner to move up to the middle bunk.

"Above!" he shouts, tapping the middle bunk with his pen.

Then he beckons to the westerner to hand over his passport: "Passport control!"

The guard fingers the westerner's passport with something like love. You could touch it that way too. The passport irritates you. The prancing lion and unicorn on the shield are pompous and stupid. The wording is ridiculous. *Her Britannic Majesty's Principal Secretary of State for Foreign and Commonwealth Affairs Requests and requires ...* But the passport also seduces you. You don't have a passport. Even if you did, it wouldn't be like this one; it wouldn't allow you to go pretty much wherever you please. The guard gestures to you for your papers. There's a flicker of surprise when you hand over your identity card. He takes out a notebook and writes something down. If he only knew. He'll be playing right into your hands if he reports this trip.

"He wasn't very friendly," the westerner says, getting back into the bottom bunk. You put the light out and join him under the blanket. "No."

A moment later, there's another rap at the door. The Czechoslovak guard. "Above!" he says to the westerner when he's checked your papers.

"I'll go," you say. "I like the top bunk." You climb up past the middle bunk to the top, lie down and smile at the guard, who is young and handsome. He scowls, knowing he's being mocked.

"Good nacht," he says, mixing languages.

"Dobrou noc, kamarád," you say, as he slams the compartment door shut.

Prague Central Station smells of perfume, pastries and petrol. The sun is up, and you jump down from the train in high spirits. You'd forgotten how much you love it here. You take the westerner's hand and steer him towards a café where you know you can get breakfast.

You push through the doors into a large room lit by dusty chandeliers and find a table that looks on to a dirty little square where pigeons peck round a waterless fountain. Against one wall is a long bar, where waiters with starched cloths over their arms lounge, ignoring the customers, who are mainly construction workers enjoying their first beers of the day.

Eventually, a waiter ambles across and cocks an eyebrow at you. This is his way of asking what you want. They don't much like Germans here in the Czechoslovak Socialist Republic, least of all East Germans. West Germans at least bring Deutschmarks. You order fried eggs with bread and coffee for two.

"The coffee is very good here," you tell the westerner, who can't find coffee he likes in Leipzig.

The waiter comes back and sets the table with exaggerated care. He's working you out. It's the westerner he's interested in. The westerner is speaking German and has a copy of the local Leipzig newspaper on the table in front of him, but the waiter has him pegged. He leans across, flicks away an imaginary crumb and says, "Change money?"

The westerner looks confused. "No," you say. The waiter looks at the westerner. "No," you repeat, and that's when you hear a rasping sound behind you. You turn round. The sound is coming from a heavily made-up old woman in a fur coat at a table in the middle of the room. She's pointing at you and muttering something under her breath. Her voice gets louder and louder, and eventually you catch what she's saying.

"Naciste!" she shouts across the restaurant.

The workmen look up then quickly away. Perhaps they

know her. The old woman heaves herself out of her seat and hobbles towards you, balancing on a walking stick. At your table, she steadies herself, lifts the stick and waves it in the westerner's face.

"Nacisté!" she shouts. She stinks – a mixture of sweat, stale face powder and urine. Everyone in the café is watching now, and the room has fallen silent. The westerner tries a casual laugh.

"She's calling me a Nazi, right? Listen," he says in English, "I'm not even German. I'm from Scotland. Skotsko, yes?"

The old woman pulls her ratty fur coat tighter round her billiard-ball body and glares at the westerner. "Pah!" she says, spitting on the ground. Then she wheels round and points at you. *"Nacisté!"* she hisses.

The westerner jumps up. "That's enough," he says. The old woman sticks her chin out, looks down her nose at him, and screams, *"Nacisté!"*

The westerner's face darkens. "Why don't you just fuck off you disgusting old bag?" he shouts, poking her on the shoulder. "Eh? Fuck off! Go on!"

You jump up and pull him away. "Sit down," you say. Then you take the old woman's hand and speak to her in Czech. "Mother," you say, stroking the back of her hand, "calm down. Be at peace, mother."

You take some coins from your pocket, put them in the palm of her hand and press her fingers around them. The westerner is standing over you, glowering at the old woman as you give her the coins: Deutschmarks. Maybe he'll ask about this later. The old woman harrumphs but takes the money and shoves it in her coat pocket. Then she shuffles back to her table, muttering under her breath. The room relaxes, and the clatter of crockery and the hum of conversation start up again.

"Silly old bitch," the westerner mutters, sitting down at last. Then he meets your eye and says, "John Bull-Halifax said your Russian was good, but I didn't realise you were so fluent."

"Russian?" you laugh. "I was speaking Czech."

"Czech? You didn't tell me you could speak Czech." His voice is sharp. He's angry because he let a confused old lady rattle him.

"Well, I can. Russian!" you laugh. "And you the great linguist." You look into his eyes. "That's what John Bull-Halifax says anyway."

He smiles warily, but he's pleased. That's how it is with him. He doesn't believe in himself, and so it's easy to flatter him.

"So, how come you speak Czech?" he asks.

"My aunt taught me. She came from here. After my parents got divorced I used to go to her house every Saturday afternoon for lessons."

"Magda?" he says and for a moment you think he's going to ask you about the Deutschmarks, but he just smiles and says, "Where should we stay?"

You lean across and point to the convent hospital on his map. "This is a good area to look," you say. "I stayed round there the last time I came here with Kerstin.

"Okay," he says. "Shall we go and have a look?"

In bed that afternoon in a pension on a side street near the convent hospital, you hear screams. You'd forgotten that the convent hospital is a mental hospital. You get up and look out of the window at the nuns scuttling past in their long black habits and white wimples. What do they do to the patients to make them scream like that?

"So tell me about your aunt," the westerner says, sitting up in bed. "Is she still alive?" His voice is sharp. He's asking this question instead of others.

"Very much so." You think of Aunt Vladka's colourful clothes, hennaed hair and big, throaty laugh.

"Does she live here? Can we visit her?"

"No, she lives in Berlin."

"But she's Czech?"

"Yes. She was married to my father's older brother, but he's dead now. She met him during the war. She was a nurse, and he was a German soldier."

"Did she bring you here, then, when you were a kid?"

You pull on some clothes and light a cigarette. "No. She hasn't been back to Czechoslovakia since 1968."

"But you seem to know this place like the back of your hand." He jumps out of bed and starts to get dressed too. He's very different from Marek. Square and strong with pale freckled skin. You like the way he is.

"Yes, well, I lived here for a while … a few years ago."

"Oh yeah? What were you doing here?"

"I came here to get away. It was – " You have to stop. You're welling up – just like that night at Shakespeare Street after the concert.

"Sweetheart," he says, "what's the matter?"

And there's that simple concern in his voice again that pulls at your heart. Suddenly – perhaps because you know he'll be shocked – you want to tell him what the matter is. What harm can it do?

You sit down on the bed. "You remember I told you my brother had an accident?"

He nods. "Yeah, John Bull-Halifax told me that too before I even met you."

"Well, here's the part John Bull-Halifax doesn't know.

It wasn't really an accident. Jürgen was an athlete. He threw the javelin. One day he had a seizure at the training ground. He collapsed and had to be rushed to hospital. He was in a coma, and we thought he was going to die. He didn't die, but something almost as bad happened. Part of his brain shut down. When he woke up, he couldn't walk and he could barely speak."

"God, that must have been terrifying," he says. "How long did it take him to get better?"

Tears prick your eyes again. "That's just it. He didn't get better. The doctors still say they haven't given up hope, but – "

"My God, that's awful," he says, sitting down beside you on the bed. "I'm really sorry. I had no idea it was as bad as that. What caused it? Was it like an embolism or something?"

You shake your head. "No. I wish it had been. His training partner, Olaf, took me aside at the hospital and told me he was pretty sure it was caused by doping."

The westerner's eyes widen. "No!"

"Apparently, Jürgen's coach had been giving him steroids and telling him they were vitamins. Olaf got suspicious after Jürgen's seizure. Eventually, he found proof. It seems Manfred, Jürgen's coach, had upped the dose because they were preparing for the Olympic trials. Jürgen had a real chance of gold in Los Angeles, and Manfred wanted to make sure he got it. More glory for him that way. We didn't even bloody well go in the end because of the Soviet boycott."

"Jesus," the westerner says. "That's unbelievable. What did you do when Olaf told you?"

"I told him I'd tell my father and that he'd press for an investigation. But he said he'd already told my father, and he didn't want to do anything. He wanted to hush it all up."

"Christ. Why?"

"I've asked myself that many times. We're not close, but I would never have thought that he would let something like that happen to his son and do nothing about it. To begin with, I thought maybe he was scared. But I don't think it was that. I think he wanted to save his career. He'd been at the Ministry for Foreign Affairs and had hoped to make State Secretary. That didn't happen. He went out of favour when Honecker came to power and was moved to the Ministry for Light Industry. But he was still a fairly important man. I think he wanted to keep his position."

"Maybe he just couldn't handle it," the westerner says. "Maybe he just kind of blocked it out."

"Maybe." He has no idea. He's never met someone like your father, someone who has spent his entire life manipulating his way to the top in a system where favour counts for everything and merit for very little.

"That must have been really hard," the westerner says. "What did you do when Olaf told you about your dad? Did you take it further yourself?"

"No. That would have been impossible. I ran away. I couldn't deal with it ... I came here." You smile. "That's why I know this place so well. I left without a word to anyone. A friend organised a visa, and Aunt Vladka spoke to people here who got me a job in a private café and a bed in an apartment a bit like the one at Shakespeare Street. I never meant to go back."

"Then why did you?"

"My father fetched me, and I had to go. I was living here illegally. And he said Aunt Vladka would be expelled from Germany if I didn't come back."

"What happened to you then?"

"I dropped out. Hung around in Prenzlauer Berg. I couldn't go on with my studies."

"You probably needed time to adjust to the shock. You don't get over something like that in a couple of months."

"It wasn't just that. I used to believe in our system, you see. I thought we really were building a better society, where everyone would be equal. When Jürgen had his accident I realised overnight that it was all a lie. What's the point of going to university if everything you learn is a lie?"

He leans across and touches your cheek. "But you're at university now."

"Yes, well, a point came when ... I guess I changed my mind."

"Really?"

You shrug and light another cigarette. "Kind of."

"Have you never thought of leaving?"

"No, we never think about this."

"*We?*"

"I never think about this."

He looks into your eyes and smiles. "We could get married, you know." He takes your hand. "I mean, I love you, so why not?"

I love you. For a moment, you're tempted. There are thousands of East German girls who pray for an offer like this every night. But it's impossible. You have Marek to think about. You stub out your cigarette, though you've only smoked half of it. You've told the westerner too much. It's time to stop talking.

"I'll think about it," you say, leaning over and kissing him. "Thank you for the offer."

*

You spend the next days sightseeing. The westerner takes hundreds of photographs with the second-hand camera he paid too much for in the camera shop on Schloss Lane, not thinking about the cost of developing the films. You eat in cafés, and the westerner pays. Each time a waiter sidles over and says, "Change money?" but the westerner, having learnt from you, says: "No."

On the second to last day, you're drinking coffee on the terrace of a café near the National Museum when a movement on the street opposite catches your eye. At first you're not sure it's her. But then she moves again, and you see her more clearly.

Jana has followed you to Prague. Your plan is working.

CHAPTER EIGHTEEN

I forgot about my dad's illness when I was in Prague, but guilt plagued me as soon as I got back to Leipzig. I wrote home asking how he was and received a reply from my mum, which said: *much the same*. Towards the end of term, I made the journey to the central post office again and phoned home. This time Shona, my sister, answered. She set out the situation for me with a bluntness my mum could never have mustered. My dad hadn't just been unwell, she said, he'd had a heart attack.

"Mum didn't tell you because she didn't want to worry you."

"A serious heart attack or a mild one?"

She didn't dignify this with an answer. "Our dad is fucking dying, and where the fuck are you, dickhead?"

"He's not dying, Shona. He's had a heart attack. People recover from heart attacks. Calm down."

"You should be here. You're such a selfish wanker. If it was Chris O'Driscoll's dad you'd be here."

I hung up on her. If our dad was as ill as she was making out she wouldn't be yelling down the phone at me, I reasoned.

Nonetheless, I made some changes to my plans. I'd intended to spend the summer with Magda. There had been talk of trips to Hungary or Bulgaria when we were in Prague. I now decided I should go home for at least ten days at the end of term, which by then was only a week away. I booked a train ticket and asked Hencke to organise a new exit visa for me at our weekly Monday morning meeting.

I never understood the purpose of those meetings. Initially, I assumed we'd discuss my DPhil research, but we never did. No doubt Hencke knew there was nothing to discuss. Researching the topic in Leipzig was a non-starter. There was plenty of material, but it was all rubbish. *The GDR is the part of Germany in which Heine's testament, the ideas for which he lived and struggled as a poet, have been realised, wrote one East German critic.* Fine. But he couldn't back it up. He couldn't back it up because it wasn't true. I had a pass for the section of the library that housed western books and newspapers – known colloquially as a 'poison certificate' – but it wasn't well stocked.

Instead, Hencke usually asked me about the students in my Friday discussion class. "Ah, the lovely Gaby!" he'd say with a little cynical smile. "She has interesting views about Great Britain?" I never knew if he was pumping me for information or just taking the piss. Perhaps he thought Kevin and I were both screwing Gaby. Some people said Hencke was screwing her. Maybe he was.

Sometimes he asked me about Jana. The little smile would appear again, though this time, presumably, for different reasons. "Such a diligent girl! Really most remarkable. If only they were all like that."

And sometimes he probed me for my opinions on the GDR. "Now, tell me honestly, how do you find it here? There are things you like? Maybe some things you don't like at all?"

Only a cretin would have honestly told Hencke anything. I made polite noises. It was interesting. The people were friendly. I appreciated the cheap cinema and theatre tickets.

"Ah yes," he'd say. "The cultural aspect."

But the morning of what turned out to be our final meeting, he was in a less jovial mood.

"Another visa?" he snapped. "What is the point of all these comings and goings?" I didn't dare tell him that I hadn't used the previous exit visa. "There will be no problem obtaining an exit permit but how am I to persuade our authorities to issue you with yet another entry visa? What with all these trips to the non-socialist abroad, they might conclude that you don't like it very much in our little republic."

"I'd be grateful if you could try," I said. "My father's not well."

He peered at me through his jam-jar glasses and drummed his fingers on his insanely tidy desk. "Is that so?" he said.

"He's had a heart attack. My sister told me it's quite serious."

He stared for a moment at his bookshelves, which were lined with leather-bound volumes of *Capital*, the complete works of Lenin and Honecker's *From My Life*, all looking as though they'd never been opened. "Very well. I'll see what I can do."

"Thank you."

He fixed me with a malicious little smile. "By the way," he said, "I bumped into one of our brighter students yesterday. A certain Magda Reinsch."

I froze. "Did you?" I managed.

A sly look came into his eye. "Do you know her? She isn't in your discussion class? No? What a pity! Such a delightful girl. But then even if she were in your discussion class, I don't suppose you would know her socially, would you? Contact with westerners isn't encouraged among our interpreters and translators. Perhaps you think that's a lot of nonsense. But then you, dear Robert, are from a NATO country, and our German Democratic Republic is a Warsaw Pact country –"

I stared at him. He'd gone mad. No contact with westerners was an unwritten rule, not official policy. But he knew about us. That much was clear. And he was furious. I don't know how long I sat there, parrying his questions and enduring his snide little remarks. Eventually, I could stand it no more. I jumped up and said I had to go.

"So you must go?" he said, his eyes disappearing into tiny pins of poison. "What a pity! Well, I hope to see you again soon. You may collect your visa from the central police station on Thursday afternoon."

I stumbled for the door, banging into the book case. Something clattered to the ground, and I rushed to pick it up. It was a tin with a picture of the Moulin Rouge on it that had once contained chocolates from Paris. Hencke grabbed it from me and replaced it on the shelf with a sound something like a growl.

I scrambled for the lift and sprinted out of the building when it reached the ground floor. I had to find Magda. If Hencke knew about us she could be in a lot of trouble.

But Magda had disappeared.

*

All that week, I searched for her, but she was nowhere to be found. Suddenly, I realised that I actually had very little idea how to contact her. It was always her who got in touch with me. I didn't know which hall of residence she lived in. I had no clear idea which classes she attended. And I didn't really know any of her friends. The only address I had for her was Shakespeare Street, but she'd always told me not to mention that to anyone and never to go there unless she was with me.

By Saturday evening, I was frantic. My train was at 08:40 on Monday morning. I had to find her and fast. In desperation, I trudged down 18th October Street to the hall of residence where Dieter lived.

"I've got a problem," I said, when he answered the door. "I need your advice."

He slung on a jacket and we went to a nearby beer bar. I was tying myself in knots, trying to explain what had happened without naming names or giving too much away, when he leant across the table and said, "Listen man, I know about you and Magda. It's okay. You can be straight with me."

My mouth fell open. "You do?"

"Sure. This isn't such a big town. Don't worry. People make a fuss about contact with westerners, but that's just political crap. Nobody really cares about it." He punched me on the arm and winked. "Lucky guy. She's a lovely girl, and I hear she's crazy about you."

I beamed. "Yeah?"

"That's the word on the street. Now tell me what the problem is."

And so I told him about Hencke and my fruitless search for Magda. "You see, there's this place we sometimes go on Shake –"

He held up a hand. "Better that I don't know the name, man."

"Okay," I said. "Well, we sometimes go to this particular place, yeah? And she's always told me never to tell anyone about it and never to go there on my own. But now I'm thinking – "

"That you should go there because that's where she probably

is, right? Well, let me put it this way, if Hencke had something on me, I'd want to know about it as soon as possible."

"Do you really think so?"

"Get over there, man. That's my advice."

"Thank you," I said.

He clapped my shoulder. "You're welcome. That's what friends are for."

*

The door to the rear house was open when I arrived at Shakespeare Street, and the building was in darkness, apart from a dim glow in Magda's window. There was no light in the stairwell, and I felt my way to the top floor. I stood for a moment in front of the brown-painted door, breathing hard. When I banged the door knocker, the sound seemed to fill the building.

For a moment, there was silence. Then I heard footsteps behind the door. A lock scraped back and the door swung open.

"Hello, Bob," Magda said. She didn't sound angry – or even surprised. "Come in," she said, standing aside to let me pass. She was wearing the sleeveless green dress she'd had on the first night I met her at the train station and she had a champagne flute in her hand.

"I'm sorry," I said as she closed the door. "I know you told me never to come here, but there's something I have to tell you. It's important."

She stood on tiptoe and kissed me on the lips. "It's okay."

"It's about Hencke. Magda, I think he knows about us."

"Oh well." She giggled, and I realised she was really quite drunk.

"I wanted to warn you," I said. "I thought – "

She put a finger to my lips. "Shh! Come through and meet the others."

The others? Numbly, I followed her. Marek was lounging on the divan in black Levi's and an expensive-looking white shirt, smoking a Kent cigarette.

"Robert," he shouted. "Well, well, well."

Kerstin was sitting on the floor in the arms of a man I'd never seen before. She fluttered her mascaraed eyelashes at me and blew me a kiss. Torsten was there too with his girlfriend, and Gert, the bouncer from *The Sharp Corner*, was already pouring me a drink. Champagne. The real stuff from France. There were bottles of it packed in ice in the kitchen sink along with some bottles of vodka. Not the cheap East German stuff. *Smirnoff* from the Intershop.

"What's the celebration?" I asked.

For a moment, they all looked kind of awkward. Then Magda said, "Marek is leaving."

"Leaving?" I said.

"Yes," Marek said. "You obviously mustn't breathe a word about this to anyone, but I'm off to the Golden West. I've kind of had enough."

"How ... how will you arrange that?" I asked.

"I've found a route out in the Harz Mountains," he said, launching into a long explanation about some underground river that crossed the border, while I stared at him dumbfounded. "The tunnel is wide enough to crawl through and not guarded. The place is swarming with guards above ground, but they've completely overlooked the tunnel. Can you believe it?"

"Perhaps it's mined?" I said.

"I've looked into it. It isn't."

"How can you be so sure?"

He tapped his nose. "I have my sources. I'm amazed no one's thought of it before. Why dig a tunnel when there's one already there?"

"Maybe someone did think of it. Maybe they got caught."

He laughed "No, it's never been used. We've looked into it very carefully."

We. I froze and turned to Magda. "What about you, Magda? Are you going too?"

She shook her head. "I have my family to think about." She smiled sweetly. "And … there's you."

It was late when I got back to the apartment on 18th October Street, but Kevin was waiting up for me. He was drinking a cup of tea and he was alone. He stood up when he saw me.

"I'm afraid I've got some bad news," he said.

"Bad news?" I said. "Bloody Nora!"

He didn't smile. "Your mum phoned. Your dad's had another heart attack. I'm afraid he's in a bad way."

CHAPTER NINETEEN

The day after the farewell party, you go to the hairdressers and then to the camera shop on Schloss Lane to get your photo taken. When you return to the apartment on Shakespeare Street in the early evening the Stasi are waiting for you.

You sense them as soon as you open the door. Instinct takes over. You turn and flee, thundering down the stairs where you bang into two officers who must have been hiding in the stairwell.

"Stop! State Security!" one of them shouts.

So this is what they look like – the grey men from the State Security who everyone is so afraid of. The older officer wears tinted glasses and has the yellowed skin of a chain smoker. The younger man is thick-set with a big face and ears like cauliflowers.

In your apartment, Hencke is standing by the bookshelf. "Quite a collection of West literature you have here, Comrade Reinsch," he says. "Most interesting. But surely you can't have read all these books. Which makes it seem rather silly to have them."

He turns and smiles, showing his small, pointy teeth. "Please take a seat." He points to a chair as he tells the Stasi men to start their search.

Are you surprised? Yes and no. You remain standing, as the agents pull on their gloves and get out their plastic evidence bags.

"Sit, Comrade Reinsch," Hencke says.

"I'd rather stand."

Hencke nods to the younger agent with the cauliflower ears. He leaves his search and pushes you into the chair with a violence that surprises you. Hencke takes a bottle of water from a string bag and puts it on the table. "Glasses?" he asks.

"By the sink."

The younger agent fetches a glass. Hencke coughs and launches into what seems to be a formal interrogation. "Comrade Reinsch, information has come into my possession which indicates that you have been engaged in state-hostile activities that contravene the laws of our socialist Republic. What is your comment on this statement?"

"I don't know what you mean," you say, and a shiver of fear runs down your spine. How much do they know?

"Comrade Reinsch," he says, "I would describe you as a very fortunate person. You have been given a second chance in life, have you not? Are you grateful to our state for this second chance?"

"I'm grateful for the chance to study."

"Ah!" He fixes you with his pin-prick eyes. "But your behaviour does not mirror this." He launches then into a long, bureaucratic description of your trip to Prague with the westerner, written no doubt by Jana.

Every muscle in your body relaxes, and it's all you can do

FIONA RINTOUL

not to laugh. Even the sight of the Stasi men taking down your photographs doesn't dampen your good cheer. For a moment there you were worried. But they know nothing of importance.

"I don't know what you mean," you say, when he's finished. You mustn't admit to the relationship with the westerner too readily. That would look suspicious. "I did go to Prague but I travelled alone."

"Intelligence in my possession indicates you travelled with Herr McPherson on – " He rattles on.

"There must be some mistake," you say.

"I think there is no mistake."

After an hour or so of this, you emit a little sob. "All right. I admit it. I did go to Prague with Herr Robert McPherson."

Hencke smiles thinly. "But you are not permitted contact with westerners, Comrade Reinsch."

You sniff, and he hands you a tissue.

"McPherson is an enemy of the working class!" he spits. Then his face softens. "Magda," he says, switching from *Sie* to *du*, "I'm trying to help you here. But there's something you're not telling me. I need to know the whole story or how can I help you, hmm?"

He reaches inside his jerkin, pulls out a packet of cigarettes and offers you one. You smile. Hencke doesn't smoke. "Now, enough of this silliness," he says, reaching over to light your cigarette. "All is not lost. Far from it. Perhaps you will now be ready to reconsider the proposal I made to you some time back. But first you must tell me the whole story. What did you hope to achieve by associating with McPherson?"

You smile. What a fool he is! If he only knew that the westerner is your cover.

"It's really very simple, Comrade Hencke," you say. "I fell in love."

Hencke's nose twitches, and his eyes cloud over. What's wrong with him? He stands up and walks stiffly away. Then you get it. He's jealous.

"Conclude your search," he tells the Stasi men.

CHAPTER TWENTY

They came for me the night before I was due to leave for Scotland. I was alone in the flat, Kevin having gone to a Friendship Between Peoples music festival in Rostock with Gaby. I was sitting on the sofa with a generous measure of *Glenfiddich* in my hand, wondering whether to make the trip home or not. I knew I should. My dad was seriously ill. But what about Magda? Things were bound to get sticky for her when the police found out that Marek had fled.

The doorbell rang. There were two of them: a tall, sunken-cheeked man of about forty in the uniform of the People's Police and a slim plain clothes guy in his mid-thirties who looked a bit like a bank manager. *Here we go*, I thought, feeling irritated with Marek for putting us all in danger with his madcap escape plan. *Just as well I'm still here.*

"Herr McPherson?" The bank manager said. I nodded, and the policeman barged past me into the living room and began to pull out the sideboard drawers and dump them on the floor.

"Eh, what is this?" I said to the bank manager.

140

"Please." He pointed the way indoors. I turned to see the policeman go into my bathroom.

I marched in after him. "Excuse me, what do you think you're doing?"

He opened the bathroom cabinet and emptied its contents into the wash-hand basin.

"What are you doing?" I repeated.

He swung round, propelled me into the kitchen and shoved me into a chair. The bank manager sat down opposite me.

"I'm Captain Sander," he said. "And that was my colleague, Lieutenant Scholze. Herr McPherson, you haven't done the dishes."

I stared at him. "So?"

"I find that interesting."

"Why? Are you the washing up police?"

He smiled thinly. Scholze appeared at the kitchen door. "Nothing's ready. He hasn't packed."

"You haven't packed, Herr McPherson," Sander said. "Why is that?"

"Why would I have packed?"

A muscle twitched in Sander's cheek. "Show him," he said to Scholze. The policeman slapped a piece of paper on the table. It was a copy of my exit visa.

"Ah," I said, relief flooding through me. So this was about papers. "I'm not sure if I'll be going. I, eh, well, let's just say something came up."

"But you have an exit visa," Sander said. "Therefore you must leave."

"My understanding is that an exit visa constitutes permission to leave not an obligation so to do," I said, thinking that was rather neat.

Sander sighed. "Herr McPherson, let me come to the point.

We have reason to suspect you of assisting a GDR citizen to flee the Republic."

"What?" My mouth fell open. This was a serious matter. Even I knew that. Did they think I was helping Marek? My irritation with him turned to anger. "I don't know what you're talking about," I said.

Scholze bent down and whispered: "Passport?"

"Passport – what?"

"Sometimes foreign guests are persuaded to sell their passports," Sander said. "This is quite common and most unfortunate."

"Well, I haven't sold my passport to anyone."

"Good," Sander smiled. "Then there shouldn't be any problem."

"Where is your passport?" Scholze asked, turning away from examining postcards Kevin had taped to the fridge door: topless girls, Rome, Mallorca, places the policeman would never visit.

"In my room."

"Could I ask you to fetch it?" Sander asked.

"Certainly." I jumped up and went through to the bedroom, thinking that I'd better go back round to Shakespeare Street once the policemen had gone.

The passport wasn't there.

They bundled me into a green and white Wartburg with the words 'People's Police' written on the side and said they were taking me to the police station. They put a flashing light on the roof and turned on a puny siren. But they didn't take me to the police station. When we got to the top of 18th October Street, they cut a red light and headed for the large turn-of-the-century building on the ring road bristling with aerials that everyone knew to be the Stasi headquarters. They bustled me into a room with a table and two chairs. It was entirely bare apart from a portrait of Honecker on the back wall. After about five minutes, Hencke entered.

"Ah, Robert," he said, peering at me through his jam-jar glasses. "We meet again. What have you been up to, dear boy? What is this all about?"

"I was rather hoping you could tell me."

He clasped his hands piously and gave me a chilly smile. "I'm afraid it's all rather out of my hands now."

Sander reappeared and took me downstairs to a windowless room with a bank of tape recorders along one wall. The passport seemed to be forgotten. Instead, he pressed me about Magda. I told him I knew who she was but that we were not personally acquainted.

Sander smiled. "Really?"

"Yes, really."

I stuck to my story and felt quite proud of myself. Here I was standing up to the Stasi to save the woman I loved. Then they asked me about Marek. I was tired by then. Five hours or more had passed. I hadn't had anything to eat or drink. Sander's tactic was to wear me down, and the passport was back on the agenda.

"We know you sold your passport. That could mean several years in prison. But we might be prepared to forget about it if you tell us what Dembowski's plans are."

"I didn't sell my passport."

"Where is it then?"

"I don't know."

He leant his face into mine and said, "Listen, Herr McPherson, we know you sold your passport and we know you changed money with Dembowski. That's illegal too, by the way. So answer me this question: is Dembowski planning to flee our Republic?"

"I have no idea."

Sander sighed. "Herr McPherson, we can do this the nice way or the less nice way. Which do you prefer?"

"I have my rights," I said.

He laughed. "You're not in Great Britain now, Herr McPherson. Here in our GDR we take our national security very seriously. I'm only asking you to do what is right as a guest in our country. Answer my question: is Dembowski planning to flee?"

"I don't know."

He moved away from me and stood for a moment staring at the wall. Then he came over, put his hands on the arm rests and leant his face in closer than before. His breath smelt of cigarettes and onions. I waited for the next instalment, but it didn't come. He leant back and punched me hard in the stomach.

I screamed. It was the worst, most searing pain I had ever felt.

"That's just for starters," he said. I clutched my stomach and stared at him. "By the way," he added, "I'm authorised to inform you that no harm will come to Frau Reinsch, whom you don't know, if you share Herr Dembowski's plans with us."

And so I told him about Marek's plan to leave through the underground tunnel in the Harz Mountains.

"Thank you," he said.

"But that might not be it at all," I fabricated in a desperate attempt to salvage some dignity. "I saw his neighbours earlier, and they said he'd gone to Prague."

Sander smiled politely. "Is that so? You've been most helpful, Herr McPherson. I really do appreciate it. Now please follow me."

They put me in a cell with a plank bed and a toilet bowl in the corner. "I apologise for the conditions," Sander said. "We're not used to accommodating guests from the capitalist abroad." He laughed at his own joke. "Perhaps I can bring you something to make your stay more comfortable?"

"I'd like a drink," I said, "and I don't mean tea."

Ten minutes later, a policeman appeared with a crate of cold beer, a bottle opener and two packets of milk-cream waffles. "Please," he said and bowed like a well-trained waiter.

I opened a beer and glugged it down. Then another. The crate was half empty by the time Sander came back for me.

"We'll collect your things," he said, straightening his tie. "Then you will be driven to Berlin where you will leave our Republic for Berlin West."

It was dark outside, but the air was clammy. "What time is it?" I asked.

"It doesn't matter," Sander replied.

"Can't I take the train?" I asked when I was in the apartment packing, "I've got a ticket."

"I'm afraid your train has already left."

"What am I going to do in West Berlin?"

"That's your business."

Downstairs another Wartburg was waiting. Sander stowed my luggage in the boot.

"What about my flatmate?" I said. "I haven't even left him a note. He might be worried. And … there are other people I should tell."

"But you were leaving anyway," Sander said reasonably. He extended his hand, and like an idiot I shook it.

"Good bye," he said.

We drove east on the ring road, passing the station, and out on to the motorway. I sat slumped in the back seat, wondering when I would see Magda again, as we bumped along behind Russian lorries with no lights. I was really quite drunk and after a while I started to sing *Autobahn* by Kraftwerk as an ironic commentary on the paved road. The driver and the policeman in the passenger seat exchanged a glance, then the policeman turned round and punched me in the face.

CHAPTER TWENTY-ONE

On Shakespeare Street, a van is waiting. The slogan 'Fresh Fish' is painted on the side panel alongside a cartoon picture of a herring. Hencke walks off down Shakespeare Street without a backward glance, and the Stasi men bundle you into one of the four tiny cages inside the van, handcuffing you to the door. The doors bang shut, and you're engulfed in darkness. It's hours before the van comes to a halt again and you're released into the fresh air and can stretch your aching limbs.

You're in a high-walled courtyard, and dawn is breaking. (Years later, you learn you were still in Leipzig. They drove around to disorientate you.) A young guard grabs your elbow and propels you up some stairs and along a corridor that stinks of disinfectant. Halfway along, he stops outside a cream-painted door.

"Wait!" he tells you and knocks on the door

Behind the door is a small square office. The blinds are drawn and a man of about fifty sits at a desk. He has the lined and puffy face of a *bon viveur*. His thinning hair is dyed black and plastered with hair oil. He wears a grey uniform with braided epaulettes and claret lapel stripes. A row of medals marches across his chest pocket, and his cuff bears the name of the Stasi guard regiment.

The guard lets go of your arm and salutes. "Colonel," he says.

The colonel looks up, as if he has only just realised you're there. "Won't you sit down, Frau Reinsch?" he says, nodding to the young man, who pulls up a chair for you. "Cigarette?" he asks.

You nod. You're gasping for a smoke. "Ashtray for the young lady," he says.

The guard brings a red glass ashtray etched with the shield of the Ministry for State Security. "Dismissed," the colonel says, and the guard salutes and withdraws.

The colonel sits back in his chair and sighs contentedly. "Ah!" He smiles. "Now, why do you think we've brought you here today, Comrade Reinsch?"

"I suppose it's about Herr McPherson."

He nods. "Ah-ha! Yes. Very good. By the way, would you like a coffee?"

You say you would and – encouraged by his relaxed tone – ask if you might also have a glass of water and something to eat. "It was a long journey," you say. "I'm dying of thirst."

"Is that so?" The colonel's brow creases in concern. He lifts the telephone receiver and orders two coffees and a carafe of water.

"We'll sort out something to eat later," he says, Then he leans across the desk, hands clasped in front of him, and looks you in the eyes. "I once had the pleasure of meeting your father, you know. I'll let you into a little secret. I thought he was a wonderful man. A true hero of socialism! He's been an inspiration to me."

You smile. "That's nice."

You see now how it's going to be. A paternal chat. A little light admonishment. You'll admit to your mistakes and offer to write a self-criticism. Then the colonel will ask you to write out and sign a commitment to work as an unofficial collaborator for the Ministry for State Security. And this time you'll do it, because in three days you're going to be in Budapest. The passport photos are in your trouser pocket. All that matters now is to get out of here quickly and without being searched.

There's a knock at the door.

"Enter," says the colonel.

The young guard wheels in a hostess trolley, and you suppress a smile. The colonel pours you a glass of water and arranges the coffee cups on his desk.

"Milk?" he asks. "Sugar?"

You gulp the water. "Could you tell me what time it is?"

"Don't you have a watch?"

"They took it off me before I got in the van."

"Really?" He sounds shocked. "I'll find out for you in a moment." He rubs his hands together and sits down. "I suppose we'd better get on with the interview."

"Yes." You take a sip of coffee. "Might as well get it over with."

The colonel smiles and presses a button on the reel-to-reel tape recorder on his desk. He states the number of the interview room and your name – Reinsch, Magdalena Maria – smiling apologetically at this bureaucratic inversion. Then he turns towards you, and the expression on his face abruptly sours.

"You're quite an arrogant young lady, aren't you?" he says. "Rather convinced about yourself?"

He tells you then some of the things he knows about you, and you realise how stupid you've been.

CHAPTER TWENTY-TWO

I'd been back at my parents' house in Calderhill just two days when I found out that Marek was dead. One morning, a letter arrived from East Germany. I rushed upstairs with it, but my excitement faded to horror as I read it. It was from Magda's friend Kerstin, the girl with the black hair and the sultry eyes. She said that Magda was too upset to write personally. Marek had been discovered crossing the border. He didn't stop when the guards shouted out to him, and so they shot him. He'd been betrayed. She hoped she didn't have to say any more.

I sat down on the bed and wept. Not for Marek. I was still angry with him. And a big part of me was thinking: *I told you so*. I cried for myself. And for Magda. I couldn't bear the thought of her hating me, as she now must. What would happen to her?

Until the letter arrived, I'd been trying to find a way to get back to Leipzig. After the East German police dumped me out of the country at the Sonnenallee checkpoint, I'd spent a fruitless week in West Berlin trying to find a way to contact Magda. Basically, I'd been checkmated. I didn't have a passport and so I couldn't get a visa to return to East Germany, not even a day visa for West Berlin. The British Consulate would only issue me with an emergency passport to make a single trip back to the UK. In the end, I had no choice but to give up and go home.

In London, I visited the East German Embassy. They told me they couldn't start a visa application until I had obtained a full passport. I was running out of money – and excuses as to why I wasn't yet home – and so I got a cheap coach ticket back to Glasgow. I got a new passport there quickly enough, limited to one year because I'd lost the previous one, and restarted communications with the embassy in London. I'd been waiting for a reply when the letter arrived from Kerstin.

Now there was no point to any of it. I'd been such a fool. Why hadn't I seen that this would inevitably happen? Why hadn't I been braver? Why hadn't I stood up to Sander? He was just a jumped-up policeman.

I had no idea what to do next but I knew I had to do something. I couldn't stay at home. Downstairs in the living room my dad was sitting slumped in front of the television in a high-backed hospital chair. The second heart attack had left him a virtual invalid. He was a bag of bones, and his hand shook when he reached for his glass of Lemon Barley Water.

"It's that hardening of the arteries," my mum whispered to me in the hall.

"No, it's not," Shona said. "It's the smoking."

"Smoking causes hardening of the arteries, Shona," I said.

"What do you know about it? You haven't even been here." It would be her constant refrain for years to come.

"Everyone knows smoking causes hardening of the

arteries," I said.

"Oh do they. What, like everyone knows you talk pure pish?"

"Pet," my mum said. "Language."

It was unbearable. I wished to God that Chris were around. Then I could have gone over to the O'Driscolls and hung out there. But he was Inter-railing round Europe with his new girlfriend, a second-year chemistry student called Joanna.

The day after Kerstin's letter arrived, I rang John Bull-Halifax at his flat in Edinburgh, in some desperation. He wasn't in, and I assumed he'd gone away for the summer, but the following morning he rang back. He was full of a production of *Zoyka's Apartment* by Mikhail Bulgakov that he was putting on at the Edinburgh Festival Fringe. It was fascinating to see how people reacted to it. The student actors were absolutely brilliant and had really got the text. And so on. It was like speaking to a visitor from another planet.

"John," I interrupted. "I was wondering if I could pop over and see you sometime."

"Sure," he said. "That'd be great. I'd love to hear how's it all been going in Leipzig. Why don't you come to the play?"

I made an arrangement to meet him in a pub at the Grassmarket in Edinburgh the following lunchtime. The place was full of colourful festival goers and Bull-Halifax walked in beaming one of his film star smiles. Never in my life have I seen anyone's face cloud over so fast.

"Dead?" he said. "Marek? What do you mean?"

"I mean … he's, eh, dead," I said.

He look around him wildly. "But – "

I told him the whole story. I saw no alternative. Apart from anything else, I wasn't going to be able to complete my DPhil at Leipzig University now. In any case, I was much too jangled to come up with any plausible lies.

I knew he'd be angry, and he was. "I thought I told you," he spluttered, his handsome face suddenly a twisted beetroot mask of fury. "No western contacts. Why didn't you listen to me, you stupid little prick?"

For a moment, I thought he was going to hit me. But he just banged his fist on the table, then turned his head away from me and glared at the door as if he couldn't stand the sight of me.

"I'm sorry," I said. "I didn't … I never thought this would happen." He sighed and dropped a napkin he'd been scrunching in his fist down on the table. "I feel terrible," I said.

"As well you might." He glared at me. "Christ, we don't normally get many casualties on our student exchanges."

"I'm sorry," I repeated.

He ran a hand through his red-gold curls and rubbed his face. "Well, I suppose you didn't pull the trigger," he said at last. "It's really the system to blame. I do struggle with it a bit, you know. And it does sound like a completely madcap plan. What was he thinking of? I mean, he's an intelligent guy." He looked at the pub door, as if expecting the answer to walk through it. "There's been absolutely nothing about it in the press here or in the West German press. The East German authorities must have managed to hush it up. They're getting better and better at that." He sighed. "What I don't understand is why he didn't just apply for permission to leave. He'd probably have got it. His sister's already in the West."

"I've no idea," I said. "I don't really know how it works."

"Apparently not." His anger simmered back up to the surface, and he glared at me for a moment. "Well, this is a bloody disaster. What are we going to tell the Arts & Humanities Research Council? Expelled from the Republic. Jesus Christ!"

I looked at the table. "I don't know," I said. "And to be

honest I don't care. I think I'm done with academia. I just want to know how Magda is. I know she probably won't want much to do with me now, but I'd still like to know she's okay." I met his gaze. "I know I've no right to ask, but do you think you could try to find out?"

He sighed theatrically. "Yeah, sure," he said at last. "I'd kind of like to know myself. I've always been very fond of Magda. I'll put a call through to my contact at the university tomorrow. I'll let you know as soon as I have some information."

"You don't mean Hencke, do you? I don't think you should speak to him."

"Hencke? Never heard of him. I'll speak to Professor Sahr, the Head of Faculty."

I got on to the train back to Glasgow, feeling fairly optimistic. If John Bull-Halifax had never heard of Hencke, I'd never heard of Professor Sahr. John had contacts in the right places – high up. Maybe there was even a chance that Magda would come to see things the way he had in the end. It wasn't me who pulled the trigger. It was the system to blame. Maybe this whole business would persuade her that the best way forward was for us to get married.

As I went to sleep that night under the candlewick quilt in my childhood bedroom, I imagined waiting for her at Berlin Zoo. I'd spot her immediately like I had in the Mitropa. She'd run into my arms and I'd whisk her off to a new life. There would be sadness about Marek, of course. But we'd get over it.

John rang back three days later. Professor Sahr wasn't at the university, it being the holidays, but he'd been able to get a call through to his summer house by the lake in Markkleeberg.

"It's not good news," he said. "Magda's no longer a

matriculated student at the university. Sahr was actually rather exercised about the amount of paperwork he'd had to process at the end of term because of her. It delayed his departure to his dacha. He's none too pleased with you either."

I swallowed hard. "What does that mean?"

"Beyond the fact that she's lost her university place? I don't know exactly. And there's no way Sahr would ever tell me. He was doing me a big favour telling me as much as he did."

"Did he say anything about Marek?"

"No, but then I didn't ask him. Bit of a tricky subject to broach and I wanted to keep him sweet so I could get as much information as possible about Magda."

"Do you think she's all right?"

"Well, I wouldn't be surprised if she's been detained for questioning because of Marek."

"Fuck," I said. "That's terrible."

"Try not to worry about it too much. They'll probably release her pretty quickly. After all, it's too late now, isn't it?"

"What can I do?"

"I'm afraid there's not much you can do. I don't think you'll be allowed back over there, and even if you were it would just cause Magda more problems if you tried to get in touch with her. The best you can hope for is that she applies to leave and her application is granted, and she then gets in touch with you."

"I don't see that happening," I said.

"Frankly neither do I. Look, Bob, I'm afraid your only option is to forget all about Leipzig and get on with your life."

"But – " I began.

"It's another world over there. We can't really influence what happens. I don't fully understand how it all works and I've been working with them for years. You certainly don't understand it. I think that's abundantly clear. And you've made yourself *persona non grata.* If you want to help Magda the best thing you can do is to get on with your life and leave her alone."

The following day, I received a communication from the Embassy of the German Democratic Republic in London, refusing my visa application. It was stamped with the words: 'Decision Definitive'.

It seemed Bull-Halifax was right.

CHAPTER TWENTY-THREE

Whoever is in the next cell lets you know where you are by knocking on the wall. One knock means A, two knocks mean B, three C, and so on. You are in the Stasi remand prison in Berlin. You shudder and wrap your arms around yourself. Like everyone else, you've heard stories about this place that is a grey blank on the Berlin street plan.

You knock back: *thank you*. Then you curl up on the plank bed with the blanket tucked tightly round you, as close to the wall and your new friend as you can get.

A couple of minutes later, the guard pulls the bolt back on your cell door, letting it go with a clang. He orders you to change position. Prisoners must sleep on their backs with their arms outside the blankets.

You lie on your back and stare into the overhead light bulb, letting it hurt your eyes. Impossible to sleep like this. But you must sleep. You're exhausted from the long drive here in the fish van. Tomorrow or sometime very soon there will be more questions. The guards who strip-searched you when you arrived, took the passport-sized photographs. You'll be asked about them.

You're so tired. Your eyes close. Then in the corridor another bolt clangs and you jerk awake.

Your interrogator is a man of about forty with one sticky-out ear and buck teeth. His accent tells you he is from the Valley of the Clueless – that part of Saxony where it is not possible to receive West TV.

He paces about the small, windowless room, while you sit in the blue jogging suit and slippers that were issued to you on your arrival with your hands under your thighs. He doesn't ask you about Hungary. They know everything about Hungary. The colonel made that clear. How you don't know. Maybe Jana is cleverer than you thought. It's because of Hungary that you're here. Fleeing the Republic. A very serious matter.

The colonel quoted Comrade General Secretary Honecker: *Those who let themselves be recruited, objectively serve West German reaction and militarism, whether they know it or not.*

But the interrogator doesn't ask about that. Instead, he asks you about the westerner, addressing you by your cell number.

"We know he sold his passport, 128," he says. "It is up to you to tell us whom he sold it to."

"I don't know," you say. "I didn't even know that he'd sold it."

He slams his fist down on the table and glares at you. "You do know, 128. Tell me."

After the interrogation, a guard takes you back to your cell through the traffic light system in operation in the corridors. You try to walk tall, but it's impossible not to shuffle in the oversized prison slippers, and each time a red light flashes and the buzzer sounds, the guard screams "Eyes down!" and orders you to wait. That's one of the worst parts. Standing in the corridor, looking down, as though you're ashamed of yourself, waiting for the guard, who is about your own age, to yell: "Walk!"

One day, a colleague bursts into the interrogation room to invite your interrogator to the pub.

"Comrade Captain Pankowitcz," he says, "won't you join us for a beer later at the *Adler*?"

It's a tactic to torment you. But it's backfired. Now you know your tormentor's name. You think about this during the long, monotonous hours in the cell. You repeat his name to yourself. *Pankowitcz, Pankowitcz*. And your own name. You are Magda. You are Magdalena. You are not a number.

Repeating the names keeps other thoughts out of your head. How do they know the things they know? Where is Marek? Has he been arrested too? Pankowitcz tells you he's gone. That he's in the West. But that can't be. He wouldn't go without you. And they know every detail about Hungary so they'd have stopped him.

The next interrogation is not conducted by Pankowitcz, but by a little round man of about fifty with a high-pitched voice. He offers you a cigarette and says, "Let's just have a friendly chat. We're not monsters, you know, my dear. Now, tell me, what did your friend Herr McPherson do with his passport?"

You can't tell him, and the smile freezes on his face. "I suppose you think you're very beautiful, 128. Well, you're not so beautiful. And every day you spend in here you'll lose a little bit of your beauty. It won't come back. I've seen it before. Pretty soon you'll be as ugly as me," he laughs. "But beauty is so much more important in a woman than in a man. Don't you agree?"

After that, they leave you alone for five days. It's so lonely in the cold, damp cell that you're pleased to see Pankowitcz when next they take you to him. This time, he keeps you up all night. He wants you to sign a confession, saying that you organised the sale of the westerner's passport.

You don't sign. Although you are dropping with fatigue, you don't sign. Pankowitcz is angry. He accompanies you back to your cell.

"The sentence will be much more lenient if you sign the confession."

"I know your name," you say. "It's Pankowitcz."

He slaps you then on the face and storms out, clanging the door shut behind him.

Two days later, a young guard collects you from your cell. He takes you down corridors you've never seen before. His voice is quiet, and his touch on your elbow is light. You risk a question. "Where are we going?"

He chews his mouth. "Family visit," he mumbles.

Family visit! Your heart leaps. Your skin tingles. You're going to see your mother! For all her faults you cannot wait to see her. Will you be allowed to hug her? Will she have something for you? Cigarettes or soap? A message from Marek or Kerstin?

The guard stops at a door marked 'Visitors' Room'. The room is freshly painted and has a clean linoleum floor. A second guard stands under a portrait of Honecker that hangs in a black frame on the back wall. At the window, oatmeal-coloured curtains flutter in the breeze. As always, they're drawn. In the middle of the room is a cheap wood veneer table with a vase of plastic flowers on it. Sitting at the table, wedged into a padded brown chair, is a portly man in his sixties. For a moment, you cannot think who he can be. Then you realise: it's your father. He stands up, and you see him flinch as he takes in your slippers and the way you have to hold up your oversized jogging trousers.

"Hello, Magda," he says.

"What are you doing here?" you blurt.

"I wanted to see my daughter."

"Where's Mama?"

"I told her to come next time."

He sits down. *I told her to come next time.* You imagine your mother meekly accepting this instruction. You slump into the chair opposite him.

"Sit up straight! Hands on the table!" snaps the guard under Honecker's picture.

"How are you?" your father asks. "You are being looked after correctly." It's a statement, not a question. Despite all the disappointments and demotions he's endured, his faith in the socialist fatherland is undimmed. "You look well," he says and smiles.

"Rubbish," you say.

His eyes flash. "I hope I don't need to tell you how difficult this has made things for me and your family. You might think of others."

You stare at him. When did you last see him? Months ago. He's put on weight. The bags under his eyes are starting to slide down his cheeks. The skin on his neck is loose. Suddenly, he's an old man.

"I'm sorry," you say, surprising yourself.

He glares at you then lowers his head. When he looks up again his eyes are shining. A single tear meanders down his left cheek. You reach out a hand to him. He takes it and holds it in his. It's the closest you've been in years.

"You must co-operate, Magda," he says. If you co-operate with our authorities, I believe this matter can be cleared up with reasonable haste. You will not of course be able to go back to university, but it might be possible to find another ...

opening. All you need to do is to tell them who bought the British man's passport. That's it. I've spoken to several people, very important people in the Party, and they say —"

"But I don't know who bought it."

He sighs. "Listen to me, Magda. You'll have to make your peace with our state sometime. This is your home. You belong here. You have your whole life in front of you. Do you want to spend it fighting useless battles or do you want to make something of your life? Maybe everything isn't perfect in our GDR, but do you suppose it's any better over there?"

You stare past him. There was a time when you believed in your country as much as he does. It would be so pleasant to slip back into that. To watch the red flags fluttering on May Day and feel your heart swell with pride. To belt out rousing choruses and believe them. To snuggle down among the collective certainties of international socialism. But it's impossible.

You stand up, clutching the waistband of your jogging trousers. "Thank you for coming. Will you ask Mama to come next time?"

The following week, you're moved to Gera for the trial. The judge is an elderly man, one of the 'People's Judges' trained and appointed after the war to replace former Nazis. His expression when he addresses you is that of a disappointed grandfather.

"Our socialist fatherland has done so much for you," he says. "We have educated and nurtured you, and you have thrown it all back in our face."

The highlight of the trial is your confession, which Pankowitcz reads to the court. It contains every detail of the Hungary plan – things you had forgotten yourself – and a dissertation on how you helped the westerner to sell his passport.

You look at your defence lawyer, Herr Giesler, a small, dapper man with a goatee beard.

"I didn't write that," you say.

He laughs. "Come, come, my dear. Let's not play the fool, shall we? Your signature is clear to see."

As he reads out his verdict, the People's Judge looks beyond you to the corn and compass shield of the GDR on the back wall of the court.

"We recall the words of Comrade General Secretary Honecker," he says in summing up. "Both from the moral standpoint as well as in terms of the interests of the whole German nation, leaving the GDR is an act of political and moral backwardness and depravity. In the name of the People, I sentence you to a term of two years and eight months."

He bangs down his gavel. The trial is over.

CHAPTER TWENTY-FOUR

Calderhill was closing in on me like a storm. I had to get away. Chris was in Amalfi, his ancestral home. I'd had a postcard from him, saying that Joanna had gone home and he'd be back soon too. Briefly, I considered joining him in Italy for a day or two. But I wasn't Chris. If I'd learnt one thing in my young life it was that. And I wasn't really in the holiday mood. And so I decided to flee to my ancestral home: the Isle of Harris.

The house in Geocrab had been sold when my grandma died, but there was still a shieling out on the west coast. I used to go there as a boy with my granda, chugging up the sea loch in his friend Norman's boat. We'd spend days at the hut, fishing and fixing the place up in companionable silence – peaceful times away from the womenfolk. What better place to get away from it all and take stock? I assumed it was still there. Even if it wasn't, what did it matter? Such was my mood.

There was just one problem: money. I'd spent everything I had getting back from West Berlin. I found myself knocking on the O'Driscolls' door.

"Bobbie!" Mr O'Driscoll exclaimed, pumping my hand. "Back from your travels, eh? Come in."

He steered me into the living room. Mrs O'Driscoll appeared and kissed me on the cheek.

"How's your dad?" she asked, her brown eyes full of concern.

"Oh, you know. *Fine.*"

"You should have phoned us," Mr O'Driscoll said. "We could have had you round for a meal. We'd love to hear all your tales. But maybe there's still time? When are you going back?"

I cleared my throat. I wanted to get this over as quickly as possible.

"Well, yes, certainly," Mr O'Driscoll said. "If it's an emergency, then of course I can lend you some money, Robert." He'd never called me Robert before. "How … how much are we, um, talking about?"

Back at my parents' house, I stashed the hundred quid in my money belt, and packed a rucksack ready for the off. I left the following morning. Shona had a summer job at an accountancy firm in Motherwell and my mum was at the shops. My dad was asleep, snoring noisily in his chair, as I closed the door softly behind me.

On Harris, my plan was to take the post bus out to the furthest settlement on the west coast and then walk over the hill to the shore of the sea loch where the shieling was. Only as the bus turned off the main Stornoway road and laboured up the first hill, did I realise what an undertaking that was going to be, especially with all the provisions I'd bought when I got off the ferry at the terminal in Tarbert, which included several bottles of whisky.

When I got out of the bus, I dumped my bags on the turf, lit a cigarette and wandered over to the beach. Two families were playing there, and one of the fathers waved to me. I'd played on this silver sand beach as a boy too, swum in the turquoise waters. Once I saw dolphins in the sound. My dad held the binoculars steady so I could watch them, and my mum, young and pretty in a blue spotted headscarf, laughed as the wind whipped the lettuce off our picnic plates.

As I watched the children playing, I thought about turning back. What was I doing here? Surely, there must be a way out of the mess I was in, a way to get back with Magda and make everything all right again. I imagined bringing her to this beach. She'd love it. Then I remembered. Marek was dead. There was no fixing that.

I stubbed my cigarette out and wandered down to the couple of houses by the jetty. How was I going to get to the shieling with all my stuff? A dinghy with an outboard motor was moored at the jetty. Perhaps it belonged to the people in one of the houses. Maybe I could get them to take me up the sea loch. But I didn't want anyone to know where I'd gone. And, anyway, it looked like there was no one in the houses.

Suddenly, I had an idea. Why not take the boat? I could putter round to the shieling in it no problem. I'd be there in less than an hour and I'd be able to take all my supplies. I knelt down by the boat and shook the tank. Half full. That would get me round to the shieling. It was stealing, of course. But I'd bring the boat back. I looked along the sound. The sea was calm.

When the families had gone and night was falling, I loaded my supplies on to the boat. As I changed into my walking boots and waterproof trousers, the boat swayed in the swell and the whisky bottles clinked noisily. I glanced up at the houses. No sign of life. I lowered myself into the boat, unfastened the mooring, and pushed the boat away from the jetty with an oar.

I turned the choke and yanked the starter cord, and the motor leapt into life with an angry rattle.

I steered the boat out into the inky sound. A crescent moon cast a ripple of light on the water, and the stars were coming out. The sea was choppier away from the jetty, but the dinghy chugged along comfortably enough. I began to relax. Then, I came to a point with a small islet opposite. I took the boat round the islet's eastern shore, which meant passing through a narrow channel. As I rounded the point, the boat was pushing against the current pulling through the channel, and the sea suddenly became much rougher. A massive wave lifted it clean out of the water and when it slapped back down, I was much nearer to the islet than I wanted. The motor stalled with a grinding sound. For one terrifying moment, I thought I'd had it. I let out a single sob. I saw Marek's face then. And his lifeless body lying in the raked sand of the death strip, faraway in Germany. This was what I deserved. My just desserts.

A moment later, another wave came and swept the boat back out into the channel. I grabbed the starter chord and restarted the motor. I cranked the throttle handle and clung to the gunwale until the boat was round the point. From there it was a straight run out to the more sheltered waters of the sea loch. I eased back on the engine and steered the boat into the mouth of the loch. The dinghy chugged along between the steep-sided hills towards the head of the loch and the shieling.

*

I'd been there nearly a week when Chris came to get me. That's what he told me. I'd lost all track of time. I cracked open a bottle of Safeway's whisky at the shieling, and that's the last thing I remember. It was my first proper binge – the beginning of something.

Although he was meant to be in Italy, I wasn't the least bit surprised to see him striding across the bog towards me.

"I killed him," I shouted. "It's all my fault."

He stumbled on a boggy tussock and swayed for a moment, the wind whipping his hair.

"Be with you in a minute, wee man," he shouted.

I slumped to the ground and began to cry.

Now someone else was dead. My dad. A third heart attack had killed him instantly. Chris had been brought home from Italy to fetch me back, my mum having worked out where I'd gone.

We didn't make it home in time for the funeral. My mum was very good about it.

"You weren't to know," she said, though it had been obvious to anyone that my dad was on his last legs. I was just too self-absorbed to notice.

She was more concerned to know what had gone so wrong in my life that I felt the need to run away like that in the first place. But of course I couldn't tell her. I mumbled some rubbish about 'girlfriend troubles'.

"You weren't even at your own father's funeral," Shona hissed at me in the hall. "You're a disgrace."

After the funeral, I went back to St Andrews with Chris. He was working on a research project on advanced polymers over the summer and had kept the flat on. It was a bleak time, and he saw me through it, cooking for me every night, making sure I didn't drink too much. One evening, when we were eating spaghetti with meatballs at the dining table in the bay window overlooking the sea I told him about the interrogation with Sander.

"It wasn't you fault," he said. "You stood up for your girl. That's the main thing."

"But I betrayed him," I said. *Betrayal.* It was an ugly word.

"You were under a lot of pressure, wee man. I would have done the same."

That made me feel better, though I didn't think it was true. Chris would have held out. Christ, he'd probably have charmed Sander into taking him on a sightseeing tour of Leipzig.

Oddly enough, I got to quite like St Andrews that summer. I took a lot of long walks on the beaches. When Chris was off, we went for cycle rides round the East Neuk, taking sandwiches and a flask. These were the kinds of times I'd envisaged when I first accepted the place at St Andrews, but in term time they had never happened. At home, I sat in the bay window reading and listening to the sea crashing on the rocks.

But I knew I'd have to leave when term started. Bramsden wrote me a flattering letter urging me to complete my DPhil at St Andrews. It seemed I was cut from the right cloth after all. But it was no use. Heinrich Heine was a closed book to me now. It was time to move on. And what was more I needed money. I'd been signing on over the summer, and I still owed Chris's dad a hundred quid. Gerard Kelly from St Ignatius' was by then working for Liebermann Brothers in London. He told me that the asset management arm was about to take on Europe and needed an investment writer with fluent German.

"Liebermann Brothers is really going places in the City," he gushed down the phone from. "Investors really value that US style of money management. They want to work with people who are tough, you know, focussed."

I knew nothing about asset management and cared less, but the job paid well and sounded about as far away from

Heinrich Heine and my previous life as you could get. I applied and I got it. None of the other candidates could match my language skills, apparently.

I packed up my room at the flat in St Andrews. In Prague, Magda had bought me a small wooden box that I'd admired in a second hand shop. It was about half the size of a shoe box and locked with an Art Deco key. It was the only thing she'd ever given me. I put all my mementos of East Germany in it. The photos I had of Magda. My train ticket from Glasgow to Leipzig. My East German tourist guide with its beautiful line drawings of famous landmarks. The keys to Marek's apartment in Berlin, which I'd forgotten to return after the party at *Café North* and which were now useless to anyone. I locked the box and stowed the key in a pocket inside my suitcase.

Chris drove me to the train station at Leuchars. On the platform, we hugged.

"Take it easy, wee man," he said.

CHAPTER TWENTY-FIVE

In a sleepy mediaeval town in the furthest corner of the Valley of the Clueless lies Malschwitz, the Stasi's secret prison. Like the remand prison in Berlin, it is not marked on the map.

The female lieutenant in charge of the women's section is waiting for you on the steps when you emerge blinking from the van into the glare of the searchlights. She is a woman of about fifty with a substantial bosom and thin, stick-like legs. The prisoners, you soon learn, call her the witch. "Take her to the medical room," she says and stalks off.

The guards hand you over to two female warders, who grab you and propel you upstairs. "The prisoner will undress and lie down on the table," the doctor says, his face a blank behind his black-framed glasses. The warders stare as you remove your clothes and the cold-fingered doctor examines you. "Hmm," he says when he's done. "Remove the prisoner."

They take you to an office, where you're fingerprinted and issued with a uniform: trousers with a yellow stripe running down the outside leg and a matching top. The female lieutenant comes into the office and stands back to look at you, one hand on her hip. "Not so pretty now," she says. She leads you up the central iron staircase to your cell. You are to share with Margit, a woman in her forties with an apologetic manner.

"Explain the rules, Prisoner Fahl," the lieutenant says.

"Yes, Madam Lieutenant," Margit says. "You must always address the lieutenant as Madam Lieutenant and you must always address the warders as Madam Warder," she tells you as the lieutenant slams your cell door shut and locks it. "Breakfast is at five 5 and roll call is at 6.10. Work begins at 6.45."

The next day, a youngish woman called Gisela sidles up to you in the work room, where the women prisoners sew all day long. "Sharing with Margit?" she asks. "Watch out. Former colleague."

She means a former colleague from the Ministry for State Security. A proportion of the prisoners at Malschwitz are ex-Stasi men and women who broke the rules. Margit's crime, you soon learn, was to get too close to a *Stern* journalist she was supposed to be watching in West Berlin. "Silly old bitch," Gisela smirks.

That evening, after a meal of potato stew, you are taken for the first time to the exercise yard for your allotted thirty minutes in the open air. As you pace up and down in the wedge-shaped enclosure, you try to work out how you're going to get through this. Courage – that's what you need. You must stay strong and hold on. On the outside is Marek. He must be working for your release. Perhaps he has already met up with Uncle Ivan. Perhaps Uncle Ivan will arrange for you to be bought free by the West German government. Perhaps you and Marek will soon both be in the West after all. You'll go out to dinner with Uncle Ivan on the famous Kurfürstendamm in West Berlin to celebrate. Then you'll begin a new life, just as planned.

You look up at the sky. It's windy and a cloud is scudding past. A moment later, the wind blows an oak leaf down into the exercise yard. You grab it and shove it in the waistband of your trousers. It's from the world outside where Marek is. And Uncle Ivan. And Kerstin. All your friends who surely cannot have forgotten you.

After one month, you are permitted a family visit. This is it, you think. Now I'll find out what's happening on the outside, what Marek is doing to get me out of here. A warder of about thirty-five nicknamed Blondie by the women takes you to the administration wing. Your mother is sitting at one end of a long table divided by a 25cm high barrier. When she sees you she stands up.

"Stay in your seat," says Blondie. "You may exchange a handshake with the prisoner at the end of the interview."

Your mother drops back into her chair, and Blondie positions herself in line with the barrier.

"Hello," your mother says, clutching at her white handbag. She's brushed her hair and she smells of her old favourite perfume, *Queen of the Night*.

"Hello, Mama." A lump forms in your throat. She's made such an effort. Travelled here all the way from Berlin. Tidied herself up.

But the visit is a disappointment. Your mother hasn't been in touch with Marek or Kerstin. She has nothing for you but some cigarettes and soap. Maybe that was to be expected. She's not a reliable messenger. Perhaps they didn't trust her. Perhaps that was wise. Nonetheless, your heart is heavy when Blondie tells you your time is up.

At mealtime, Gisela asks you how the visit went. You run a piece of bread round your bowl to mop up the potato mush and shrug. "She didn't have any information. I still don't know what's happening on the outside."

Gisela leans across the table as if to brush a crumb from your arm. "If you need to get a message out, I can show you how," she says in an undertone.

You've heard about these kinds of messages, which the prisoners call 'Kassiber'.

On Sunday evenings, the women are allowed to watch TV. That Sunday, Gisela asks the warder on duty, a woman near retirement, if she can show you her books instead. Gisela has a couple of novels in her cell sent by relatives, which she has been allowed to keep.

The warder nods. "Twenty minutes," she says.

As you look through the books, Gisela slips you a vial of invisible ink she keeps among her toiletries.

"Write your message with this and let it dry. Then write your letter on top. Try to use a fine-tip pen. Find a way to let your mother know about the message underneath. For example, you can write a phrase that spells 'use a match' with the first letter of each word to let her know that she should run a match under the letter to bring out the secret message."

You compose your message to Marek and Kerstin in your head. When you are next issued with a sheet of paper on which to write your monthly letter home, you scribble the Kassiber down while Margit is in the TV room.

Dear M & K, you write, please send news. Have you spoken to Uncle Ivan or taken other steps? I am well, but I need news. All my love, M.

Weeks pass before the next letter from your mother arrives. It's full of banalities, but you devour them. The weather has been cold, but it is improving. Aunt Helenka is well despite a bout of flu. Rosa, the cat, brought home a mouse.

At mealtime, you tell Gisela about the letter. "I'll distract Margit," she says. "Don't forget not to hold the match too close to the paper or it'll catch fire."

Your hand shakes as you run the flame under the paper later that night. Back and forwards. Not too close. And it works. Hidden words come into view:

Dear M, you read, *I think about you every day —*

The cell door flies open. The witch stands in the doorway and behind her, smirking, are Gisela and Margit.

Your punishment is twenty-one days in the isolation tract. You have passed the reinforced metal door with the words 'Forbidden Zone' written on it in black letters that leads to the isolation tract several times but have never seen the so-called tiger cages that lie behind it.

The tiger cages have no furnishings apart from a plank bed, and the toilet is separated from the cell by an iron-barred gate that can only be opened from the corridor.

"Push this button if you need to go to the toilet," says the witch. "A lamp will come on in the corridor, which will alert the guard. The guard does not like to be disturbed too often."

The first day, the guard does not come for twenty-four hours. "Look at you, Prisoner Reinsch," says the witch. "You dirty pig."

It's not your fault that you've soiled your cell. But your face burns as the witch clangs shut the door marked 'Forbidden Zone'.

The witch really does look like a witch, and during your imprisonment at Malschwitz you have sometimes amused yourself by picturing her flying through the sky on a broom stick with a big black hat on her head, shouting one of her favourite slogans: "The victory of Socialism is assured!" Once you made a drawing of her for Gisela and the two of you laughed yourselves silly.

You try to summon that image now and fail.

During the twenty-one days you spend in that windowless cell, you come close to madness. Not simply because of the privations and petty humiliations. But because you saw what was written on the Kassiber before the witch snatched it out of your hand. Kerstin has had no contact with Marek. She knows of no plans to get you out. You are entirely alone now. Marek has forgotten you. Where will you find love now? You think of what the second interrogator said at the remand prison. *Every day you spend in here you'll lose a little bit of your beauty. It won't come back.* You don't want to lose your good looks but you know that you will. The last time you caught your reflection in the window it was already happening.

On your final day in the isolation tract, the witch visits you again. "So you wanted to make contact with your friends," she says. "It wasn't worth it, was it, Prisoner Reinsch? He's in the West, you know. Your special friend. The Jew. He's forgotten all about you."

When she's gone you weep silently for what feels like hours. And for the very first time, you wonder if what she said might be true.

CHAPTER TWENTY-SIX

Much to my surprise, I fitted in well at Liebermann Brothers Asset Management. I was from the wrong kind of background, but Americans don't care about stuff like that. I was good at my job. They cared about that. And I was funny. A lot of my best successes at Liebermann Brothers were scored in the *Bunch of Grapes* round the corner from our European headquarters on Ironmonger Lane. Guys who ran portfolios worth millions of dollars were always thumping me on the back at the horseshoe bar and saying, "Christ, Bob, you're so fucking funny!"

One of my most notable successes in the *Bunch of Grapes* was Annabel, the younger sister of Jeremy Richardson, a rising star in the European equities team. She often used to come over from her job in Mayfair to join us for a drink on Friday evenings.

Annabel was blonde and glossy with plummy vowels and a light, easy laugh – the kind of girl who used to look through me at St Andrews. But now I had a job and money and I was a right laugh, and Annabel rather took to me. One Friday evening, we were sitting next to each other at the bar. As the punters piled in and the noise rose, we got pushed closer and closer together. I let my hand rest on her shapely stockinged thigh. She didn't push it away, and so I let my fingers creep up her leg. It was as I'd thought. She was wearing stockings and suspenders, and I knew they were for me. I leant across and whispered an invitation in her ear.

Back at my flat, I tore off her blouse, unhooked her bra and pushed her down on the sofa.

"Bob. Goodness," she whispered as I nuzzled her neck and fumbled with her pants.

Now I had a beautiful girlfriend as well as a job and money and lots of mates. Well, drinking buddies from the trading floor. The traders were just a sea of faces to me, as anonymous as the numbers that scrolled down their computer screens, and I interchanged them the way a farmer rotates his crops.

But there was a dark side to my new life in London – my drinking. One Friday night about six months after I'd started seeing Annabel it all came to a head.

I left the office around eight with a couple of bond traders. It had been a bitch of a day. Corrections had come through from Jens Müller, the new VP in charge of Germany and Eastern Europe, and he wanted the file back before the weekend. It was a relief to collapse on to a bar stool in the *Bunch of Grapes* beside John or Dave or whatever their names were. We were drinking pints, but I was having whisky chasers too – one of my little ruses. The pub was rammed. It stank of booze and fags. Beetroot-faced traders bellowed obscenities. Girls in silky work blouses, a couple of extra buttons undone for the pub, downed G&Ts. The jukebox vied with the *Nine O'Clock News*.

"What do you think of that?" one of the traders asked me. The lead story was about the killing of three unarmed IRA suspects by British soldiers having been ruled lawful by a Gibraltar jury.

"Fucking IRA scum," I said, though I hadn't followed the story in any detail.

"But they were unarmed. I mean – " He launched into a long, theoretical argument.

"Who the fuck cares?" I said. "Let's get another fucking drink."

I got down from my stool and banged into a bloke holding a full pint. A girl got covered in beer. I tried to daub it off her blouse, and her boyfriend objected. There was a brawl and the last thing I remember is Annabel's brother Jeremy pushing through the pub's engraved glass doors with a shocked expression on his handsome, public-schoolboy face.

I woke up the next morning in Chiswick Police Station. I'd been picked up on Chiswick High Road and charged with drink driving.

"What was I doing there?" I asked the sergeant on duty. Then I remembered: Annabel lived in Chiswick.

It was my first blackout. A warning.

The following Monday, Gerard Kelly came to see me. Liebermann Brothers was a US firm, and Americans are pragmatists. Gerard had been detailed to tell me that if I wanted to get blind drunk and have a punch-up I should do it somewhere further away from the Liebermann Brothers' office than the *Bunch of Grapes*.

"It wasn't a fight, Gerry," I said.

"That's not what I heard." He met my gaze. There was a flash of anger in his eyes but also a beat of concern. "Everything all right, eh, generally?" he asked.

"Yeah," I piped. "Everything's fine."

"Because, you know, there are, um, resources available."

"Resources?" I said.

"Yes. You know, uh, assistance. Help."

The crease on his trousers was razor-sharp, and his black brogues were polished to a gleam. He hadn't shone at school or university, but he was soaring through the ranks at Liebermann Brothers. He expected to be made VP soon, he'd told me the previous week in the company restaurant (always a restaurant, never a canteen).

"Assistance?" I said. "What, you mean, like, secretarial assistance?"

"You know what I mean," he snapped. "Think about it, Bob. You don't want to lose your job. Not now you've got a company mortgage."

Ah yes, the preferential-rate company mortgage: that was a honey trap and no mistake. I'd used it to buy an expensive little pad overlooking the canal in Maida Vale.

Gerard was right. I did not want to lose my job. And so I thought about it, and I decided I need to curb my drinking. Annabel had been on at me about it too. She said the one thing she didn't like about me was how much I drank. But assistance. Help. Resources. There was no need for that. All I had to do was cut down.

CHAPTER TWENTY-SEVEN

One Saturday morning in December, the witch unlocks your cell door at 4.30 in the morning. You stare at her. She never opens up, and anyway it's too early.

"I'm sorry the beds are not made, Madam Lieutenant," simpers Margit. "I had no idea it was so late."

The witch ignores her and hands you a cardboard box. Inside the box are the clothes you were wearing when the Stasi picked you up at Shakespeare Street. They are neatly pressed and smell of prison detergent.

"Put them on, Prisoner Reinsch," says Blondie.

"But – " you begin. It was summer when you were arrested. The clothes are not warm enough.

"Put them on!"

You pull off your prison clothes, step into your old jeans and T-shirt and stand by the bed, shivering. Margit stares as Blondie hands you a buff-coloured envelope and tells you to put your personal items in it. Already inside the envelope are all your mother's letters to you in prison that you had to hand back a month after you received them.

The witch grabs the envelope and says, "Follow me, Prisoner Reinsch."

"Is something happening, Madam Lieutenant?" Margit asks.

Because of her special position among the prisoners, she is sometimes allowed to ask questions or make comments. But not today. "Stand by your bed, Prisoner Fahl," says the witch.

You follow the witch down the central iron staircase to the administration wing, where she shows you into a room. The curtains are drawn and standing by the window is a man.

"A man!" you gasp. You haven't seen a man since you arrived at Malschwitz. Men and women are strictly segregated in the prison, just as the West Germans prisoners are kept apart from the East Germans.

"Follow the comrade's instructions," says the witch, slamming the door as she leaves.

The man is about fifty with thinning, slicked-back hair. He's wearing a cheap brown suit and a padded overcoat and in his hand is a camera. A good one. A Praktica MTL3 with a maximum shutter speed of 1/1000 of a second. He tells you to stand against the back wall and puts the Praktica MTL3 on a tripod.

"Look at my thumb," he says, "and now keep looking where my thumb was."

He presses the shutter. The camera is almost noiseless. "Look at the window," he says, "and now look at me." When he's done, he knocks twice on the door.

"All done, Comrade," he says to the witch.

"Thank you, Comrade Martin." She shakes his hand and smiles. Have you ever seen her smile before?

"Perhaps you should get her a coat," he says, nodding in your direction. "She's freezing in those clothes. This building isn't, eh, very warm."

The witch's smile fades, but she shouts down the corridor for someone to bring you a coat.

"And maybe some socks," the man says, glancing at your bare feet which are turning blue in the Bulgarian leather sandals you were wearing when you left Shakespeare Street. Then, to your astonishment, he winks at you.

Something is wrong. That is very clear.

You put on the coat and socks, and the witch leads you down the corridor to a small, unheated room that contains a single table and chair.

"Sit down and wait here, Prisoner Reinsch," she says. You wrap the coat around you and thank God for the photographer. The curtains are drawn and you briefly consider getting up and peeking behind them. But it's dangerous. The witch will know and then there will be trouble.

When the witch returns several hours later, she gives you a sandwich. "Eat," she says. Then she takes you to the staff toilets.

"You are going on a journey, Prisoner Reinsch," she says. "Use the lavatory."

Unlike the toilets the prisoners use, the doors in these toilets have bolts, but you don't dare bolt the door. The witch will go mad if you do.

"Hurry up, Prisoner Reinsch," she shouts through the door. "I haven't got all day."

She taps her foot impatiently as you wash your hands at a basin where, presumably, she has washed her own hands many times. Above it is a sign that reads: *Together we will secure Peace and Socialism!*

She leads you then to the prison entrance. The door is open, and you can smell the cold outside air. A warder comes up to you and shoves two buff-coloured envelopes into your hands.

"Get a move on," the witch says, pushing you down the steps to where a van is waiting.

When you step down from the van many hours later and slip on an icy pavement, you are in Berlin. You know this because you glimpse the red light at the top of the Television Tower blinking above the 1970s' apartment block in front of which the van is parked.

A guard steadies you. "You go that way," he says, pointing to the apartment building entrance where a tall man in a sheepskin hat and coat is waiting in the shadows.

You follow him up two flights of stairs. *Home Sweet Home,* reads the doormat in front of the apartment door where he comes to a stop. Inside, the apartment is stuffy and crammed with ornaments. Among the glass animals and porcelain ladies you spot a number of Party gongs. Perhaps this is what is known as a safe house: a normal apartment loaned to the Stasi by its owner for meetings. Probably this one belongs to a Stasi widow.

"Please go through," the tall man says, holding open the living room door.

On the brown vinyl sofa sits Pankowitcz. Next to him is your father.

Your father stands up. "My dear," he says. Pankowitcz shifts in his seat and coughs.

"Please sit down, Frau Reinsch," says the tall man, indicating a free armchair.

Please. It's the second time he's said that. You drop into the vinyl armchair, which feels unbelievably soft and comfortable. He called you 'Frau'. You smile. *Frau.* It sounds so friendly, so nice. And you know then that it's true. What you suspected when the photographer winked at you. You are no longer a prisoner. You are to be released.

"Ahem," says Pankowitcz. "We have some important information to convey to you, Frau Reinsch." He forces his big, ugly face into a neutral expression, then tells you what you already know.

The interview is brief. There are documents to sign. The tall man explains what each one is before you sign it. Confirmation that your personal items have been returned to you. Confirmation that you agree not to disclose any information regarding the location and conditions of your detention in return for your early release.

Your father smiles encouragingly. He has organised this, pulled strings at the Ministry for State Security. That is very clear. "Sometimes western journalists – " he begins.

"The enemies of socialism are cunning," says Pankowitcz. "Therefore, silence is mandatory."

Silence is mandatory. Your father looks nervous. Perhaps he thinks you will resist this demand. If so, he has no idea what you've been through.

"I understand," you say and sign the paper. The tall man picks it up carefully and places it in a file.

"For that same reason there can be no question of an exit permit," Pankowitcz says, shifting his thick lips into a smile. "In case any such notion had entered your head."

You shrug. Leave. Stay. What does it matter? The conversation you had with Dieter in *Café Riquard* is like a whisper from another world. You no longer dream of visiting Paris or London. A walk in the park, a cup of good coffee, a warm soak at the public baths: those are the things you dream of now.

The tall man slides another document on to the coffee table. "Your new identity card," he says.

You stare at the photograph. It was taken this morning. Perhaps they developed it while you were waiting in the unheated room. You haven't seen a photograph of yourself in a long time. You wonder if you recognise the girl in the picture. Yes and no. Then you notice a mark in the top right-hand corner of your new ID card: M12.

Pankowitcz follows your eye. "This particular kind of identity card must be renewed every twelve months," he explains.

You nod slowly. Your father looks at the carpet then at you. "It's a small matter."

"Quite so," says Pankowitcz. "If everything is in order, it will be a straightforward procedure."

You look across at the imitation fireplace that dominates the room. It's crammed with photographs of a young man, presumably the Stasi widow's son. As a small boy. In the uniform of the National People's Army. In a lounge suit with a girl in a white dress on his arm. You'll never get a job with this ID card. But perhaps it doesn't matter. What kind of job could you do anyway?

"That's it," says Pankowitcz. "You may go home."

"Home?" You stare at him.

"I have the car with me, Magda," your father says.

So they expect you to go with your father to the villa in Lichtenberg where you grew up. You look across at him. It's wonderful to hear him say your name. Really it is. But can you go to Lichtenberg with him?

Pankowitcz stands up and stretches out his hand. The interview is over.

"Stand up, Magda," your father whispers, and you scramble

to your feet.

Pankowitcz grasps your hand and shakes it. "Goodbye," he says and walks out of the room.

"Frau Reinsch?" The tall man is standing in the doorway. It's time to go home with your father.

CHAPTER TWENTY-EIGHT

Perhaps you think that I forgot about Magda when I moved to London? Not so. Though Liebermann Brothers could have been a wonderful place to forget.

By the late 1980s, Liebermann Brothers was riding high. It was in tune with the Zeitgeist. Thatcher had crushed the unions. Mining and shipbuilding were the past; tinkering cleverly with money was the future. The Black Monday stock market crash was, as Gerard Kelly liked to put it to clients, 'in the rear-view mirror'. A flight to quality was underway that could only benefit a pedigree Wall Street firm such as Liebermann Brothers. We were hiring and building a new European headquarters on Cheapside. It was a glitzy tower with a vast glass atrium: empty space that told the world how little we needed to worry about money.

As an investment writer, I wasn't part of the cut and thrust. I was just a Putzerfisch feeding on the fringes. But I put in the hours and reaped the benefits. A salary my parents could only have dreamt of. The pad in Maida Vale. Exotic holidays and big nights out.

But I didn't forget. Even when Annabel moved in with me in Maida Vale, and we became what people call 'a lovely young couple' (lovely apart from the shadow of my drinking), and everyone assumed we'd get married, I never stopped wondering where Magda was and what had happened to her.

The memory of the letter I'd received from Kertsin stung, but deep down I knew there was more to it than the words on the page. I thought, many times, about getting back in touch with John Bull-Halifax. But I never did.

I didn't tell anyone at Liebermann Brothers about my time in Leipzig, though I could have done. I could have turned it all into a great big joke: regaled my drinking chums with stories of my ejection from the GDR at gunpoint, Kevin and his string of socialist lovelies, Jana's amateurish attempts at espionage. They'd have been falling off their stools in the *Bunch of Grapes*, choking on their Californian Chardonnay in *Balls Brothers'* Wine Bar. *Bobbie, you're such a fucking laugh!*

But I didn't want to talk about it with my new colleagues. It was too precious for that. Instead I carried what had happened inside me like a knife twisting in my guts. Sometimes I had nightmares about it. I saw Marek being shot in the back, lying lifeless on the death strip. Or Magda being punched in the guts by Sander, as I had been.

"Don't dwell on it," Chris said. "It's in the past. There's nothing you can do."

He and John Bull-Halifax were the only people who knew what had really happened in Leipzig. I'd told Annabel the odd snippet but not the whole story. Annabel was basically a very nice, middle-class girl from Godalming, who wanted to get married and have kids and didn't really know where East Germany was. And, yes, okay, I knew the story wouldn't make me look very good in her eyes.

When I was drunk, it was different. Then the knife in my guts would stop twisting, and I'd imagine that Magda was fine. I'd see her striding across the Naschmarkt in her green velvet miniskirt or cycling back to Shakespeare Street late at night. I even imagined I might see her again one day.

Sometimes I think that's why I drank. For those blissful moments when I believed she was fine.

But when I sobered up what came back wasn't just a thumping headache and a greasy stomach but the bitter taste of regret – the dreadful realisation that I'd screwed up and there was no way back. My courage had failed when it really mattered.

And so I did nothing, although there were things I could have done. I didn't get back in touch with John Bull-Halifax. I didn't try to write to Magda at Shakespeare Street. I didn't contact Amnesty International. Instead I brooded on it all – quietly and privately – and sought oblivion.

CHAPTER TWENTY-NINE

You sit with your brother for over an hour in the old people's home in Pankow, holding his hand.

"I've been away," you say. "That's why I didn't come to see you. I'm sorry."

He stares straight ahead. Saliva dribbles down the side of his mouth. As his case is now officially hopeless, he had to be moved from the rehabilitation centre in Brandenburg. The only space available was in this old people's home. You wipe the saliva away, and a new droplet starts to form.

"Leave it," your mother says. "There's no point." You glare at her and dab your brother's mouth. A fresh droplet forms. "See?" she says.

"Hush, Elena," says Aunt Vladka, squeezing your hand. "Can't you see how hard this is for her?"

"He's much worse," you tell your father when you flop into the passenger seat of his waiting Wartburg saloon. "Why didn't you tell me?"

"He's not worse. You're imagining it."

"How do you know if you don't visit him?"

He shoots you a look. "I speak to the doctors." He puts his sunglasses on. It's just gone four o'clock, and the December sun is low in the sky, slanting through the windscreen. "Fasten your seatbelt," he says and starts the engine.

"Stop. I think I'll walk."

"But – "

"I'll be fine." You get out and slam the door.

Dark is falling as you trudge along Müller Street, and it's bitterly cold. You tuck your scarf into your collar. A few flakes of snow drift down – not enough for it to lie. You walk carefully, watching your step, looking neither left nor right. You can do this. You know you can. *Keep walking,* you tell yourself. *Stay calm.*

Nothing is more frightening to a former prisoner than freedom. The previous week, you went for a walk and had to turn back. It was too soon. People bore down on you in the street like a herd of wildebeest, and you retreated, whimpering, into a doorway. Men brushed past, uttering dark, hostile words. You half-expected them to pick up stones and throw them at you. You forced yourself to leave the doorway and sprinted home. People stared as you flew past. When you got to your father's villa you were shaking. He came out of his study and put his arm round your shoulders. He led you through to the living room, where he settled you on the sofa with a blanket over you.

"Shall I stay with you a while?" he asked when he brought you a cup of hot chocolate.

You shook your head. "I'll be fine."

You sat for a long time in your father's living room,

decorated (against your mother's wishes) in the hunting lodge style popular with his friends in the upper echelons of the Party. A room with so many memories, most of them bad. You stared at the stag's head above the fireplace – a memento from a shooting trip with Ulbricht – and wondered what was to become of you. What is the point of freedom if you can't walk down the street?

You keep walking east along Müller Street, heading in the direction of your father's house, looking neither left nor right, forcing one foot in front of the other. If you were to turn back and walk south you would eventually come to Schönhauser Allee. From there it isn't far to Marek's apartment on Pflaster Street. That's where you were headed last week when you panicked and sprinted home. You need to go to Pflaster Street because you need to see Marek. He doesn't yet know that you've been released. No one does apart from your parents and Aunt Vladka.

Suddenly, you stop. It's dark now, and the snow is getting heavier. What are you afraid of? You remember the saliva dribbling from your brother's mouth. You have to be strong. Someone has to be strong. You turn and head back towards Schönhauser Allee. You walk quickly, scared you'll lose your nerve, covering your face with your scarf. You don't want anyone to spot you. The further south you go, the more familiar the streets become. You know so many people who live here. There's *Café North*. You sprint across the road to avoid it, almost colliding with a tram.

Your heart thumps as you push through the heavy brown-painted doors into the main hallway at Pflaster Street. Marek's apartment is on the third floor of the front house. You recognise every chip and scrape on the apartment door. The card you made for him with 'Dembowski' printed on it in

Gothic script is still pinned to the architrave.

You knock on the door.

Silence.

"Marek!" you shout. "Marek, it's me. It's Magda. I'm out. I'm free."

No reply. You knock again. And again. You keep on banging on his door. "Marek!" you scream.

Upstairs a door opens. A man appears on the stairs. You recognise that big, mangled face. It's Marek's neighbour Gert. The last time you saw him was at *The Sharp Corner* in Leipzig.

"Magda!" He runs down the stairs two at a time and takes you in his arms.

"Where's Marek?" you ask. "Has he gone out? Do you think he'll be back soon?"

Gert strokes your hair. "He went away, Magda. It was quite a while ago now. Seems like everyone's leaving, doesn't it? Soon there'll be no one left in our little Republic."

You gaze up at him. "Where did he go?"

Gert shrugs. "People say he's in the West, but I don't know for sure. He disappeared overnight. Pouf!" He snaps his fingers. "Just like that."

You lean back against the apartment door. "He is in the West," you say. "The Stasi told me."

PART TWO

CHAPTER THIRTY

The package arrived one Monday morning in August. I should have been at work, writing reports on high-yield corporate bonds or some such nonsense. But I wasn't. I was sitting on the sofa at home watching TV and having a couple of drinks. I'd told Gerry Kelly I had a meeting first thing.

For one precious week, I had the flat in Maida Vale to myself. Annabel was in New York for an old school friend's hen party. (When would it be her turn?) I wanted to take advantage of the unaccustomed freedom by extending the weekend a little. Then the office would be more bearable when I eventually got there.

Except I never made it to the office because the package threw me off track. Food poisoning, I told Gerry. "That's the second time in two weeks," he said. "Maybe you should see a doctor."

I recognised the handwriting on the address label straight away. Big, slanting script written in black fountain pen. Bit pretentious. Reeked of money and privilege, just like the writer, whatever his politics might be. I'd received quite a few letters in that handwriting when I was in Leipzig. John Bull-Halifax used to write to me once a month.

Dear Bob, I trust you are well ... And so on. He was a diligent chap. It was a side to him not many people saw. He seemed to prefer everyone to think that he'd become the youngest ever lecturer in Soviet Studies at a British university by flashing his film star smile.

I stared at the package. It was postmarked London, NW5. I had a dim memory that Bull-Halifax's parents lived in Hampstead. If I wasn't mistaken, his beautiful mother was a psychotherapist. I hadn't heard from John since he phoned me at my parents' house in Calderhill. I think we both felt it would be better if we kept away from each another after that. The last news I'd had of him was years back when Chris was still doing his PhD at St Andrews. He told me that Bull-Halifax had taken up a lectureship at Edinburgh University.

"Good for him," I said. "Plenty of posh girls in the corridors there too."

I grabbed the parcel and ripped it open. Inside was a book entitled *Leipzig – City of Heroes*. It was about the Monday demonstrations that took place there in 1989, precipitating the fall of the Berlin Wall. John had marked one of the pages with a clipping torn from a newspaper. I turned to it.

There was a full-page black and white photograph taken at a night-time demonstration. Thousands of people packed into the square in front of the Nikolai Church, each one holding a candle, and strung across the centre of the crowd a home-made banner that read: WIR SIND DAS VOLK, meaning WE ARE THE PEOPLE. It had been taken with a telephoto lens, but the faces in the crowd were clear to see. Magda was standing near the front of the crowd holding one end of the banner.

In that moment, I saw her again so clearly. Her perfect pale skin and almond-shaped eyes. Her gorgeous slender body. I smelt the musk of her sweat and felt the touch of her skin: cool, creamy and smooth. I'd never had it with anyone like I'd had it with her.

I put the book down on the coffee table. I'd never believed that things would change in the GDR. Like so many people, I thought the system was set in stone. When change did come, I didn't like it.

"It won't come to anything," I told Annabel as we watched the TV coverage.

I found it hard to watch the news from Germany that year. It brought it all back in a sickening rush. It was as if the police had finally unearthed a body I'd buried in the garden fourteen years previously.

Annabel couldn't understand why I wasn't more interested. We had a lot of fights that year. In fact, we nearly split up. How could I explain what I was feeling? The Wall was open. I could go to East Germany any time I wanted. But what was the point? Marek was still dead, and I was still to blame.

I poured myself another whisky. Well, Magda had obviously survived. That was good. She looked well. Beautiful as ever. Hopefully, she'd found her way in the new Germany.

I picked up the envelope and shook it to see if there was a note. There was. It was written on a University College, London compliments slip:

Dear Bob,

I hope this finds you well. I thought you might like to know that both our East German friends are alive and well.

Perhaps you know already? In case not, please take a look at the enclosed book and newspaper cutting. If you want to discuss it further, don't hesitate to give me a call here at UCL.

Kind regards,

John

Both our East German friends? I grabbed the newspaper cutting and smoothed it out on the coffee table. The article was about a Polish-language film festival that had taken place the previous month in New York. And there was a photograph of the organiser, his black hair now more chin length than shoulder length: Dr Marek S. Dembowski, Associate Professor at Columbia University.

CHAPTER THIRTY-ONE

It's a warm Saturday afternoon in early September. You're brewing a pot of coffee on the stove and listening to the radio. Prints of the photographs you took the previous week at the Hamburger Bahnhof art gallery are laid out on the kitchen table. Photographing exhibits for museums and galleries has been a lifeline for you, even if it does steal time from your own work. You haven't looked back since Kerstin got you a first commission at the Pergamon Museum just before the Wall came down.

Your son, Kwan, is sitting at the far end of the kitchen table, drawing a picture of an aeroplane. He's just back from his Saturday morning visit to his father and paternal grandmother at the apartment they share in Friedrichshain. Just as the coffee pot starts to whistle, the ring of the telephone in the hall makes you jump. The telephone's been there for over two years now but you still haven't got used to its harsh ring. Sometimes you wish the authorities hadn't poured so much energy into sorting out the utilities in the eastern part of Berlin.

You don't much like having a telephone, and the long wait for a connection here used to help to keep rents down and put a brake on the deluge of West German lawyers and businessmen moving to Prenzlauer Berg.

You go into the hall and pick up the receiver. "Reinsch," you say. As soon as you hear your father's voice you know it's bad news.

"It's amazing he lasted this long," your father says when he's told you the news. "That's what the doctors say. They did a wonderful job. We should send something to Dr Langmann. You remember him. He's one of the ones from before."

"He lasted this long because he was so strong," you reply, infuriated by his cool tone. "He was always so incredibly strong physically. Don't you remember? He was one of the finest athletes of his generation, until – "

"Of course, I remember," your father interrupts. "But he also had a great deal of help from the doctors after his accident. Especially before. Now, of course, in the wonderful market economy it's all a little different."

Especially before. You hold the receiver away from your head and stare at the wall.

"I was wondering," your father says. "Would you mind telling Elena?" These days, he always calls his ex-wife Elena. "Her place is closer to you than to me."

"I don't mind telling her," you say. "But let's not pretend it's because her apartment is closer to me."

"Who was that, Mama?" Kwan asks, when, in a daze, you wander back through to the kitchen where he's still drawing an aeroplane.

"Grandpa," you say, sitting down opposite him.

"Did he get me my kite?"

"Your kite?"

"He said he would get me a kite, remember?"

Now he says it, you do remember. You reach across and touch your son's hair: so black and soft.

"You might have to wait a little while for your kite," you say. "I'm afraid Grandpa had some very bad news for us."

Kwan picks up a red crayon and starts adding tail lights to the aeroplane. "Is it about the kite?" he asks.

"No, it's about Uncle Jürgen." Your voice catches, and you touch his hair again. This time he pulls away. "I'm afraid he's dead."

Kwan carries on drawing and doesn't look up.

"Kwan? Did you hear me?" You reach across and still his drawing hand. "Look at me. Uncle Jürgen is dead. He died this morning."

"Dead," he repeats, as if experimenting with saying it. Then finally he looks up. "Are you sad?" he asks.

"Yes, I am."

"Poor Mama. Did you cry?"

"Not yet. But I expect I will."

He picks up his crayon and finishes colouring in the tail lights, pressing down very hard on the paper. "Do you think you'll cry a lot?"

"Probably, yes."

He nods and then starts to cry himself. Not the kind of tears he normally cries that are over almost before they've begun. A quiet, dignified trickle. "He had a sad life," he says, sniffing and wiping his nose with the back of his hand.

"That's true. Though it wasn't all sad."

You try to remember Jürgen as he was before: sprinting down the track, every sinew straining, the javelin perfectly poised in his right hand. But it's so long ago now that the memory is fading.

You dab the tears from Kwan's eyes, and find yourself uttering the same platitudes your father said on the phone to you. *It's for the best. He didn't suffer.*

"We have to go out now," you say. "We have to go up to Pankow to tell Granny about Uncle Jürgen."

"I don't want to. I want to finish my drawing. Look, it's nearly done."

From the radio comes the sound of Madonna singing Beautiful Stranger. You march over and turn it off.

"I don't want to either. But we have to."

On the way to your mother's apartment, you pop into the café across the road to tell Gert the news.

His big mangled face crumples, and he comes round from behind the bar to hug you. "Magda, I'm so sorry," he says.

You press against him. "Thank you."

He bends down and ruffles Kwan's hair. "And how are you feeling, young man?"

"I'm okay, thank you," says Kwan with an earnestness that breaks your heart.

"Will you be in later?" Gert asks. "Shall I come round when I've finished my shift?"

You nod. "That would be nice."

The doorbell rings just after 22.00, and you see Gert's face in the spy glass. He hands you a bottle of red wine filched from the café cellar.

"Some medicine for the patient," he says, squeezing your shoulder. "How are you doing?"

You shrug. "I knew it was on the cards. And it's probably better this way. He's been practically a vegetable for more than fifteen years. I wouldn't wish that on my worst enemy.

But it's still sad."

"How's Elena?" he asks as you uncork the wine in the kitchen and fetch two glasses from the cupboard.

"She took it better than I expected. I think she was trying to be strong for Kwan. He was very upset, although he's only ever known Jürgen the way he was. Aunt Vladka came over later in the afternoon. She's going to stay with her tonight."

You go through to the living room and sit down on the big tan leather sofa in front of the bookcase. This battered sofa is almost the only thing that still remains from when Marek lived here. Over time, you've transformed the apartment on Pflaster Street and made it your own. It's strange now to think back to when Uncle Ivan gave you the key when he met you in Berlin after your release from prison. Back then, you never thought you'd use it. You were living in Leipzig again with Kerstin at the apartment on Shakespeare Street. You had a part-time job tending the graveyard near Torsten's gallery. That gave you enough money to get by, and in your spare time you took photographs. Some of them are now hanging in this apartment. You didn't want to take the key. You'd found a simple kind of happiness back in Leipzig and wanted to keep your life uncluttered. Sometimes in your kind of situation people crumbled. But you were getting stronger every day, and your photographs were getting better and better.

However, Uncle Ivan insisted. "You never know," he said and slipped the key in your pocket.

Gert pours the wine. "When is the funeral?"

"We don't know yet. Probably next week."

"I'll come with you."

"Thank you."

"It goes without saying."

He's always been there for you ever since that day when

he found you knocking on Marek's door two weeks after you got out of prison – now your door. It was him who came to fetch you from the Stasi Museum on Normannen Street on that bleak afternoon in 1993 when you finally went to see your Stasi files, having always said that you didn't want to see them, that there was no point. And afterwards, he helped you to move into the apartment here.

You sip your wine. It's from Romania. Gert knows you still prefer products from the old brother lands. "You know," you say, "sometimes I feel like I'm on a ghost train at a fairground. I never know when the next ghoul is going to come leaping out of the darkness at me. Back in 1989, I really thought the worst was over. I thought we'd won. We, the people. I was so stupid."

"You weren't stupid. Just hopeful."

You sigh and light a cigarette. You need to stop smoking now you have Kwan. You've changed to a milder brand and you keep it to ten a day, but it would be better to stop. Perhaps after the funeral.

"I don't know about that," you say. "Even before 1989, I thought I'd worked it all out. I was so naïve. I remember when I first went back to Leipzig after I got out of prison. My father took me to the train station. I told him that I'd be fine and that he should go home. When he'd gone I decided to get a Currywurst from the stand outside the station. But when I got to the front of the queue, I couldn't say the words. I couldn't say, 'A Currywurst, please,' because I didn't really believe that the woman in the van would give me a Currywurst in exchange for a couple of coins. Why would she? I was a piece of dirt, a number, Prisoner Reinsch. That's what had happened to me in prison. I no longer believed I was entitled to anything."

You take a deep drag of your cigarette and laugh. "The woman got absolutely furious, the way people did back then, remember? I suppose it was an outlet for all kinds of frustrations. 'What's wrong with you?' she yelled. 'Are you some kind of freak?' I ran back into the station and found a corner to hide. I was shaking and crying. I was a complete wreck. But somehow I got myself on to the Leipzig train. And when I got out at Leipzig and saw Kerstin waiting for me, it was like it all lifted off my shoulders. And I thought to myself: *it's been awful but I've come through it.*

"I was so happy when we were sitting on the tram together and I saw the University Tower and the New Town Hall. It was a dump, the New Town Hall. Black with soot. But I was glad to see it because I thought I'd come home. I thought the dark days were over. And I promised myself that I would never have another moment like the one I'd had at the Currywurst stand. That I would not let them defeat me. That I would be strong. And later that night when Kerstin told me that Marek was in the West, I kept my promise to myself. I didn't crack up. I found a way to deal with it. I was half expecting it, of course, by then."

"It's not naïve to try to come to terms with things. You had to. There was no support."

"I know. I just didn't realise how much more there was to come. My release was only the beginning."

"Did you ever find out how Marek got out?"

"No. I still don't know."

Gert laughs. "Maybe he really did find a tunnel in the Harz Mountains. Remember your British friend's face? *But won't it be mined?* And Marek: *Na!*"

You smile. "Maybe." You told the westerner so many lies. You think about that sometimes and wonder how he is. "But it's more likely that he'd just applied to leave without telling me."

"Well, it doesn't matter," Gert says. "The important thing is that you kept your promise to yourself. You found a way to deal with it."

You shake your head. "I was so proud of myself at the time. *They've thrown everything at me,* I thought, *and I've survived.* But that was arrogant."

"It wasn't arrogant, Magda. We've all had shocks. That's what it's like to live in a country that's had a change of system. You've had more than most and you've coped with them."

You smile. "I wonder what's next. I'll need to phone Jürgen's old training partner, Olaf, and tell him that Jürgen is dead. I expect he'll want to come to the funeral. Maybe my father will finally express some regret. What do you think?"

Gert takes your hand in his and squeezes it. "Maybe. And then maybe the last ghoul will be put to rest and you'll be able to get off the ghost train."

CHAPTER THIRTY-TWO

Times were not as good as they had been at Liebermann Brothers. There was downwards pressure on fees. Margins were tight. Our campaign to penetrate Europe was costing more and taking longer than head office had bargained for, the Europeans having mysteriously failed to grasp how much better our Anglo-Saxon style of asset management was than their own. Therefore, the Liebermann Brothers Thanksgiving press lunch was to be a more sober affair than in previous years. Where was the value-added in a bunch of journalists in cheap suits getting pissed at our expense?

The lunch was chaired by Julian Collins, Vice President, Global Head of Sales, Europe Middle East and Asia, a standard-issue, moderately handsome, public schoolboy in his late thirties. He straightened his Bulgari cuff links, and a brittle smile danced across his lips as he broke the bad news to the journos.

"Welcome to the Liebermann Brothers' Thanksgiving Lunch," he began, bathing the journalists in his gaze. "I know

I speak for every single one of my colleagues when I say how very pleased I am to see so many of you here today. Some of you will have joined us last year for our Thanksgiving press lunch. Now, on that occasion we had a very general kind of chat. Which was absolutely fantastic. However, on reflection, we did feel that last year's discussion was perhaps a little unfocussed in nature. So, this year, we thought we'd conduct a guided discussion round the table during lunch. The topic we've chosen is European distribution in a cross-border context. As you know, this is a key theme in our industry at this point in time."

He fixed the journalists with a steely gaze – he didn't have a very high opinion of their intelligence – as if defying them to disagree with him or yawn openly. "I'd now like to invite my colleague, Tony Bardolucci, who, as you know, is our Head of Third-party Distribution, to outline some of the initiatives we've been involved in this year on the institutional side. We'll then open the floor up to a general discussion and at a later point, probably after the main course, I'll bring in Mark Bradshaw, who'll outline our recently revamped cross-border distribution strategy targeting retail investors."

The journalists' faces fell. Mark Bradshaw, a nerd in his early forties who'd once been an independent financial adviser in Wantage, smiled grimly, as Tony Bardolucci, a meaty-faced New Yorker who always looked as if he was being strangled by his own necktie, cleared his throat.

"Thank you, Julian. Hello everybody and great to see you all here today. Now, as an organisation, we have seen very significant expansion of our investment management operations in mainland Europe over the past five years. As you know, Europe is a highly competitive and highly fragmented marketplace – "

The journalists reached for their drinks, and so did I. It was going to be a long afternoon. I'd arrived at the office late and in a bad mood because of an argument with Annabel. She wanted me to 'see someone' about my drinking. "Like who?" I yelled. "Why don't you see someone about your nagging?"

I'd finished my first glass of Pouilly Fumé and was on to my second before Tony had even finished his preamble, which had washed over me like a wave on the seashore, leaving behind only the odd pebble: *best of breed ... strategic partnerships ... client-focussed solutions ... portable alpha.* There was a time when I'd been very careful about drinking at work. But shortly after John Bull-Halifax's parcel arrived, I'd stopped being quite so careful and once I'd stopped I found I couldn't start again. I nudged the wee girl journalist on my right and whispered to her to pass me another bottle of Pouilly Fumé. Julian Collins flicked me a glance, and his lips tightened. I pretended not to notice and filled the journalist's glass and my own.

"Golly," she said. "That's quite a ... generous measure."

"This is Liebermann Brothers," I whispered. "No expense spared."

I was on my fifth glass by the time Tony Bardolucci and Mark Bradshaw had wrapped up their contributions to the cross-border distribution discussion. Dessert had been served – pumpkin pie with Chantilly cream – and the girl journalist had gone to the toilet, I suspected to puke. My neighbour on the other side, Bill Smythson, Jnr, a visiting luminary from our San Francisco office, chose this moment to engage me in conversation.

"So, it's, uh, Bob, isn't it? How's business, Bob?"

Bill Smythson was a tall, slender man in his mid-fifties with a full head of silvering hair and a slight stoop. I'd met him once before at an internal 'Strategic Influencer' seminar in our Chicago office. He fulfilled a lofty function in our alternative investments division, the exact nature of which was not entirely clear to me. He was not noted for his sense of humour. He liked money and not much else. His role at Liebermann Brothers seemed primarily to involve being driven up and down the Pacific Highway in an expensive automobile seeking out other guys who liked money and not much else – or hedge fund managers as they call them in the business.

I struggled gamely to bring Bill into focus. He was wearing an expensive-looking dark blue Italian suit, a white shirt and a yellow Hermès tie clipped with a gold tie pin. In his breast pocket was a Mont Blanc Meisterstück fountain pen – the regulation accessory of the successful fund manager. Mineral water sparkled in his wine glass. I eyed him malevolently and spat out the word "Crap" along with a mangled piece of pumpkin pie.

Bill froze, a forkful of cream-laden pie suspended halfway between his plate and his mouth. "Crap? That's not what I expect to hear from a senior member of our executive marketing team."

All of sudden, I felt very drunk. "I'm hardly fucking senior, Bill," I slurred.

He winced at the expletive. "You're senior enough, Bob, senior enough." He put a hand on my arm. "Let me tell you a story."

Perhaps he wanted to help me. He wasn't to know I was beyond help. Or perhaps he just wanted to shut me up. Either way, he began his story. He talked in the booming tones of over-confident white American males everywhere. He'd gone to Harvard, and it showed. His delivery was that of a prosecuting attorney summing up for the jury in an open-and-shut homicide case. Soon everyone round the table was listening in. The gist of the story was this: a highly successful hedge fund manager of Bill's acquaintance ("I don't mind telling you I have quite a bit of my own money with this fella") lived in a luxury villa in an exclusive suburb of San Francisco. This man was a millionaire many times over. He had everything he could possibly want. He'd just turned fifty-five and was planning to retire. Then he discovered his neighbour, also a successful hedge fund manager, had $30 million worth of assets more than him.

"Well," said Bill, "Sam – that's my friend – he turned right round and cancelled his retirement when he heard that. He launched a whole new hedge fund strategy and made a whole new pile of money. Then he had more than the other guy. Then he retired. How d'ya like that? Now, do you think Sam said, 'Crap' when I said, 'How's business?' Let me tell you: he did not. Sam always said, 'Business is just great, Bill'. Because if business wasn't great, he made it great. That's the kind of guy he was. Isn't that something? Huh? Isn't that remarkable?"

A smile played across Bill's handsome face. The story was meant to amuse. The polite thing, the sensible thing, would have been to laugh and turn back to the girl journalist who had now returned from the toilets looking ready for round two.

But I was in a sour mood. I hadn't yet come to terms with the shocking contents of John Bull-Halifax's package, and the argument with Annabel had rattled me. There was something new in her attitude towards me, something that smelt suspiciously like contempt.

"That really is something, Bill, yes," I said. "I think your friend sounds truly remarkable. He sounds like a very remarkable wanker indeed." Bill blinked. "Wanker is British for asshole," I supplied helpfully. "You know, dickhead. Twat."

The table fell silent. Then Brian McNeil, an old drinking

buddy of mine from *Investment Digest*, gave a loud, forced laughed. "Ha, ha!" he bellowed, catching my eye and mouthing, *Shut the fuck up!*

Julian Collins flashed the journalists a 24-carat smile. "Well, now that we've consumed our, eh, pumpkin pie, maybe it's time to get back to the topic of cross-border distribution. Kurt?" He turned to the second-in-command at our Frankfurt office, a tedious young German in a charcoal suit who'd recently joined from Deutsche Bank. "I don't think you've yet shared your thoughts on the distribution landscape in Germany. I'm sure we'd all be fascinated to hear your insights."

And I think they might all have been willing to leave it there. But I was on a roll. "Pass me the wine, would you, love?" I said to the girl journalist.

She looked at me with frightened eyes. "Go on," I said, nudging her playfully.

She reached across the table for the one remaining full bottle of red. Julian coughed and gave me a warning look. I ignored him. Reasonably decorously, I poured some wine for the girl journalist and me.

"In Germany, the distribution of units in retail investment funds is heavily dominated by the branch networks of the leading universal and savings banks," Kurt began. "Approximately 84.6% of sales of units in retail investment – "

"Approximately 84.6%," I said, leaning into the girl journalist. "I wouldn't like to hear the exact figure."

She giggled nervously. Julian glared.

"German investors, both retail and institutional, exhibit a strong preference for bond-based products," Kurt continued. "At the end of the second quarter, assets under management in bond investment funds –"

"Fuck's sake," I muttered, loud enough for everyone to hear.

Julian's eyes widened. He coughed and ran a finger across his lips to indicate that I should shut up.

I nudged Bill. "Here, have a drink."

"No, thank you," he replied stiffly. "I never drink at lunchtime."

"Oh, go on. Live a little." I sloshed some wine in the direction of his glass but missed and got his trousers.

He pushed his chair back. "You – " he snarled.

"Sorry," I slurred.

Kurt stopped mid-sentence. Everyone looked at Bill and me. The girl journalist scrambled for a napkin. I jumped up and started dabbing at Bill's trousers.

"Would you just – ?" He pushed me away.

"I'm sorry," I repeated. And in that moment I truly was.

He rounded on me, his face puce. "Do you know how much these pants cost?"

"I don't," I said, "but I tell you what: I bet your friend Sam could afford to buy you a new pair." I picked up my glass. "Let's drink to him, eh? Let's drink to Sam. He moves money around better than the other guys. What a hero!" I drained my glass and thumped it down on the table.

"Will you excuse me?" Bill said to Julian Collins.

"Of course." Julian jumped up. "I'm, eh …" He smiled uncertainly.

Bill waved his hand, signalling both acceptance of Julian's unspoken apology and an undimmed desire to leave the room. With a last contemptuous look in my direction, he strode towards the door.

"I'll, eh …" Julian said to Kurt.

Kurt nodded. Julian followed Bill out, and Kurt cleared his throat.

"As I was saying, the German investors prefer bonds."

He looked round the table, smiling at his own joke. There was a ripple of relieved laughter.

"Investment in equities by the German investors currently accounts for only …"

I slumped back down into my chair.

"Are you all right?" whispered the girl journalist.

Suddenly, I felt like crying. What the fuck was I doing? "No," I said, "I don't think I am."

The next day I was called in to see Arnold Black, Senior Vice President, Investment Management, Europe, Middle East and Asia. I knew what was coming. It was amazing I'd lasted as long as I had at Liebermann Brothers. Even before I stopped being careful about drinking at work, there were days when I was too hung over to think straight. There had been sickies. Unguarded remarks. I wasn't fooling anyone any more. My scores in the peer review the previous year had been shocking. In the 'citizenship' category – basically a measure of how into the whole idea of Liebermann Brothers you were – I'd scored just 20%. It was an all-time low. I'd survived for three reasons. First, when I was on form, I was really good at my job. Secondly, Gerard Kelly had protected me. I hated to admit it but I knew it was true. By then he was an important man at Liebermann Brothers with a window office and a pretty, young Cambridge graduate for his PA. The third reason was Cordelia Schuhmacher, the well-padded brunette who acted as Arnold Black's PA. Once, a couple of years previously when I'd been working late, I'd walked into Arnold's office to leave some papers to be greeted by the sight of Arnold with his trousers round his ankles. His bare arse was pistoning up and down above Cordelia, who was sprawled across his antique desk, her face a picture of dawning shock, her lolling right breast half-obscuring a tasteful black and white photograph of Arnold's wife Samantha and his two young sons. Arnold turned. His face was beetroot. His eyes widened and he made a violent shooing gesture.

I closed the door quietly behind me, shaking my head. Shagging his secretary: what a cliché. Cordelia wasn't even that attractive. The next day Arnold invited me to lunch at *Zucchinis*, an expensive Italian restaurant near St Paul's Cathedral. Being a US firm, Liebermann Brothers didn't endorse drinking at lunchtime, but that day Arnold ordered a bottle of Saint Emilion to wash down our steaks and brandy with the coffee. No direct mention was made of the events of the previous evening, but I was given to understand, ever so subtly, that if I were to keep absolutely schtum, Arnold would always be happy to do whatever he could to advance my cause at Liebermann Brothers.

Arnold looked distinctly uncomfortable, then, when I arrived in his office. He cleared his throat and met my eyes only fleetingly. I saw him glance at the photograph of Samantha and the boys. If I was going to play that card, now was the moment. But what was I going to do? Tell Samantha? Then I'd be fired and Samantha would be sad.

Arnold laid his cards on the table pretty swiftly. We could go through all the standard human resources procedures, in which case I should consider our conversation to be an initial verbal warning. Or we could expedite things, in which case he could offer me a substantial pay-off in return for me signing a confidentiality agreement, relinquishing any future claims against the company and agreeing not to take up an equivalent position with a competitor for six months.

"Gardening leave," Arnold said brightly, and we both laughed as if we believed I could get a position with a competitor, as if we didn't both know that I was a drunk and my career was over.

"Right," I said. "When do you want me to go?"

Arnold pressed his fingertips together. "I always think it's best not to drag these things out, don't you? Much better for all concerned to move swiftly."

"Yes," I agreed. "Strike while the iron's hot and all that."

Arnold nodded and laughed, a stagy sound entirely devoid of warmth. Then he fixed me with a sudden, cold stare. "How does right now sound?"

I swallowed hard. "Right now?"

He pressed his fingertips together again and said no more.

"Okay," I said. "I guess I'll just, eh, go and clear my desk."

Arnold reached behind him and produced a glossy paper bag emblazoned with the Liebermann Brothers logo encircled by holly, one of a consignment we'd had made up the previous Christmas for client gifts. "I took the liberty of asking Cordelia to do that for you. Gerard has kindly deactivated your computer password. If you'd like to hand over your electronic pass and sign these papers, we'll be all set."

CHAPTER THIRTY-THREE

A brief funeral ceremony is to be conducted at the graveside by a humanist celebrant. "We don't want a priest," your father said when he told you about the arrangements on the phone. "We have never been religious."

It's true. Your family has never been religious. It's a political family. And you are not religious, but you somehow do want a priest: white robes fluttering in the wind, arms raised high as he says, "Ashes to ashes, dust to dust."

Your father is sombre in a black overcoat, and your mother is dressed in an old navy blue suit you haven't seen her wear in years. She walks behind your father, arm-in-arm with Angelika, a young nurse from the old people's home who was fond of Jürgen. You know they arrived separately, but for a brief moment they look as though they are together, united in grief.

Aunt Vladka is waiting at the cemetery gate. She hugs you and Gert in turn, and her scent of cigarettes and hairspray catapults you back to those Saturday afternoons you used to spend learning Czech in her little apartment full of colourful cushions and candles in glass bottles. Jürgen often used to collect you at the end of the afternoon, and Aunt Vladka would sometimes treat you both to an ice cream at a local milk bar.

"This is Olaf," you tell her, turning to the tall, slim man at your side. "Jürgen's training partner."

She clasps his hand. "Thank you for coming."

When the hearse arrives, you see that your father has spared no expense. He's burying his son in a heavy hardwood casket with brass handles. He still has money. Under the terms of the treaty of reunification the pensions of former government officials have been preserved. His is generous, and he still receives the extra allowance accorded to him in the GDR as a Fighter Against Fascism.

The celebrant is introduced to you as Joachim Witzlack. He wears a shiny dark blue suit and tinted glasses, and his hair is plastered to his head with hair oil. He has the grey complexion of a chain smoker, and it doesn't take much of an effort of imagination to picture him with a microphone hidden in his lapel and a recording device in his pocket. The old members of the state security service pop up in all kinds of places, but humanist celebrant is a new one on you.

You clutch Gert's hand as the coffin is lowered into the ground and try to block out Herr Witzlack's rasping monotone. Your mother sobs and lurches forward, supported by Angelika, to throw a rose into the grave. Olaf throws in an old photograph of him and Jürgen in front of the sports academy in their GDR tracksuits. What was that term the old regime had for its sportsmen and women? Ambassadors in tracksuits. And those who defected were traitors in tracksuits. Your father picks up a handful of earth, throws it on to the coffin and bows. You do the same, and that's it.

"Ladies and gentlemen, the ceremony is over," Herr

Witzlack says. You wonder what he did before. You can just see him sitting at one of the long interrogation tables in the Stasi remand prison, smoking cigarettes and quizzing prisoners about their sex lives. "Herr Reinsch would now like to invite you for lunch."

The meal is at an inn on what is still called Karl Marx Street. Since reunification, the street names have been changing all the time in the new states of the Federal Republic. You sometimes wonder who decides which names can stay and which must go. Dimitroff Street, named after the Bulgarian communist leader, has been renamed Danziger Street, and Ho Chi Minh Street is now Weißenseer Way. But Rosa-Luxemburg Platz remains the same, as does Paul Robeson Street. Perhaps it is only those who held political office whose names must be expunged from the street map.

In the restaurant, your mother sits at one end of the table with Angelika, and your father sits at the other with Herr Witzlack. Despite all the time that has passed since their divorce, your parents barely speak. You suspect that somewhere deep down inside, your father still loves your mother but can't admit it, even to himself. And while your mother might find it in her heart to forgive him for exposing her affair with the second violinist, she will never get over the loss of her musical career.

You order bratwurst with puréed potatoes and cucumber salad and a vodka to steady your nerves. It's good, but your mouth is dry and you can only pick at it.

"You look well," Aunt Vladka says and squeezes your hand across the table.

"So do you." It's true. She's chic in a long purple coat and strawberry coloured scarf. You know she struggles financially. She probably got these clothes at a flea market or as a hand-me-down from a friend. Like so many decent people, she has lost out in the new system.

"Can I get you anything, Frau Reinsch?" Gert asks your mother. "Salt? Pepper?"

She shakes her head and asks you if Kwan will be all right. "He's with Gert's sister. He'll be fine."

"Another beer," you hear Herr Witzlack call to the waiter. "I hope you were happy with the service, Ewald," he says to your father. "It was kind of you to give me the job. Things aren't what they used to be. I sometimes think the world's gone mad. Good men who worked hard for their country are being persecuted. That's the only word for it. Still. Some old colleagues like us still stick together, don't we, Ewald?"

"It was a very nice service," your father says.

You realise then that your father has employed this ex-Stasi man to bury your brother because he's down on his luck. Maybe he's even the subject of a prosecution. He reminds you powerfully of the colonel who interviewed you at the Stasi HQ in Leipzig when you were first arrested. Suddenly, the memories from that terrible day when Olaf came to see you about your brother come flooding back and you can stand this quiet lunch no longer.

"Papa," you say, "as we have Olaf here today and we haven't seen him in such a long time, I wonder if I can I ask you a question?"

Herr Witzlack coughs and lights a cigarette. "Uh-huh," he says. "Here we go."

Your father looks up. He's caught your tone, and his face hardens beneath the soft, fleshy contours imposed by age.

"Ask away," he says.

"Why did you cover up for Manfred?"

"Ha!" He laughs, but his laugh is hollow. "My dear, this is all very much in the past. And I hardly think it's the right topic of conversation for this occasion."

He doesn't say "Manfred who?" or "What do you mean?" though you haven't spoken of Manfred in years.

"Why not? We can talk about these things now. Times have changed. I want to know, Papa. Why did you cover up for him?"

"I did not cover up for him, as you put it. I don't know what you're talking about. And this really isn't the moment."

"Magda," your mother says in a small, tired voice that infuriates you because you remember it so well from childhood. "Your father is right. Now is not the best time to discuss these things."

Your father is right. How many times did you hear that when you were growing up? Even after the divorce, she often supported his decisions with regard to you and Jürgen.

"You're just as bad," you say. "You didn't do anything either. I'm not saying you knew they were giving Jürgen steroids before the accident," you say to your father. "But afterwards. When Olaf told you what had happened. You covered it up. Why?"

The table is silent. No one has ever talked about what happened in this way. No one has ever uttered the word 'steroids.' Not even you.

"My dear," your father says, "sometimes life deals us a tough hand. The best thing we can do then is to accept our situation. The worst thing we can do is to look for someone else to blame. We don't want to become like the Americans and start looking for someone to sue every time we experience a misfortune."

He laughs, and Herr Witzlack joins in. "Indeed no," he says. "We wouldn't want to get like that."

"A misfortune? Is that what you call it?"

"There's no evidence it was anything else."

You stare at him in disbelief. "Yes there is. Olaf told you Manfred was doping the athletes. He'd been doing it for years. Then he upped Jürgen's dose, and that's when he had his so-called 'accident'."

'Doping.' That's another word that has never been spoken among the family.

"But he couldn't prove it."

Olaf coughs. "I could prove it, Herr Reinsch. I had the confidential medication records. I removed them from the training centre at considerable risk to myself. As I recall, you didn't want to see them."

"I'll thank you to mind your own business, young man." Your father dabs at his mouth with his napkin and glares round the table. "What is this? Some kind of plot?"

"I didn't know that Olaf had obtained the medication records," says Aunt Vladka. Why didn't you look at them, Ewald?"

"I'll thank you to mind your own business too," your father snaps. "As I recall your main contribution at a time of family tragedy was to smuggle my daughter out of the country entirely against her best interests." He juts out his chin and addresses the table. "The medication records had been obtained illegally."

"Jürgen was being doped illegally," you say.

"You don't know that's true," your father says.

There are tears in your mother's eyes, and she pats Angelika's arm sorrowfully. "Why does everyone keep rehashing the past?" she says. "Can't they see how painful it is for me? I was his mother."

"Hush, Elena," Aunt Vladka mutters. "This is not about you."

"It was true," you say. "You know it was."

"I don't know it. It might have been true and it might not."

"So if it wasn't true, what happened to Jürgen, in your opinion?"

"A person can become ill for many reasons."

You stare at him. "But, Papa, I think it's all very clear. There have been newspaper reports, television programmes. Our athletes were given steroids manufactured by Jenapharm and told they were vitamins. Their coaches deceived them. Coaches like Manfred."

"It is not clear at all," your father says. "Perhaps some of our athletes were given steroids. I don't know about that. But there's no evidence this happened to Jürgen. First point. And, even if it did, there's no evidence that this is what caused his accident. Second point. Just because something is reported in the newspapers doesn't mean it's true. The western media loves to run down our Republic. For your information, West German athletes were given steroids too. It happened everywhere."

"That's true, Herr Reinsch," Olaf says, "but they knew they were taking them. They had a choice."

Your father waves a dismissive hand. "It was illegal."

You look at him. *Our Republic.* You remember being in the stand at the Gymnastics and Sports Festival in Leipzig the year before your brother's accident, listening to a successful female athlete addressing the crowd: "*People ask what the secret of our sporting success is. There is no secret. It's all because of actually existing socialism. The future is on our side: on the side of socialism.*" The crowd cheered, and you cheered with them. Back then, you scoffed at the things you'd heard people in the West said about the East German athletes. About doping. You thought they were jealous of your country's athletic prowess. But it was all true.

"Papa, there have been court cases. Coaches have been given prison sentences."

"Not Manfred."

"No," Olaf mutters. "Manfred got away with it. He had friends in high places."

"There have been any number of court cases since 1990 in this area and in other areas too," your father says. "It's called victor's justice. That's how it is in the wonderful new Germany. Personally, I think we've paid a very heavy price to have bananas in the shops and shiny new cars on every street corner. I look around me and I see young people with no jobs and no hope. I see homeless people. Did you ever see a homeless person in our Republic? Were you afraid to go out at night?"

He's jutting his chin out again. It's odd. You agree with much of what he says. It's true that things are not so wonderful in the new Germany. The West Germans are arrogant. They think they know it all. People like you have become strangers in their own country. Everything from the past has been swept away, whether it was good or bad, without anyone asking if that's what people want. The old regime blamed everything on the West Germans. *The trail of blood leads to Bonn!* In the new Germany, the East Germans are the ugly ones with their thick accents, poor English and badly cut clothes – the butt of jokes and an endless source of resentment because of the cost of reunification. All the dreams from 1989 of building a better kind of GDR, creating a new kind of socialism, are long forgotten.

"We don't want to be a Kohl plantation," people shouted after the Wall came down. But that's exactly what your country became – and you do still think of it as your country. The slogans you chanted at the Monday demonstrations in Leipzig sound hollow today: WE ARE THE PEOPLE. Now you think:

227

WE WERE THE PEOPLE. For a few weeks. Not longer.

"Think about our women," your father continues. "Before there was a Kindergarten place for every child. Every woman had the opportunity to work. Even if a woman didn't have a husband, she could look after her children."

You look at your plate, where the half-eaten bratwurst and potato purée lie uneaten and congealing. When you were pregnant with Kwan your father said you were behaving as if you still lived in the GDR.

"The child has no father. How will you pay your way?" When it became clear you were going to keep the baby, your father's advice was to marry Dong-Sun, Kwan's father. "You can't bring up a child on your own in this new Germany."

And you did think about marrying Dong-Sun for those kinds of economic reasons. But it would never have worked out. Dong-Sun is a gentle soul. That's what initially drew you to him. Your short affair began not long after you saw your files at Normannen Street. You and Dong-Sun were united in confusion. You were confused by what you'd seen in your files, and he was confused by life in the new Germany. Although Dong-Sun grew up in Germany and didn't see his North Korean father from the age of ten, when, like so many North Korean men, he was sent home, there is a lot of the North Korean in Dong-sun. You know he misses the certainties of the old GDR. That's why it would never have worked between you.

You rub your face. It's been a long day. You look across at your father. He's still jutting his chin out, looking round the table defiantly.

"You know," he says, "when the border was sealed in 1961 people were happy. It meant no more sabotage from the West. No more doctors and dentists disappearing over the border to earn more money. No more disruptions to production because essential workers were being lured away by capitalist bribes. It gave us a firm base on which to build the fairer society we were trying to create. That's what people wanted. You probably can't even begin to imagine what it was like back then. We'd come through the bloodiest war in history. Our country had been brought to the brink of destruction by National Socialism. We wanted to build something better: a new Germany based on the principles of equality and socialism."

He smiles and you try to smile back. What he says isn't untrue. But it's not the whole truth either.

"But you didn't create a better, fairer society," you say. "That's the problem."

"Well, I won't deny there were problems. But there are problems in every society. At least we tried to make something that was better. At least we had something to believe in and work towards. We were working towards communism and we were happy. What do people believe in today?"

You look at the table. You don't have an answer to that question. "Things happened that can't be excused," you say.

"Well, you're entitled to your opinion." He pats your hand. "You've always had firm views."

"Huh," says Herr Witzlack, lighting a cigarette. "All women have firm views."

Your father appears not to hear him. Instead, he looks into your eyes and, speaking very quietly, says, "I'm sorry."

You nod. "I know."

Suddenly, you feel sorry for him. He's been lying to himself all these years. Imagine the strain.

And what about you? Haven't you been lying to yourself too. You've been telling yourself that you're fine now, when you're not. That it's better to live privately than to confront the demons from your past. But isn't that what you refused to do in the GDR? To live only in the private sphere. Why have you never spoken to your father about doping before? The same reason that you've cut yourself off from all political engagement. Because you're afraid.

Well, maybe it's time to stop being afraid.

CHAPTER THIRTY-FOUR

"This is the hardest thing I've ever had to do," Annabel said when she left me three weeks after I lost my job at Liebermann Brothers.

"Well, don't do it then."

"It's not that simple." She smiled sadly. "I can't go on like this."

"Like what?"

"You know what I mean."

And that was it. All of a sudden after all those years of brave faces, she'd had enough. She said she couldn't talk to me. She said she wanted a baby. She said I left the room every time she said this.

Before I was fired, she'd wanted me to go to AA. They have these special meetings in the Square Mile for City executives. They start at 6.30am so all the City alkies – and believe me, there are plenty of them – can be back at their desks flexing their Bulgari cuff links by 8am on the dot. She begged me. *Please go. If not for yourself then for me.* And I did go along a couple of times to please her, but it wasn't for me.

She was very decent about everything when the end came. There was no shouting, no more nagging. She left the money for her share of the bills in the kitty jar and insisted on paying a month's rent in lieu of notice. I never had got round to remortgaging the flat in both our names. That was something else she was always moaning about: *I have no financial security.*

"Financial security is like religion," I used to say to her. "It's all an illusion."

Her brother Jeremy came to collect her in a hired van. He didn't come into the flat. There had been an incident at the *Bunch of Grapes* when I still worked at Liebermann Brothers, and we no longer got on. Annabel assembled all her packed boxes and suitcases in the hall by the front door and took them out one by one on to the metal staircase that led down to the car park where Jeremy picked them up.

When she was ready to leave, she kissed me on the cheek and told me to look after myself. Then she picked up the one remaining suitcase and walked towards the door. She was wearing a green skirt I liked – it swished about her knees in a nice, feminine way – and a fitted leather jacket that showed off her slim waist.

"Annabel?" I said.

She held up a hand. "Please don't, Bob."

I heard the click of her heels on the metal staircase, and I wandered into the hallway feeling utterly desolate. A moment later she was back. I felt a surge of joy. She'd changed her mind! Then I took in what she was saying.

"Did you hear me? I said I forgot to give you the keys. I'll leave them on the telephone table, shall I?"

I scratched my head. "You can hold on to them if you like. They could come in handy. You might want to ... pop round some time."

She put them down. "No thanks."

That's when I finally realised it was over. We'd been together for over ten years. We'd talked about marriage and kids, and now it was over. What was I going to do without her? She cooked my food. She cleaned the house. She kept up with our friends.

"Annabel," I said, "listen – "

"Shut up, Bob," she interrupted. "Please. There's nothing left to say."

"What do you mean? Of course there are things left to say."

"I have to go."

I grabbed her arm. "Look, Annabel, I'll sort myself out. I promise. I know I've been a pain lately, but now I'm out of Liebermann Brothers things are going to change. That place was getting me down. I'm going to cut down on my drinking and make a fresh start."

"Cut down on your drinking? Don't you understand, Bob? You can't cut down on your drinking. You need to stop. You're an alcoholic!"

I glared at her, hurt. "All right, all right. I'll stop drinking altogether then if that's what you want. It's whatever you want, sweetheart. Just say the word."

She sighed. "I need to go. Jeremy's waiting."

"Don't do this to me, Annabel." My voice cracked. "I can't manage without you. I need you, for fuck's sake. I love you.

"If there was any hope, I'd stay, but there isn't." She picked up her suitcase and left.

A month later, I put the flat on the market. I couldn't stand living there without her. It was like a ghost flat. Lighter squares on the walls where her pictures had been. Empty drawers and hangers in the bedroom. Rotting food in the cupboards and fridge.

After the sale went through, I rented a bachelor pad on Noel Road in Islington. I liked it because it had a garden, it looked on to Regent's Canal and it was near *The Island Queen* pub. *The Island Queen* is the kind of pub that makes you feel good about drinking. It was full of arty types lubricating their creative machinery.

I added the money I'd made from the sale of the flat to what was left of my pay-off from Liebermann Brothers and opened a business account. It came to a tidy sum, which is why the bank allowed me to have a business account. Apparently, my credit rating was shot to pieces because of some unpaid bills.

"It's been a difficult time," I told the business account executive. "My fiancée and I have unfortunately split up."

"I understand," he said, ogling the zeros on the cheque.

I bought a state-of-the-art iBook laptop and got some business cards printed in the name of City Savvy Translations. *Managing Director: Robert J McPherson*, they read. That sounded good. For a couple of weeks I stayed moderately sober during the day and sometimes spent several hours at a stretch sitting in front of the iBook tap-tapping on the keyboard, *formulating a business plan*.

But it didn't last long. Pretty soon, I was desperately lonely. And when you're lonely, you need a friend; you need your best friend. In the flat on Noel Road, I began to drink more than I'd ever drunk before.

It all came to a head one early spring evening. I'd begun to feel embarrassed buying booze in my local off licence, and so I was on my way to Sainsbury's in the car. I didn't see the Range Rover bowling down Colebrooke Row, and I smashed headlong into the passenger door. It was a woman driver. She took one look at me and got straight on her mobile to the police.

"He's drunk," I heard her screaming. "He's not fit to drive. My son could've been killed. Killed!"

"She was going too fast," I told the police when they arrived.

"Have you been drinking, sir?" asked one of the officers, a tall sandy-haired Scot who looked about 19.

"I had one glass of white wine with dinner. That's not a crime, is it?"

"White wine is alcohol, sir. Could I ask you to step into the back of the car for me?"

They did a breath test, and I was charged with drink driving. It was a second offence, so I knew I'd lose my licence. But that wasn't the worst part. The worst part was when I looked out of the police car window and saw the woman I'd driven into comforting her wee boy. He was shaking and his face was smeared with tears, and it was all my fault.

The following week, my cleaning lady resigned. Radojka was a good-looking young Serbian woman with long black hair and dark soulful eyes. I looked forward to her visits. She called me Mr McPherson and smiled sweetly when I paid her.

She came on Tuesday mornings and I was always careful to take it easy on Monday nights so I could be up and at the iBook when she let herself in. But that week I forgot and spent Monday evening with a bottle of whisky. The next thing I knew Radojka was slapping my face and saying, "Mr McPherson, are you okay?"

Slowly I came to. *What is Radojka doing here in the middle of the night?* I thought. For a brief moment, I thought I'd got lucky. Then I saw the sun slanting through the blinds. It was daytime. I looked down. I was lying on the bed half-naked. I pulled the duvet up and fumbled for the alarm clock on the bedside table:

11 am, the time Radojka came round each Tuesday.

"Mr McPherson?" Radojka said.

"I'm, eh … Christ."

I tried to sit up. Then something happened. Maybe I reached out a hand to her, and she got the wrong idea. I don't know. Her tone changed. Suddenly, she was putting on her coat and swapping her work trainers for her high-heeled street boots.

"Where are you going?" I asked as she headed out of the bedroom door. I pulled the duvet round me and scrambled out of bed.

"Stay where you are," she ordered, grabbing her bag from the hall table.

She marched to the door. I stumbled after her, tripping over the duvet and banging hard into the wall.

"I haven't paid you," I said.

"I didn't do the job. I don't want to be paid."

She let herself out, slamming the door behind her. My keys came flying through the letterbox, and I heard her thumping down the stairs in her sexy boots. *Radojka has left the building*, I thought, slumping to the floor, and that's pretty much the last thing I remember about that week and the one that allegedly followed.

*

I woke feeling like someone was shaving bits of bone off my skull with an angle grinder. A woman I didn't know was bending over me. She was young and sweet with a shiny complexion and fine blonde hair cut in a short bob.

"Can you hear me, sir?" she asked.

I blinked and tried to bring her into focus. She was wearing a white coat and a badge that read: Dr S. J. Henderson. I glanced round. I was lying on a trolley between two green screens in the middle of a noisy room.

"I don't feel well," I said.

"That doesn't surprise me, sir."

"Where am I?"

"Homerton Hospital, sir. You were admitted to accident and emergency at – " She consulted a chart. "2.35am." She smiled brightly. "Are you able to stand up, sir?"

"What day is it?" I asked, easing my legs over the edge of the trolley.

"Friday."

I put my feet on the floor and heaved myself up to standing. I was as weak as a kitten. I stood by the trolley clutching on to my trousers, while the doctor listened to my heart beat and took my blood pressure.

"I meant what's the date?"

She gave me a sharp look. "10th of March. Any blood in your stools, sir?"

10th of March. I tried to work back. What was the last date I could remember?

"Sir? Any blood in your stools?"

"No. Eh … I don't know."

She looked at my chart again. "Your friend who called the ambulance told the paramedics that you're an alcoholic and had been on a drinking binge. How much had you been drinking, sir?"

"I … eh …. I'm not sure, doctor."

"A bottle of spirits a day? Two bottles?"

"A bottle," I lied.

She made a note on the chart. "Right, sir. Your friend said that you had been vomiting blood. You have stated that you are uncertain if there has been blood in your stools. A rectal examination is therefore indicated to rule out an anal fissure. I'll just pop outside for a minute. If you'd like to remove your trousers and lie face down on the trolley, we'll get that done."

She began to pull the screens. A rectal examination? I didn't want some young girl shoving her finger up my arse.

"Is that really necessary?" I asked, tears forming in my eyes. She smiled grimly. "Yes, sir, it is."

After the examination, I was left on a trolley in A&E for three and a half hours before an orderly arrived to take me upstairs. I was put in a ward full of old men with bladder problems. I have never felt so ill or so ashamed. The DTs were starting, and although the doctor had given me a Diazepam, they were still pretty bad. My mouth felt like a gerbil cage, but I wasn't allowed a drink because I was nil by mouth until they could work out why I'd been vomiting blood.

I was seeing things I knew weren't there. Spiders the size of a cat crawling up the screens. Maggoty creatures erupting from the skin on my arm. Hallucinations. I wanted to scream, but forced myself to stay quiet. I didn't want that girl doctor to come back. The determined look on her face as she pinged on her latex gloves had made me shudder. As I lay on the trolley, weak, dehydrated and juddering from the DTs, snatches of memory from the previous days came back to me. Lying on the living room floor at Noel Road, wet and shivery with a paramedic crouching beside me saying, "I'm concerned about your heartbeat, sir. It's very fast." Jeremy standing in the living room door, his lip curled in disgust, saying, "Christ, he's not even dressed. Get him some trousers, would you, Bel?" And behind him, Annabel, pale and anxious, asking the paramedic if I was going to be all right.

Two days later, Chris visited me in hospital. I hadn't seen him in over a year. I must have been asleep when he arrived because I woke to find him pacing by my bed.

"Big man!" I yelled.

"Hiya!" he replied with manufactured brightness. "How are you?"

"How do I look? I saw myself in the mirror yesterday and I looked like an old jakey. Too bad because they sent this girl round to see me and she was quite fit. Sally her name was. But I've had some nutritionally complete drinks since then. Maybe things have improved?"

"To be honest, you don't look too good."

"Suppose not. How did you know I was here?"

"Long story. Here's the short version: Annabel phoned your mum, and your mum phoned me."

"My mum *phoned* you?"

"Yup."

"Why did she do that?"

He pulled up a chair and sat down by my bed. "She was worried, wee man."

"Annabel shouldn't have phoned her. I'm going to have a word with her about that when I get out of here."

Chris rubbed his face. "She didn't know what else to do. You know it was her who called the ambulance? She'd been phoning you and getting no answer and she got worried. She went round to the flat with Jeremy and he broke the door down. Apparently, it was a bit of a mess in there. Piss and puke everywhere. She was quite upset."

I stared at the bedclothes. "She shouldn't have phoned my mum," I repeated.

"I don't think she felt she had a choice."

I swallowed hard. "Didn't you bring me any grapes?" I asked.

Chris didn't smile. "Wee man, we need to talk."

He told me that he wanted me to try AA. He had some leaflets with him and everything. Fucking AA. It was everyone's solution to everything. No one understood. Like the alcohol counsellor who'd come to see me earlier with her swishy blonde hair and shapely tanned legs. She'd looked impossibly healthy, like a visitor from another world. What could she possibly know about the dark places I'd been on the bottle? How could she counsel me?

"Who put you up to this?" I asked.

"Nobody."

"Look, I don't want to go to AA. It's full of crackpots. It's not for me. And you don't need to worry about me. This whole business has been a massive wake-up call. Did I tell you they gave me an endoscopy? It was horrible. I thought I was going to choke. There's no way I'm going through that again. I won't be drinking again when I get out of here. That's it. It's all over."

"So, you're going to stop?"

"That's what I just said."

"What? Just like that?"

"Yeah. Just like that."

"It won't work. You've been there before."

"Not like this I haven't. This is different. I've had a shock this time."

He put the AA leaflets down on the bed. "Look, I've come all the way down from Edinburgh to see you. I've taken time off work. I've left Joanna on her own with the kids, which, let me tell you, she wasn't too happy about. You've had shocks before. I'd like you to promise me you'll at least give AA a try."

"What is this? Did you promise my mum you'd get me to go or something?"

He didn't say anything. So that was it. He had promised her. They'd all been madly in touch. Making plans for Bobbie. It was a conspiracy.

I pushed the leaflets towards him. "Away with you!" I said, trying to be funny.

But again, he didn't laugh. He'd changed since he got married. No longer the black-eyed rogue I'd known as a kid. He stood up. "I've got to go," he said, and there was a whole subtext in those words. The long journey back to Edinburgh. Joanna at home on her own with the kids. All the trouble he'd been put to. All the trouble everyone had been put to.

I didn't fucking ask you to come, I wanted to say. Instead, I rallied my forces and said, "Thanks for coming to see me, big man. I appreciate it."

He stood for a moment looking at the floor, then bent down and picked up a wisp of blood-stained cotton wool. "Hospitals are filthy these days," he said, dropping it absent-mindedly into the bin. When he turned back to me, his face was as bleak as a rainy day in Glencoe and there were tears in his eyes.

"I'd like you to know that I miss you," he said. "You're my best friend. We've known each other since we were five. You've been like a brother to me. I'm asking you to please sort yourself out. I'll help in any way I can, but it's got to come from you, wee man. You're the only one who can fix this."

When he left I felt like I'd been kicked. My body started to shake, and a yelp of pain rose from somewhere deep inside me. He was my best friend. I loved him. I couldn't make him laugh any more but it seemed I could make him cry. The next day I told the nurse that I would like to have another appointment with the nice lady from the South Islington Alcohol Advisory Centre after all.

CHAPTER THIRTY-FIVE

District Administration
Leipzig,
25.11.1985
for State Security
stern-rö
L e i p z i g
Evaluation and Control Group

OPK "Hamlet" - Registration Number: VI/946/83
Department XX/9 – Comrade Pankowitcz (2514)

The OPK investigation of:

REINSCH, Magdalena Maria (16.06.64) – "Coralie"

was initiated on 10.10.1984. The main reason for the Operative
Personenkontrolle (Operative Control of an Individual) was
"Coralie"'s previous unstable political-cultural attitude, which
manifested itself in the form of a distorted understanding of the
conditions in socialist countries, leading "Coralie" to abandon

her studies at the Karl Marx University Leipzig (KMU) and seek out links with negative-hostile elements. "Coralie" has since been rehabilitated and readmitted to the Party and to the translation and interpretation study programme at KMU.

The operational plan is to use three IMs (unofficial collaborators) to monitor "Coralie"'s progress from a political standpoint while she is participating in study at KMU. In the further investigation of this case, the information of IMS "Babylonia" should be taken into account; according to this information "Coralie" 'often ponders her future in the GDR' and 'expresses hostile opinions'.

You flick forward to one of the reports "Babylonia" wrote:

District Administration
Leipzig, 30.04.1986
for State Security
stern-rö
L e i p z i g
Department XX/9

Report from IMS "Babylonia" on recent meetings with "Coralie"

Two meetings took place between "Coralie" and me in the past week, and further to these meetings it was possible to establish and elaborate on the following information regarding the surveillance object's proposed actions and state of mind:

On 15.05.1986 she intends to travel to the city of Prague in the Czechoslovak Socialist Republic in order to participate in a touristic excursion with the individual named MCPHERSON, Robert James ("Highlander"), a British research student currently resident at 2034 Leipzig, 18th October Street, No 8.

This touristic excursion is not to be understood as indicative of a romantic intention on the part of the surveillance object. Her objective is rather to create the impression of a romantic intention in order to deflect attention away from other planned negative-hostile activities whose end purpose is to facilitate an illegal crossing of the state border.

At the bottom of the report, there is this:

Expenses:
1 pot coffee	8.75 M
2 pieces cheese cake	à 3.50 M
1 bottle red wine	9.00 M
	24.75 M

There was also a stipend of 225.00 East Marks per month. Was that the motivation?

You close the folder and put the file back on the top shelf of the metal store cupboard. The other shelves hold your developer, film processing tanks and old negatives. You created this workroom cum darkroom not long after you moved into the apartment on Pflaster Street.

Before, it was a kind of dressing room off the main bedroom. The walls were painted a dark shade of plum and there was a divan against one wall. Above the divan hung a framed black and white photograph of Marek in a trench coat on the Marx-Engels Bridge that you took, which had appeared on the fashion pages of *Sibylle* magazine. You still have it, tucked away in a drawer somewhere. His hair was long then. Past his shoulders. He's staring moodily into the river, a burning cigarette in one hand. So handsome. So in control.

He brought you to this room the first time you made

love. He opened the heavy velvet curtains and sat you on the window ledge as he undid your blouse, lingering over each button. "You're so beautiful," he said, as he caressed your small breasts. "So strong and firm. Not like a woman at all. Like a boy, only better." He turned you round and eased down your jeans and pants. "I love you," he whispered, as he moved inside you. "What we have is special. It's not like other loves. We'll always be together in our own way."

In our own way. You knew what that meant. And you didn't mind. You didn't mind at all. You wanted a love that was special and like no other.

Now you understand how damaged you were by your brother's accident. But back then you thought this special love from Marek would see you home.

At your trial, they knew everything, and you didn't understand how that could be. You were so naïve, ducking Jana and thinking you were very clever. Organising a decoy. You had no idea how intensively you were being watched. Perhaps no one did. People suppressed their suspicions about those closest to them. Otherwise, how could they have gone on?

You reach up and take the file back down from the metal store cupboard. This is the first time you have looked at your Stasi files since the day when Gert picked you up from Normannen Street.

It's time to look again. Time to be brave. You've known that since your father's stunted apology at Jürgen's funeral. You open the file and spread the contents out on the floor. There you are sunbathing with Marek in the garden at the hut by the lake. Here's a photo of you walking along Shakespeare Street in the rain.

There are other photos too. From later. They never stopped watching you. Here's one of you and Uncle Ivan in the Hotel

Metropol (freely convertible currencies only). You met him there after your release. A newspaper contact of his had told him you were out, and he wrote to you at Shakespeare Street suggesting a time.

He strode across the hotel foyer towards you in his crumpled, seersucker suit and took you in his arms. He didn't notice the way the young man standing under the clocks behind the reception desk that showed the time in Moscow, Havana and Beijing turned to watch you in the mirror as he steered you towards the elevator, saying, "You have time for dinner, right? Is here okay? The restaurant in this hotel is not at all bad."

The restaurant was a festival of plastic East German luxury. You shrunk into your chair as Uncle Ivan scanned the wine list.

"I'll take a beer," you said, choosing an eastern brand. When the waiter came, you opted for the cheapest thing on the menu: pork schnitzel and chips.

After you'd ordered, Uncle Ivan took off his glasses and looked into your eyes. "Are you all right?" he asked. "We were so worried about you when we found out what had happened."

You didn't really know how to answer that question. Were you all right? The week before your periods had started again, having stopped when you were in the tiger cage, and so you said, "Yes, I'm all right."

"I feel so responsible," he said.

"It wasn't your fault."

"I really thought we'd considered everything. I still don't know how they found out."

"Neither do I."

"And then, you were gone and we had no information. Nothing. We just had to keep hoping you'd be able to get a message out."

"I did try, but somehow it didn't get through."

"If only we'd got it. Marek left a bit later." He glanced over at you a little warily when he said that. Perhaps he thought this news would make you angry. But you were beyond anger by then.

"I know," you said.

Uncle Ivan didn't tell you how Marek got out, and you didn't ask, not least because of the waiter standing just inside your field of vision, who had been polishing the same glass for the past five minutes.

"If we'd had more information we could have done something for you from over there."

You shrugged. "I'm out now."

"I have a message for you from Marek."

You put a finger to your lips. "Let's take a walk."

You walked from the hotel down Unter den Linden, stopping at the Marx Engels Bridge, where you looked into the River Spree just as Marek does in the photograph from *Sibylle*.

"You've changed," Uncle Ivan said.

You shrugged. "Maybe."

"Marek is in West Berlin," he said. "He stayed there because he didn't want to be too far away from you. He can't come over. He's still an East German citizen in the eyes of the government here. He asked me to tell you that he thinks about you often and that we're at your disposal if you want to try again."

You looked into the river. He thinks about you often. What had he said when you first made love at Pflaster Street? *We'll always be together in our own way.*

In Leipzig, you had been talking to Torsten about putting on an exhibition of your photographs. You and Kerstin had joined a pressure group called Alliance 88 and were hosting regular meetings at Shakespeare Street. Mrs Dannewitz hadn't been well and relied on you to get her shopping.

"I want to stay here," you said.

You lay the photograph of you and Uncle Ivan at the Hotel Metropol down on the floor. They weren't as good with a camera as you are, the grey men from the Stasi. But that's okay. You have your own photos too. You can do something with this material. Something that will take you outside of the private sphere. It's time. You owe it to Jürgen. And to yourself.

Tomorrow, you'll phone Torsten at the gallery.

CHAPTER THIRTY-SIX

I landed at Tempelhof Airport on a dark, wintry evening in early December, back in Berlin for the first time since I was thrown out of the GDR at the Sonnenallee checkpoint. I'd been to West Germany a couple of times in the intervening years. There had been trips to Frankfurt when I was at Liebermann Brothers. But I hadn't been east of the River Elbe in fourteen years.

I stared out of the window as the S-Bahn snaked eastwards through Kreuzberg and into Friedrichstraße on elevated tracks. Across the river spun the circular neon logo of the Berliner Ensemble. I'd gone there once with Kevin to see a production of the second part of Goethe's *Faust*, an impenetrable and noisy rampage which served only to prove that those who said *Faust II* couldn't be staged were probably right.

My hotel was on Unter den Linden. I'd booked it because I knew it. Back in the day, it had been an Interhotel for western tourists and I'd sometimes drunk coffee in the downstairs restaurant, which looked on to the street. The restaurant was almost empty when I checked in, and when I'd dumped my luggage in my room I went back there and ate a meal of Wiener Schnitzel, fried potatoes and cucumber salad. When the waitress asked me if I'd like to see the wine list, I answered "No" rather more emphatically than was perhaps strictly necessary. It was one of the things I was learning: how to refuse alcohol without making a big deal of it.

"Could I have a sparkling mineral water with lime, please," I said, glancing up at her. She was called Kristina and her hair was pulled back in a glossy blonde pony tail. "Lime, not lemon."

My plan for the evening was to take a walk and then to get an early night. The next day, I was to take the train to Leipzig, where I had an appointment at the Federal Authority for the Records of the State Security Service of the Former German Democratic Republic.

I scrunched up my napkin, pulled on my coat and headed out into the night. I walked briskly past Friedrichstraße in the direction of the Brandenburg Gate, breathing in the smell of roasting chestnuts and the freezing night air. I stuffed my hands in my coat pockets, cursing myself for forgetting to bring gloves, and turned up my collar against the biting cold.

At the Brandenburg Gate, I stopped for a moment to watch people ambling across what had once been the most heavily fortified border in the world. Fourteen years previously, when I was in West Berlin trying to find a way to get back to the East, I'd huddled on to a viewing platform on the western side with a bunch of tourists. *So grey*, they'd said as we gazed into East Berlin. *Look at the tiny little cars!* But my eyes were fixed on the slender Television Tower which glinted to me in the sunlight like a beacon.

Later, I took the U-Bahn to Wedding, passing through the ghost stations patrolled by armed guards. There were fewer tourists at the viewing platform there, and I stood for a long time staring at the sign that read 'FIN DU SECTEUR FRANCAIS'. Beyond the watchtower, where guards could be seen moving about, were the blocked-up apartment buildings on Bernauer Street. Marek's apartment on Pflaster Street was just a few streets away.

Now the only reminder of that time was a double line of cobblestones threaded through the tarmac interrupted at intervals by a brass plaque that read 'Berliner Mauer, 1961-1989'. I turned and headed back through the bare lime trees on Unter den Linden towards the river, where I crossed the bridge and headed down Karl Liebknecht Street. It was like a visiting an old friend who's been very ill: familiar but different. The brown windows of the Palace of the Republic were strewn with graffiti. The cathedral had been tarted up. Shiny new trams trundled along the tracks, occasionally coupled to renovated cars from the old days.

Suddenly, I felt sickened. My old friend wasn't going to make it. The city had lost its heart and soul. Abruptly, I turned into a side street and marched blindly away from the iconic buildings of the city centre. I'm not sure how far I walked. Several miles at least. Soon I was away from the centre in the streets of Prenzlauer Berg, where freshly renovated apartment buildings painted in bright colours stood side-by-side with dilapidated edifices like the one Magda used to take me to on Shakespeare Street in Leipzig. As I rounded a corner, I caught sight of a café bar that looked familiar. On impulse, I went in.

"A sparkling mineral water," I said to the waiter. "With lime, not lemon."

I picked up the menu. *Café North*. I peered into the interior and recognised enough to know it was it was the same place where I'd seen Magda and Marek kissing on the dance floor to the strains of *Mack the Knife*. I sighed. I'd been such a young fool.

As I waited for my mineral water, I examined the other drinks on the menu: the ones I couldn't have. Red wine. White wine. Prosecco. Sekt. Lager. Dark beer. Malt beer. Vodka. Gin. Whisky. What wouldn't I have given to have one? Just one glass of wine. Or one beer. Something to take the edge off. But it was impossible. I knew that. I'd finally learnt my lesson.

The previous week, I'd celebrated six months of sobriety. Phil shook my hand as I walked through the door of the consulting room at the South Islington Alcohol Advisory Service and gave me a card. It was from Sally. *I'm so proud of you!* it read.

I sat down in the orange plastic bucket chair and stared at the card. "Tell her, tell Sally, I'm sorry," I said, a sob rising in my throat. "Tell her – " I couldn't go on.

Phil squeezed my shoulder and gave me a hankie. "It's all right. She knows … "

I downed my sparkling mineral water, threw some money on the table and got up to go. Time I was safely back in my room at the hotel on Unter den Linden.

*

I woke with a start and sat bolt upright, sweating. My mouth was dry and my head hurt. I'd been drinking. I'd had a beer at *Café North*. Just a small one for old time's sake. *Ein kleines Bier, bitte.* So easy to say. And to drink. Golden liquid in a stem glass glistening with bubbles. Ice cold beer sizzling on my tongue and shimmering down my throat. It was only a beer. Christ's sake. What was that? Four, five per cent? Big deal. But then I wanted a whisky. *Waiter! A whisky, please! Bring me a fucking whisky!* A big continental measure in a thick-bottomed whisky tumbler. I weighed it in my hand, swirling the liquid round, watching the oily traces slide down the glass, then I knocked it back. It stung like fuck and it was beautiful.

I collapsed back on the pillows and closed my eyes. Dreaming that you've had a drink is a normal part of the recovery process, but I hadn't had a dream like that in weeks. I rolled over. The alarm read: 04.39. I jumped out of bed and went over to the minibar. The door clinked as I opened it, and cold light streamed on to my feet. I knelt down and looked at all the little coloured bottles in the door: blue, green, red, amber. I picked up a miniature of Johnny Walker Red Label. The frock-coated man strode jauntily across the label, manufactured in Kilmarnock, about thirty miles from Calderhill. *Keep walking.* That was the Johnny Walker slogan. *Keep walking away.* That was mine. I took a bottle of sparkling mineral water from the bottom shelf, kicked the door shut and got back into bed.

I woke again just before six with the spare pillow clutched to my chest. For a moment, I imagined it was a woman, warm and fragrant and kind. I knew I wouldn't get back to sleep, and so I got up, took a fruit juice from the minibar and pulled back the curtains. I looked out on to the city waking up. The street lights made fuzzy pink and orange dots in the spreading dawn. Breakfast started at seven. My train to Leipzig didn't leave until after ten. I had time to kill. I got the wooden box from Prague out of my suitcase and laid the contents out on the bed. I looked at the photograph of Magda and Marek that Sally had admired. So Marek was in New York. But where was Magda? What had happened to her?

Perhaps I was about to find out. By lunchtime I'd be back in Leipzig, where I had an appointment with a certain Frau Martin at the Museum and Records Office in the former Stasi

HQ. John Bull-Halifax had organised it for me, pleading that I was a special case and should not have to wait the normal time to see my Stasi files.

It was Phil who had persuaded me to get back in touch with Bull-Halifax.

"He might be able to help you find out more," he said. "I know you were angry that you'd been deceived when you found out that Marek was alive and well. But you must have been relieved too. Now you don't have to keep beating yourself up about that, wouldn't it be good to know that things worked out for Magda too?"

"I think he's probably told me everything he knows," I said.

"Even if he has, wouldn't it be good to talk it over with someone who understands?"

I emailed Bull-Halifax at UCL and got a reply straight away. We agreed to meet for lunch the following week at a gastro pub on Farringdon Road called *The Falcon*.

"Bob!" he called as he strode towards me across the pub's fashionably distressed floorboards, flashing his big film star smile. The NHS glasses had been replaced by designer specs and his red-gold curls were shorn, but he hadn't changed much. "Fancy a beer?" he said.

"I'll stick to mineral water."

He smiled across at me, puzzled, I think, for a moment, then said, "Okay. I'll get the menus."

"I'm so glad you got in touch," he said, when we were munching our way through pan-fried Toulouse sausages on a bed of Puy lentils. "You've been on my conscience for months."

He told me he'd hummed and hawed about whether to send me the newspaper cutting, unsure if it would make things better or worse. "When I didn't hear from you, I thought maybe I shouldn't have sent it."

"No," I said. "Overall, I think it made things better. Best on the whole not to go around believing you're responsible for someone's death. But I had to … well … sort myself out a bit before I got in touch."

"You were never responsible for his death," he said. "I said that even at the time. It was the system."

"I felt I was."

"I know you did. That was the worst thing about the Stasi. They really fucked with people's heads. Made them believe things that weren't true, destroyed them from the inside out. They're acknowledged now as masters of a technique known as *Zersetzung*. It means decomposition. They broke people down by destroying their self-confidence and their relationships."

"But it wasn't the Stasi who sent me the letter. It was Magda's friend Kerstin, presumably at Magda's behest."

"I don't believe that," he said. "Magda wouldn't have done that."

"I don't know. Maybe she wanted rid of me."

"Even if she did, she wouldn't have done that. I reckon the Stasi staged the whole thing. Either that or she really believed that Marek was dead."

"What makes you say that?"

He took a slug of his beer with the glorious nonchalance of someone who doesn't care whether they have a drink or not. "There's something I have to tell you," he said. "I did see her once before the Wall came down. It was back in 1988. I thought about getting in touch with you but as I didn't learn anything useful, I never did. I went over to the GDR to talk to Professor Sahr about the Student Exchange Programme. He told me Magda was still living in Leipzig, and I managed to get in touch with her. I took her to the *Auerbachs Keller* for a meal. I asked her about Marek. If it was true that he was dead. I had started to suspect that it might not be because there was never anything about it in the West German press. Not a whisper. Anyway, she said that it *was* true."

I stared at him. "God," I said. "You saw her. How did she look? Was she all right?"

"She'd changed. She was rather reserved. I think something had happened to her, but she wouldn't crack a light. She was no longer at the university. She was living with Kerstin in that old apartment they had. She seemed to be spending most of her time taking photographs."

"I'd love to know what happened to her," I said. "And it would be good to think that you're right about the letter. But I suppose I'll never know."

"Well," he said. "There is a way you could find out. You must have heard about all the East Germans who've been requesting their Stasi files. You could do the same."

He told me then about Frau Martin. I realised that he'd been waiting for me to get in touch ever since he sent me the package. He'd planned it all, just as he'd planned our chance meeting on the stairs of the modern languages building in St Andrews.

"Well, yes," he said, when I questioned him. "I am working on a book in this subject area. But it's your decision. That's why I didn't follow up with you. I don't want to force you. But it might give you some peace of mind. Are you busy at the moment?"

I shook my head and took a sip of my sparkling mineral water. "Not really. I'm kind of between jobs."

"Well," he said. "I'll be happy to fix up a meeting if you want."

I put the photo back in the wooden box from Prague. Soon

I would find out more.

I showered and went down to the restaurant for breakfast. An old Japanese couple was sitting at a table near the door. The other tables were occupied by solitary businessmen. There was an oblong buffet laden with cold meats, cheeses, breads, cereals, yoghurt and fruit. I picked up some toast and a coffee and took a seat at an empty table by the window.

The old Japanese couple got up to leave, bowing as they passed me. They shuffled towards the lifts, wavering on their old feet. I was wondering why they weren't with a tour group when a younger Japanese woman appeared with coats and hats for them. Their daughter perhaps. I hoped she was their daughter and that she was looking after them.

CHAPTER THIRTY-SEVEN

These days, Torsten isn't just a Leipzig gallerist. He has a new gallery in the Mitte area of Berlin too. You meet him in a nearby café where he's well known and well liked. "Hey, Torsten," people shout, as he pushes through the door bundled up in an overcoat, and tips his signature Fedora at you.

"My idea is to cover as much territory as possible," you tell him when he's ordered coffees for you both. "I want to show two worlds – or two ways of seeing the same world. I want to use my images to show one side, and the Stasi's images to show the other. I suppose part of what I want to do is show what we've lost as well as what we've gained."

Torsten sips his coffee. He's a bear of a man these days. Married to Lucie. Two kids. A conventional life. But still ready to take risks.

"You know I'd love to work with you again, Magda. The exhibitions of yours we put on after you came out of prison were some of the best we ever had at Lippendorfer Street. As an artist, I trust you implicitly. I just have one concern. Isn't it going to be too painful to go back over all this stuff?"

"That's what I've always thought. But now I think I'm ready to confront it again. Did I tell you my brother died?"

"No. I'm sorry."

"Thank you. It was expected but it's none the less devastating for that. But it's also made me think. I've been living quietly for too long, snapping pictures of museum exhibits. I wonder if that isn't what certain people wanted. It's time to speak up about what happened to me. I've already pulled together a couple of triptychs if you'd like to see them."

"I'd love to." He drained his coffee and put his hand on yours. "Look, Magda, I know you and I know your work. I've always wanted to exhibit your work again. You know that. If you can tell me when you'll have it ready, I'll book it in. Then we can make a time for me to come round and see what you've done so far."

Torsten comes round to Pflaster Street one Friday evening when Kwan is at his father's house. The triptychs are laid out in the workroom and a bottle of wine is open in the kitchen.

The first triptych is called *Ode to Joy*. You've built it around three central elements: the photograph you took of Marek for *Sibylle*, a Stasi surveillance photograph of you and Marek walking down Karl Liebknecht Street together in the spring sunshine, and one of the thousands of reports written about you by IMS Babylonia. This one gives the date and time of the trains you and Marek were to take from Leipzig to Budapest and from Budapest to Vienna, the name of Uncle Ivan's contact in Budapest, the names of the Austrian couple and the number of the locker that Uncle Ivan had taken at Budapest train station.

"Do you ever hear from Marek?" Torsten asks.

You shake your head. "We haven't been in touch in years. There's not much to say. I didn't mind that he left without me. I understood that. I didn't even mind that he did nothing to help me while I was prison. Maybe there was nothing he could do. But I minded that he didn't keep in touch with me after I got out of prison. That he didn't tell me about his new life."

"About Vincent?" he asks.

You shrug. "Vincent and the rest. He didn't even tell me he'd moved. He didn't tell me anything, because he didn't have to. He knew I was shut away over here. Remember when I tried to call him that time from your gallery on the 3rd of November in 89? I wanted to tell him that I was going to the big demonstration on Alexanderplatz the next day. Things were changing so fast, I thought maybe he could come over on a day visa and join us at the demonstration. I even thought he might come back to East Germany. Help us to build a new kind of country. The kind of country the demonstrators were calling for. What did Stefan Heym say on Alexanderplatz on the 4th of November? *Socialism – not the Stalinist kind, the real kind – is unthinkable without democracy.* I thought he'd want to be part of that.

"I tried the number so many times. I kept getting a message saying it was unobtainable. I thought I must have dialled incorrectly because I'd never dialled a number in West Berlin before. But the number was out of date. He was already in New York with Vincent."

Torsten squeezes your shoulder. "He was always a complicated person."

"I know. I didn't mind that. I didn't even mind that it was over between us. We had our time together. I always knew that there were two sides to him and that he might one day choose the side that wasn't me. I minded that he hadn't been honest with me. 'Our love is special,' he used to say. But in the end he lied to me like any cheating middle-class husband might."

Torsten laughs. "In that spirit, I can only say you're better off without him." He turns to the second triptych. "What's this one called?"

"Ode to Freedom."

The subsidiary elements of the second triptych are a Stasi surveillance photograph of you and IMS Babylonia at the hut by the lake south of Leipzig, a menu from a café in Wedding and a Polaroid photograph of you and IMS Babylonia taken by the owner of the café in Wedding on 9 November when you finally crossed the border together at Bornholmer Street.

You remember how she hugged you when you stepped over the white line, which you had read demarcated the actual border. "We're in the West, Magda!" she squealed with delight. You stumbled into the first café you saw and the owner poured two glasses of Sekt.

"Here's to you, young ladies," he said, clinking glasses with you and kissing you both on the cheek.

How might you have felt then if you'd known what was to come? People talk now about reunification as though it were a victory. They listen to Beethoven's 9th Symphony with tears in their eyes. But the truth is that for people like you, the people who fought for democratic socialism in East Germany, it was a defeat.

You gaze at the portrait that is the central element of the second triptych. It was taken at the apartment on Shakespeare Street. Her hair hangs in a glossy black bob and her beautiful brown eyes are lined with kohl. IMS Babylonia holds a burning cigarette in her right hand and she is looking down at her other hand, which rests on the table.

For years, you couldn't look at this photograph. You kept it locked away in a drawer. But now you can see the beauty in it again.

"It's a strong piece," Torsten says. "I love it."

You smile and take hold of his hand. "Thank you. Thank you for trusting me. I have an idea for an even stronger one."

CHAPTER THIRTY-EIGHT

Frau Martin from the Federal Authority for the Records of the State Security Service of the Former German Democratic Republic in Leipzig was a pleasant, well-meaning woman – the sort of woman I'd no doubt one day wish I'd married: solid and sensible but not unattractive. She brought me the files, got me a cup of coffee and left me to it.

From my files I learnt that Jana, who rejoiced in the poetic code name of "Rosalinde", had not only followed my relationship with "Coralie" (clearly Magda) like a soap opera, she had written down every single word I'd ever said in class verbatim. It seemed she didn't think much of my grasp of politics and history:

"One of his principal criticisms of the socialist system in the GDR concerns the "overpowering influence of the USSR" and the "lie" of the Soviet liberation of Germany from the Nazi dictatorship in 1945. In a historical context, he returns repeatedly to the topic of the supposed rape of German citizens after the Great Patriotic War and when pressed on this topic (absence of any evidence in the archives, generous assistance provided to German citizens by the Soviet Union in the 1945-1949 period) shows himself to be completely under the influence of the threat-lies and totalitarianism doctrine propagated by the western imperialist powers."

And I learnt that John Bull-Halifax was right. Neither Magda nor her friend Kerstin had anything to do with the letter I received about Marek. It had been written and sent, under instructions from the Stasi, by an IM codenamed "Cowboy". It was clear who "Rosalinde" and "Coralie" were from the context. The same was not true of "Cowboy".

Frau Martin had told me that agents could sometimes, though not always, be identified through the Stasi's filing system. I went to her office and asked her to look up "Cowboy" for me.

"It may take a while," she said. "Sometimes the cross-referencing is quite complex. Would you like to wait or shall I phone you later at your hotel?"

"I'll wait for a bit. I still have material to read."

When Frau Martin returned half an hour later, I was staring at a report I'd just read in disbelief. I had just learnt that my passport had indeed been sold, though obviously not by me. The report was written by Sander. He was considerably vexed. The sale of the passport represented a serious breach of security – and of discipline. It had been sold by one of his own IMs: "Cowboy".

"Are you all right?" Frau Martin asked.

I gazed up at her kind face. "I think so. There's been good news and there's been bad news."

She smiled. "In this case, I found the name quickly. This agent was very active."

She handed me the index card for "Cowboy". It read: Bockmann, Paul Dieter, and there was a photograph that would already have been out of date in 1985 of a young man wearing a bolo tie with a bucking bronco engraved on the clasp. I stared at it. *Give me a train ticket out of here, man? I'd grab it like a shot. Choo-choo!*

"Wow," I said at last. "I didn't know his first name was Paul."

Frau Martin looked concerned. "I hope – " she began.

I shrugged. "He was … a friend of mine. I thought so anyway. I just found out that he sold my passport. I got thrown out of the country because of that. I lost my girlfriend. I – " I shook my head and looked at the table, unable to go on.

Suddenly, I remembered the gleam in Dieter's eyes when I told him about Magda disappearing. How eager he was for me to go to Shakespeare Street. He knew that Kevin was in Rostock with Gaby. That must have been when he took the passport.

Frau Martin smiled sadly. "People often get this kind of news. Does it say who he sold the passport to?"

"It's just another code name." I stood up. Suddenly, I'd had enough of the whole business. This trip was supposed to provide some kind of catharsis. Instead, it was opening up fresh wounds.

"Would you like me to check the filing system again?"

"No. I should get going. It could've been anyone." I stretched out my hand to her. "Thank you for your help."

She held my hand a moment longer than necessary. "Have you seen our museum?" she asked.

I shook my head. "No."

"Would you allow me to show you round?"

I hesitated. I just wanted to get out of there, but she was smiling expectantly. "Thank you," I said. "That would be nice."

She led me out of the records office and into what had been the main entrance to the Stasi headquarters. A white cloth banner put up by the citizens' committee after it stormed the HQ in 1989 still hung there: *This building has been secured by the People's Police on the instructions of the government and the Citizens' Committee.*

"The committee opened an exhibition in the original Stasi rooms entitled 'Stasi – Power and Banality' in 1990," Frau Martin said. "Many exhibits have been added since, and the exhibition has become permanent. You know what Erich Mielke, the Minister for State Security, said? That he wanted to know everything about the East German people? This museum is a kind of monument to that paranoia."

We wandered from room to room. Smell samples. Listening devices. Fake stomachs with cameras concealed inside. Suspect school homework. It seemed there were no lengths, however ludicrous, to which Mielke's ministry would go.

"They were mad, weren't they?" I said.

Frau Martin laughed. "Yes and no. They were very efficient in their own way. You should go upstairs and see the archives. There are roomfuls of files. It makes you wonder what they could possibly do with all that information. The irony is that they had all this data, but they ended up knowing nothing. They didn't see the end coming. And, you know, they were never as powerful as people thought. People used to say that every fourth person was an informer, but that wasn't true. It was more like one in fifty. I sometimes think the Stasi started that rumour themselves to scare people. And people thought they'd suffer consequences if they refused to inform on someone. But that wasn't really true either."

We were back at the entranceway. "You knew, didn't you?" I said.

"Knew what, Herr McPherson?"

"That I'd feel better if I looked round the exhibition."

She smiled. "Maybe. In this job, you become a little bit like a counsellor."

"Back there in the reading room, I wished I hadn't looked."

"People often feel like that."

A flash of pain in her eyes told me this was more than an abstract notion to her. "Did you – ?" I asked.

"My husband."

"Christ. I'm sorry." What kind of a man would betray a woman like Frau Martin, I wondered, with her pleasant curves and soft, olive skin.

She gave me a brisk smile. "It was a shock. But it's important to say that my case is unusual. In the main, family life survived unscathed. That's something to be thankful for, isn't it? So, what will you do now?"

"I don't know. My train back to Berlin doesn't leave until tomorrow morning. Perhaps I'll take a look round the town centre."

"You should. It's changed so much. All the buildings have been renovated. But that's not really what I meant. I was wondering what you'll you do with the information from your files? Is there a next step?"

Her gaze was penetrating but kind. *She knows,* I thought. *She knows I'm in recovery.* For a brief moment, I considered telling her the whole story. The weakness I'd displayed all those years ago in an interrogation room somewhere in this very building. My terrible, annihilating compulsion to drink. All the times I'd cried alone in my room because it hurt so much to carry on drinking but it hurt more to stop. Everything I'd lost: money, jobs, Annabel. The lies I'd told myself. I imagined asking her what she thought I should do next. But her expression of interest was no doubt just professional politeness. And so I smiled politely back and said, "I'm not sure. I'll have to think about it."

"All right." She handed me her card, which, to my surprise, listed both her office and home phone numbers. "If I can help you with anything just give me a call."

I wandered back towards the centre of town through Barfuß Alley. These days, it was crowded with pavement cafés, glittering with fairy lights. For a moment, I considered sitting down at one and ordering a soft drink, but I decided to head back to my hotel instead. Then, as I was walking across Karl Marx Platz, now Augustus Platz once more, I saw the number 11 at the tram stop. That was the tram Magda and I had taken when we went to the party at *The Sharp Corner* in the Südvorstadt the first night I'd met her. On impulse, I sprinted over to the tram stop and jumped aboard.

As the tram swung off the ring road on to Karl Liebknecht Street, I saw that the renovations only reached so far. Here many of the buildings looked as dilapidated as they had done the first time I made this journey. And as I sat looking out on to the once familiar street that people still affectionately called "the Karli", I realised that I wasn't yet done with this place.

Why had I come here? I'd come to find out if John's hunch that Magda had nothing to do with the letter was right. Now I knew it was. But I also wanted to know what had happened to Magda. And I was none the wiser.

I got off at the next stop and went into a café. I ordered a sparkling mineral water with lime and went downstairs to the pay phone. I thought about what Frau Martin had said. *Is there a next step?* she'd asked me. I knew now that there was.

She answered on the third ring, sounding like she'd been expecting my call. "I have a question for you," I said. "You remember the woman in my file codenamed 'Coralie'? I know who she is. Her name is Magda Reinsch. I need to find her. Do you have any idea where she lives now?"

"The names are blanked out for a reason, Herr McPherson," she said.

"I know, but – " I stopped, unsure how to explain myself to her. "It's important," I said. "I came here to find her." And as I said it, I realised it was true.

There was a pause, then Frau Martin said, "I can't give you any contact details from our records, Herr McPherson. That would be quite wrong. But I do happen to know that Frau Reinsch is a photographer, currently living in Berlin."

CHAPTER THIRTY-NINE

It's a chilly afternoon in early January. You're in the workroom sorting through some photographs that you developed the previous day, when the phone goes. These days, the phone makes you even more tense than it used to. The pre-publicity for your exhibition at Torsten's gallery has started to go out, and you worry that Pankowitcz will find out about the photographs you've been taking of him or that *she* will get in touch.

She should be scared of you, but there is a big part of you that is scared of her. You'll never forget what she said to you when you confronted her in the apartment on Shakespeare Street after you had seen your files. She knew you were going to Normannen Street. She'd tried to talk you out of it. She must have been sitting at home all day, preparing what she would say to you if your files gave her away.

"Betrayal is just a word," she said, meeting your gaze. "What does it really mean? We all had to survive those times, Magda, and that's how I survived. I don't think my activities necessarily hurt anyone."

"But I went to prison."

"Yes, and that's when I said to them that enough was enough. You must realise that I didn't know that would happen. When it did, I immediately started pushing for your release. In fact, I only continued to work for them so you would be released. You think your father organised it all, and he did play a role, but I'm pretty sure you'd have been in there a lot longer if it hadn't been for me."

You try to know as little about her now as possible, but you do know some things. She lives in a villa in Charlottenburg and has an important job at the Pergamon Museum. She's married to a West German lawyer and they have two children, a boy and girl.

Pankowitcz should be scared of you too, but he's not one little bit scared of you. That is one reason why you are creating this exhibition with Torsten.

A couple of years ago, you published some of the photographs you took after you came out of prison in the culture supplement of a Sunday newspaper, alongside an article you helped to write about prison conditions in the former GDR. Pankowitcz saw the article and wrote you a long, vitriolic letter. You still don't know how he got your address. You're not in the phone book. The buzzer at Pflaster Street still says Dembowski, not Reinsch. All your photography work is handled by an agent.

In his letter, Pankowitcz addressed you as 128. You clutched at your heart when you saw that number written on the page. Suddenly, you were back in the Stasi remand prison, exhausted and powerless. Pankowitcz said you had doctored the photographs. He said he could prove it. He said he was going to sue you for misrepresenting the past and misleading the public. The letter in your hand shook as you read on:

> You broke the law, 128. What should we have done with you? Every society is the same. Those who break the law must be punished and must accept their punishment. Now you try to make yourself feel better about your past crimes by accusing others of maltreatment. There was no maltreatment, and you know this very well. If it weren't that so many journalists seem willing to lap up your sordid lies, these accusations would be a big joke, and we would all laugh long and hard.

Pankowitcz cannot sue you. You know that. But when you read the letter, all you could hear in your head was the old man who presided at your trial, the People's Judge, saying: *In the name of the People, I sentence you …*

You tore up the letter and threw it in the bin. You tried to forget about Pankowitcz. But Pankowitcz did not forget about you. Another letter came, this time not from Pankowitcz himself, but from an organisation called the Society for Legal and Humanitarian Support: a support group for former members of the state security service of the GDR and other functionaries who believe they are discriminated against in the Federal Republic. The letter listed the names of men you had slept with, obtained from you by Pankowitcz under interrogation. *We will be publishing this list on-line if you do not stop harassing Hauptmann Pankowitcz, our honest, decent and hard-working comrade, with immediate effect,* the letter said.

There were names on that list that you did not want people to see, but you tore that letter up too.

However, Pankowitcz wasn't done. One night, he came round to Pflaster Street. You'll never forget the way your guts cramped when you heard him snarl his name into the intercom: "Don't hang up, Prisoner 128," he said. "Don't make that mistake. We need to talk."

You whimpered, dropped the receiver and clung to the wall, feeling entirely helpless.

"Release the door, 128," Pankowitcz's voice bleated from the dangling receiver. "Let me in."

You banged the receiver back in place, ran through to the living room to collect Kwan and charged upstairs to Gert's apartment. He saved you from Pankowitcz, as he has saved you so many times. Afterwards, you laughed about it together. The look on Pankowitcz's face when he saw Gert. The way Gert roared at him, and Pankowitcz drew back terrified, like a cartoon mouse. The squeal Pankowitcz let out when Gert pinioned him to the wall.

But you didn't publish any more photographs from that time after that and deep down you knew it was because you were afraid of Pankowitcz. And of *her*. That's why you've decided to take the game to her and to Pankowitcz with the exhibition at Torsten's gallery. Because you don't want to be afraid any more. This is what you learnt at your brother's funeral.

And so you've been following Pankowitcz, just as his operatives once followed you. You've worked out his schedule. You know a lot about him. And all the while you've been taking photographs. Photographs of Pankowitcz and of his cronies from the Society for Legal and Humanitarian Support. Three weeks ago, you were there when Pankowitcz and a friend disrupted a talk given by a former Malschwitz prisoner.

"I can't get a job because of people like you spreading lies about me," Pankowitcz yelled. "Who's the victim here?"

All the time you were wedged behind a pillar, snapping away. You caught the twist in his face, the righteous anger. Afterwards, you followed him home and got different pictures. Pankowitcz staring morosely into space on the U-Bahn platform at Alexanderplatz. Pankowitcz sliding a key into the front door of a bleak prefabricated apartment block near the former Stasi remand prison in Berlin, which is now a museum. He lives alone in his apartment these days, his wife having divorced him in 1995. He blames that on hostile elements too.

But the phone call is not from her or from Pankowitcz. It's from a certain Frau Martin at the Federal Authority for the Records of the State Security Service of the Former German Democratic Republic in Leipzig. Someone is trying to get in touch with you. Someone from Great Britain. An old comrade.

"What's his name?" you ask.

"John Bull-Halifax. He says he met you at a cultural exchange in the Soviet Union. He says he needs to talk to you about a mutual friend."

John Bull Halifax. It's years since you were last in touch with him. He came to see you in Leipzig not long after your release from prison and took you to dinner at the Auerbachs Keller in the Mädler Arcade. You sat beneath the vaulted ceiling eating fried chicken and red cabbage and drinking a Romanian Pinot Noir, listening to him telling you that the westerner had received a letter saying Marek was dead.

"Who told him that?" you asked.

"The letter was from Kerstin. She said that she was writing it on your behalf."

You lit a cigarette and looked across the table at him. So handsome with his red-gold curls. So healthy and well-kept. Perfect teeth. Glowing complexion. Bright blue eyes. There was something in his tone that irritated you. He expected something from you, but you had only been out of a prison a couple of months and you had nothing to give. He thought he was quite the hero tracking you down and arranging to meet you in order to help his friend. That was clear from his manner. But what did he know? He had no idea what you had been through. The comrades from the West were all the same: naïve, condescending, and in the end really rather stupid.

In Moscow, you were shocked by the poor standard of living. But John dismissed it as irrelevant.

"Socialism is a process," he said.

It was a process that he didn't have to live through in the United Kingdom of Great Britain and Northern Ireland. In Moscow, he often suggested going to a hard-currency bar. He couldn't understand why you didn't want to go there even if he paid. "We're building a vanguard for the revolution," he used to joke, when you mocked the expensive hi-fi he'd brought with him from Britain and the gold-plated fountain pen he'd paid a black market trader far too much for on a visit to Leningrad. That evening in Leipzig those jokes weren't funny any more.

"Did you get Kerstin to send the letter?" he asked.

"Is this an interrogation?" you snapped.

"Of course not.

You stubbed out your cigarette. "I don't know who sent the fucking letter, but it wasn't me."

"And is Marek dead?"

You took a slug of red wine and thought for a moment. "Yes," you said at last.

Even today you cannot explain why you said that. Perhaps because he was becoming dead to you, even then. Perhaps because you thought it didn't matter what you said. John Bull-Halifax was from another world and shortly he would return there.

He sat back in his chair. "I see," he said.

Did he believe you? You don't know. He didn't pursue the topic. If he'd believed you, wouldn't he have questioned you further? Instead, he reached across the table and took your hand.

"I still have that photograph of you that you gave me in Moscow. It's on my mantelpiece. What happened to the bright-eyed girl in that picture? You never used to be like this."

You pulled your hand away. "Well, I'm like this now," you said.

What would it be like to see John Bull-Halifax again now? He must know now that Marek is alive and well and living in New York with Vincent. He must have left the Party. It's inconceivable that he's still a Communist. You can't imagine meeting him. You can't imagine what you'd say to each other. And anyway, you're very busy. You have the final triptych of your exhibition to design and mount, the one with the photographs of Pankowitcz, the one titled *Ode to Fear*.

"I'd prefer not to see him," you tell Frau Martin.

CHAPTER FORTY

It was a freezing cold day in the middle of January when I finally found Magda. John Bull-Halifax had rung the previous day to say that he'd exhausted all possible lines of enquiry and drawn a blank.

"Maybe she likes to keep a low profile. Maybe you should come home."

"Maybe," I said.

I'd been in Berlin for over a month by then, missing what my sister termed "a normal family Christmas" in Calderhill and bringing in the New Year by watching the fireworks exploding over the Brandenburg Gate from a park bench in the Tiergarten. I celebrated with a bottle of mineral water and a paper twist of roasted chestnuts.

After I phoned Frau Martin in Leipzig, I cancelled my return flight to London, took the train back to Berlin and found a cheap short-stay apartment in the Friedrichshain area. I had no clear plan but I felt oddly elated as I hung my clothes in the wardrobe, put the wooden box from Prague on the bedside cabinet, and went to the local shop to stock up on milk, bread, butter, cheese and salami. I phoned John and told him what I'd found out.

"It's only half the story," I said. "I want to know the rest, and the only person who can tell me is Magda."

My mission was clear – to find Magda. It was less clear how I would accomplish it. Nevertheless, it was a happy time. Between bursts of activity, I spent my days pottering about town, marvelling at how things had – or hadn't – changed. Sometimes, I just sat in a café and read a book. It was a different kind of life from the one I'd had in London – more fulfilling in a way.

Nonetheless, as I wandered up Schönhauser Allee that freezing afternoon, I'd pretty much decided it was time to go back to London. I was running out of money. And I was running out of ideas. John's phone call to Frau Martin had been a last-ditch attempt to get in touch with Magda. It seemed she didn't want to be in touch. Perhaps I just had to accept that.

My goal that afternoon was to visit Kollwitz Platz. Having seen Käthe Kollwitz's sculpture *Mother and Her Dead Son* in the refurbished Neue Wache memorial to the victims of war, I wanted to see the sculpture of her by Gustav Seitz in the small park in the square that bore her name. I got a bit lost and turned into a side street to consult my map.

The street felt oddly familiar. I wandered down it, half looking at my map and half taking in the odd mix of prefabricated 1970s' apartment blocks and stucco-fronted, turn-of-the-century tenements. At the far end of the street, the road forked and there was a small triangular park where some children were playing. I'd been here before. Suddenly, I was certain of that. As I marched towards the street sign to check the name, an engine revved. I turned to look. A red VW Polo pulling out of a tight parking space. A woman was at the wheel. High cheekbones. Shapely mouth. Wide slanting eyes. A beauty. She clashed the gears and bumped the car out on to the road. As she sped past, I jumped into a doorway to avoid getting run over.

*

After I'd found Magda, I began to watch her, to find out about her life. I didn't plan it. It just kind of happened. The weather had taken a turn for the worse. It snowed almost every day, and the average temperature was minus five. I took to spending my days in the cosy café opposite the apartment building, where, I quickly learnt, she lived. It was Marek's old building. The street was Pflaster Street. That was why it had seemed familiar.

I told the people who ran the café that I was a writer. I said I was writing a memoir, which was almost true. The notes I made on the iBook I'd bought to launch City Savvy Translations amounted to something like a memoir. They treated me with a certain respect after that, asking if I had enough light and what I thought of this or that author. It was some time since I'd been accorded this kind of professional regard, and I have to admit that I lapped it up, although it was all a sham. Pretty soon, the waiting stuff knew that I liked my sparkling water with lime, not lemon, took my coffee black with two sugars and preferred my salad without vinaigrette.

The first thing I learnt about Magda was that she had a son. An Asian-looking boy. She appeared with him early each morning and took him, I assumed, to school. The second thing I learnt was that she had changed in some absolutely fundamental way. I can't really explain it. She was the same in so many ways. Still beautiful. Still graceful. Still marching down the street at top speed, even when taking her little black-haired son to school with his satchel on his back. There was, I suppose, a pall of melancholy over her that had not been there before. *Perhaps motherhood has mellowed her*, I thought. Single motherhood. There was no sign of a father. But I also remembered what Bull-Halifax had said about the time he met her in Leipzig: *She was rather reserved. I think something had happened to her, but she wouldn't crack a light.*

Apart from taking her son to school each morning, there was no fixed pattern to her days. Some days, she was gone all day, returning at 16:00 with her son. Other days she returned to the apartment after dropping him off and appeared to spend the rest of the day there. Several times, I saw her piling camera equipment into the red VW Polo before speeding off. I had to resist the temptation to rush out and help her.

After a couple of weeks, I worked out that she had one other regular weekly appointment. On Thursdays, she always left her apartment building at 14.15 sharp. One Thursday, I decided to follow her. I had it all carefully planned. I'd paid the bill in advance and stowed my iBook in my rucksack. I was lingering over a cup of coffee when she appeared in the doorway of her building dressed in a tailored coat and black beret. I put down my coffee, jumped up and headed for the door.

"Off early today?" asked the waiter, a big man with a mangled face and a tattoo of Tom of Finland on his powerful right forearm.

"Yeah," I mumbled. "Meeting a friend."

Magda had set off down Pflaster Street at a clip, and I was just in time to see her turn left on to Schönhauser Allee. I sprinted after her, reaching the corner as she disappeared into the U-Bahn station entrance. I wove across the street against the traffic, getting honked at, and clattered down the steps. There I slowed my pace. She was standing at the far end of the southbound platform. I stayed where I was until the next train squealed to a stop. When I saw which carriage she was getting in, I loped along the platform and got in the one behind. I gazed at her through the scratched panes of glass that separated our carriages. This woman who had captured my imagination like no other. Who captured my imagination still. Who had turned my life upside down, even if she hadn't intended to.

She got off the train in the centre of town at Mohren Street, near Koch Street where Checkpoint Charlie had been. She set off in the direction of the cranes that crowded Potsdamer Platz, and I followed at a discreet distance. She turned left into Voß Street, and I nearly gave myself away by rounding the corner too quickly. She glanced in my direction, and I froze. But she looked straight through me like I was water, the way the Yah girls used to at St Andrews. I slipped across the road and watched as she stopped outside a modern apartment building and pressed a buzzer. A moment later, she pushed through the door and was gone. I nipped back across the street to examine the entry system. All the buzzers were for private residences apart from two, which were for ground-floor offices. Schmidt & Lerner Cleaning Services and Dr Juliane Kranold, therapist.

The next morning, I skipped my vigil at the café and went to the local library in Friedrichshain. I looked up Dr Juliane Kranold in a directory of medical practitioners in the district of Berlin. She specialised in treating patients suffering from post-traumatic stress disorder, particularly former prisoners.

That evening I phoned John Bull-Halifax and told him what I'd discovered.

"Were you following her?" he asked. I'd so often lied in response to questions put in that tone. *(Have you been drinking?*

Is there something you're not telling me?) Perhaps because I was sick of lying, so utterly sick of it, I simply said, "Yes."

"Don't you think that's a little unethical?"

"Don't talk to me about ethics, John," I said, suddenly angry. "Was it ethical to help to prop up a system that put young women in prison for no reason because you thought it was cool to wear second-hand suits and call yourself a Communist?"

"Listen, I was as shocked as anyone else when I found about some stuff that went on. We didn't know those kinds of things were happening."

"Didn't you? Maybe that's because you didn't want to know. The first new German word I learnt when I arrived in Leipzig was 'Stasi'. It was all very well for you, wasn't it? With your cushy job at the university. None of it really affected you. You could pose around in your National Health specs with impunity and choose not to know about certain things."

"Well maybe I was a bit of a poser back then, Bob, but whatever you may think, I was also a convinced Communist. I was devastated when the end came. We all were. I still am a convinced Communist, if you want to know. Socialism has never been tried in the kinds of countries where it might work. Karl Marx did say that Russia wasn't ready for Communism. And things aren't exactly perfect now either, are they, here or there? I have friends in Russia whose lives were destroyed when the system collapsed. They hate Gorbachev."

I sighed. "What am I going to do, John? I feel like I've got to know the full story now, but I can't keep spying on Magda like this. It's not right."

"How should I know," he said, a trace of anger in his voice. "What do you need to know the full story for anyway? Is there something you've not been telling me?"

I held the receiver away from my head for a moment and

looked at the floor. "Yeah," I said at last. "I'm getting over a bit of a drink problem."

"Thought so," he said. "All that sparkling mineral water. Why don't you come home? We'll meet up again and talk about it and see if we can find a way to persuade Magda to talk to you. Anyway, you shouldn't think that talking to her will solve all your problems. If you have a drink problem, that's a separate issue and you should probably deal with that first. "

"Okay," I said. "I'll think about it. I'm running out of money anyway. I've been paying for my flat in London and the place here."

I put the phone down. I decided that the next day would be my last at the café. John was right. In my head, I'd conflated what had happened to me in Leipzig with my drink problem. If I could solve the riddle of one, I'd be able to fix the other too. But that was rubbish. They had nothing to do with each other. I'd found out what I could. It was time to go home and get on with my life, but before I did so I wanted to see Magda one last time.

Things didn't start off as normal the next morning. Magda didn't appear in the doorway with her son first thing. Perhaps it was a school holiday. I ordered rolls with butter and jam for breakfast and a pot of coffee, and got out my iBook as usual. I'd been tapping away for about two hours, keeping a weather eye on Magda's building, when she appeared in the doorway alone. Instead of turning right, as she usually did, and heading for Schönhäuser Allee, she crossed the street, weaving past her red VW. Only the little triangular park separated her from the café, and with a stab of horror I realised that she was heading my way. Why had I not considered this possibility? This was, after all, her local café. I sat frozen to the spot as she pushed through the café door, praying she wouldn't recognise me.

But she didn't even glance in my direction as she marched over to the bar, sat down on a stool and ordered an espresso from the waiter with the big mangled face. They chatted about the weather, as the waiter tamped the coffee into the filter basked, and I breathed a sigh of relief. Even if she did recognise me there was no law against being in a café. It could be a coincidence.

I tried not to stare at her as she shook off her coat. She was wearing jeans and a V-neck jumper that offered a glimpse of the dusky hollow between her breasts. Then I heard what she was saying. She was talking to the waiter about preparations she was making for an exhibition of her work.

"You should see my workroom," she laughed. "It's a total mess. All my old photographs are everywhere. And I've had to go through every page of my Stasi files. Let me tell you, it looks like Normannen Street after a bomb hit it in there."

"It'll be worth it in the end," the waiter said. "And now you have a few days off."

"Yes, thank goodness. Kwan is at his grandmother's. I haven't had a weekend without him since I don't know when. The only problem is the plumber. He wasn't able to come yesterday to fix the leak in my sink. Do you think you could let him in?"

"Sure. What time?"

"He said he'd come at 15.00 today."

I looked across as she fished in her pocket and produced a set of keys for the waiter. He walked along the bar to right behind where I was sitting and dropped them in a glass bowl.

That's when it clicked into place. I had a set of those keys too. They were in the wooden box from Prague on my bedside cabinet. The locks could have been changed, of course. But equally they might not have been. There was an intercom system on the apartment building now, but apart from that it hadn't been renovated. The waiter had told me it was the subject of a court case. A Jewish man from New York named Ivan Süsskind was claiming ownership. I waited until Magda had gone, then I slipped my iBook in my rucksack, paid my bill and left.

At 8pm that evening, I arrived at Magda's building, carrying a large bunch of flowers. I'd observed that there was an elderly woman living in the apartment above Magda's. I pressed the buzzer I reckoned was hers.

After a time, the intercom crackled into life and an old woman's voice said, "Yes?"

"Delivery," I chirruped.

"Oh, but I didn't order anything."

"I have a delivery for you, madam. Some beautiful flowers."

"I'm not expecting any flowers."

"Frau Vogelbein? Yes, they're definitely for you."

Eventually, she buzzed me in. When I reached the landing, she was peering at me crossly through a narrow gap in the door spanned by a security chain, but when she saw the flowers her suspicions seemed to evaporate. "What beautiful flowers!" she exclaimed.

"Aren't they?"

"But I wasn't expecting any flowers."

"Someone must be thinking of you, madam," I said as I shoved them into her hand.

As she closed the door, I clomped back downstairs, whistling as I went. I opened the main door and shut it again, waited a few moments, then took my shoes off and padded back upstairs to Magda's apartment. My heart pounded as I inserted the key in the lock. It fitted, but when I turned it, the lock didn't move. I felt something like relief. This madcap scheme wasn't going to work after all. Thank God! Then I tried the other way, turning the key anticlockwise and the lock clicked back. I pushed the door and walked into Magda's apartment.

The light from the street lamps cast an eerie glow in the hallway. The apartment was very changed but I recognised a lamp on the console table made from a zebra's foot. Letters were piled next to it addressed to Frau Magdalena Reinsch. As I made my way down the hallway to the living room, I glanced at the framed photographs on the walls. Each had a scrawled black signature in the bottom right-hand corner: M.R. I pushed open the living room door. There in front of the bookcase was the battered tan sofa where Marek had sat smoking the morning after the night at *Café North*.

He'd smiled when I walked into the room looking crumpled and hungover and rubbing my face. "Coffee's in the kitchen. Help yourself."

Where was the workroom? Perhaps it was in the small room off the main bedroom. Magda and I had slept there the night after the party at *Café North*. We both knew what I'd seen and we made love in a frenzy of anger, lust and excitement.

I pushed open the bedroom door. The blind was drawn and it was dark inside. I got out the pocket torch I'd brought with me and ran its beam round the room. Against the back wall was a double bed covered in a white quilt. The dressing table was crammed with make-up and jewellery. Beneath the window was a chest of drawers piled high with books. On it sat a couple of photographs. Magda's son by a lake somewhere. A black and white portrait of young woman playing the cello. A snap of a boy in a tracksuit.

The door to the anteroom was next to a large antique

wardrobe. I pulled the door back and shone my torch round the room. The divan and the bookshelves were gone. Just as I'd thought, this was the workroom now, and it seemed to double as darkroom. There was a blackout blind and a red darkroom lamp. I pulled the blackout blind and turned the light on. The floor was strewn with papers, and the walls were stacked with empty frames with numbers taped to them.

I was about to bend down to pick up one of the papers from the floor when I sensed a movement behind me. I swung round. The waiter from the café across the road was standing in the doorway.

"Fuck!" I yelled, cursing myself for turning on the light. I looked around for a way out. But the man filled the doorway. There was no way past him.

"Don't look so worried," he said. "I know who you are. I have a message for you from Magda."

And I remembered then where I'd seen him before. On the door at *The Sharp Corner*, the very first night I'd met Magda at Leipzig train station.

CHAPTER FORTY-ONE

It's a bright cold day in late February. You stand at your apartment window, watching the westerner, as he has been watching you. He's sitting at a window table in the café opposite, tapping on his iBook. He's wearing a white shirt and a navy blue pullover and he has glasses on. Gert brings him a coffee, and he smiles in acknowledgement. From this distance, he looks little changed, but Gert says there are deep lines round his eyes and that his hands shake.

You shoulder on your coat, wrap a scarf round your neck and head downstairs. The westerner stands up when he sees you in the doorway of the café.

"Hello," he says and shakes your hand, holding your gaze with those green eyes you remember so well.

"Hello," you say. He's still the same in so many ways. Square and strong. But Gert is right. His face is lined and he looks much older.

You smile at him, and he smiles back. Then you throw your arms round each other and embrace.

"It's so good to see you," he says. "I actually can't quite believe this is happening."

"It's good to see you too."

Gert brings you coffee, and you chat for a while about the weather, the way people do when they haven't seen each other for a long time and don't know where to start. And when the westerner picks up his coffee cup, you see that Gert was right about his hands too. They shake. You stare out of the window for a moment. You told him so many lies. You hope he didn't suffer too much because of those lies.

He tells you then about his trip to the records office in Leipzig and about Dieter.

"Can you believe it?"

"People can surprise you. That's one thing I've learnt since reunification. Did you know that he moved back to Frankfurt an der Oder and married a girl he was at school with? We all thought he'd head straight for Texas when the Wall came down, but no. Jana was the one who couldn't wait to get to America. She's a lecturer in American Studies now at Bochum University."

"God," he says.

"They've all done well for themselves. They got their education. That makes all the difference."

"You've done well for yourself too. You've got this exhibition coming up."

"Things are starting to come together now, but it hasn't been easy. There's been so much in the newspapers about the Stasi and what they did to people, but if you apply for a job no one stops to ask if the reason you don't have a degree is because you were in prison or you weren't allowed to study."

"And what about Hencke?" he asks, "what happened to him?"

"I believe he became a financial adviser."

"No!" The westerner laughs.

"Yes, some people are adaptable. Stasi informer today, insurance salesman tomorrow. With a BMW and a private pension plan. It's because they don't really believe in anything. You know, I met him once in Leipzig after I got out of prison. He was coming out of the international newsagents on Grimmaische Street. You remember it? You were shocked that the only British newspaper they had was the *Morning Star*. I saw him clock me and wonder what to do. He decided to brazen it out and came striding towards me. It was the summer and he was wearing shorts and sandals. I remember looking down at the black hairs curling on his toes and feeling sick. 'Well, well,' he said, 'if it isn't Miss Magdalena.' I didn't look up but when we drew level, I turned and spat in his face. It was a turning point for me. After that, I started to feel better about myself."

He puts his hand on yours and squeezes it. "You should always feel good about yourself, Magda."

You shrug. You wonder if he'll still be saying that when you've told him your side of the story. Because you've decided that you're going to help him. If you can. Something in his manner strikes a chord with you. He's been through it, just like you. That's why he's doing all these mad things. Watching you. Breaking into your apartment. Not that you ever dreamt he still had the key. You thought he might 'borrow' the key if you put temptation in his way. You wanted to see how far he'd go. Well, that's what you get for testing people.

You light a cigarette and offer him one.

He shakes his head. "Don't drink, don't smoke."

"So, how are you?" you ask.

He looks into your eyes for a moment. "Yeah, I'm okay." Then he says, "To be honest, Magda, things have been a bit difficult lately, but it's getting better."

You smile. "Good. Getting better is good." You stub out your cigarette and say, "Let's go up to my apartment. We can talk there."

You get him a sparkling mineral water from the fridge and make yourself another coffee. He's looking at the books in the bookcase behind the tan sofa when you bring the drinks through to the living room.

"I remember you always had so many books at Shakespeare Street. All that West literature and all those books by Christa Wolf that were impossible to find in the shops."

"Yes. We had our sources."

He sits down beside you on the sofa and says, "Magda, did you go to prison?"

You nod. "Yes."

"I'm so sorry.

"It's in the past. What doesn't kill you makes you stronger."

"Was it my fault?"

"Your fault?" You shake your head emphatically. "No, it was nothing to do with you."

It's funny, he told you on the phone about how he hung on in West Berlin, trying to find a way to cross back over to the East after he was ejected from the GDR by the police at Sonnenallee. How he got in touch with John Bull-Halifax and got him to phone Professor Sahr. And it provided you with a strange kind of retrospective comfort. Someone was thinking about you even if you didn't know it at the time. He could have gone home and forgotten about the whole thing. But he didn't. He tried to help you. You hardly ever thought about the westerner when you were in prison. You only thought about Marek, who did nothing, and Kerstin, who did worse than nothing.

He leans back against the cushions. "I'm glad about that. I'm glad nothing I said harmed you."

"I've thought things through," you say. "And I'm happy to tell you whatever you want to know. You can look in my files if you want. I've pulled together some material I think might be useful to you, but you're welcome to look at whatever you like. I know what it's like to be where you are now. To have found out certain shocking things. That's what the Stasi did. They messed with people's biographies so they didn't know who they were any more. You have a right to know who you are."

"I'd rather you just told me," he says. "You tell me your story, and I'll tell you mine."

You look at him. Does he understand what this will mean? "Okay," you say at last. "But I have to warn you that some of the things I did weren't very kind either. I'm not just a victim. Your turning up here has made me realise that. I deceived people too. I deceived you."

He holds your gaze. "I'm ready to hear it."

And so you tell him everything. You tell him how Kerstin betrayed you and Marek forgot you. And you tell him about all the lies you told him. All the bad things you did.

He swallows hard at certain points, and when you're done, he looks at his hands for a long time. "Didn't you like me even a little bit?" he asks.

"Yes, I did. You must believe that. That just made it harder. I'm sorry. I really wish it could have been different."

"Well," he says, "I suppose it wasn't your fault. I suppose it was the system. That's what John Bull-Halifax said when I told him I'd betrayed Marek." He looks up. "I can't believe Marek just left you sitting in prison."

You shrug. "Neither could I."

"Did you ever find out how he got out?"

"No. And it doesn't really matter now."

"That's the missing link, isn't it? That and my passport. I

292

should have got Frau Martin to look up the buyer's code name when I was in Leipzig, but I just wanted to leave by then."

"Maybe you can call her?"

"I don't think she'd want to deal with something like that over the phone." He stops. "What's wrong? You look like you've seen a ghost."

You grab his arm. "I've just thought of something. Oh, Bob, it's much worse than we thought."

You remember the momentary beat of wariness you saw in Uncle Ivan's eyes when you met him in Berlin after you got out of prison and he gave you Marek's message. *Marek went over a bit later,* he said. But that wasn't true.

"Do you remember what the code name was?"

"Yeah. It was 'Lech'."

"Shit!" You shake your head in disbelief. He must have left after the party at Shakespeare Street. Or maybe the next day. After you'd been arrested.

"Do you know who it is?" the westerner asks.

You bury your head in your hands and let out a cry of anguish. You hear Hencke's nasal lisp in your head: *And do you know what name I've chosen for Comrade Dembowski? Lech. Perfect, isn't it, for a little Polack?*

You nod and take hold of his hand. "Yes, I know who it is."

"You're crying," he says, reaching across to touch your cheek. "I always make you cry."

"No," you say. "You just always end up drying my tears."

You spend the night together but you don't make love. You just hold on to each other. You have something in common now. You were both deceived by the same person. Marek. Beautiful, bitchy, clever Marek. That's it, you think as you finally drift into sleep in his arms – the last surprise.

EPILOGUE

It's a warm summer evening, and the guests are arriving for the private view. Torsten stands in the doorway in his new linen suit smiling and greeting each guest as they enter the gallery. He points them in the direction of a table covered with a white linen cloth where two smiling young women with sleek pony tails are doling out glasses of Sekt and red wine. Inside the gallery, another two waitresses circulate with canapés, weaving between the guests who are already crowding round the exhibits.

It's a mixed crowd. Some people from the old days. Older. Chastened in one way or another. But if Torsten looks into certain corners of the room and lets his eyes drift out of focus, he can almost imagine that he's back in the gallery on Lippendorfer Street where it all began. An innocent time, that seems like now. A simple time. When the enemy was clear. Or so it seemed. And an exciting time. Romantic.

There are of course also the absentees, those who wouldn't dare to show their faces in a place like this these days. And the other ones. The unreconstructed comrades. Also immediately recognisable. Here to size up the enemy. See what they're doing now. He's spotted a couple already. (But not Pankowitcz. Not yet anyway. That's why Torsten is standing in the doorway of his own gallery like a bouncer. To keep Pankowitcz out.)

And then there are the other guests. The people who've travelled over from Charlottenburg and Spandau on the S-Bahn. They sip their drinks and say, "Hmm. Interesting." And the critics. *But isn't this theme of coming to terms with the past a little played out now?*

It doesn't matter what they say. Torsten knows this exhibition is a triumph. It's going to make his career and it's going to make the artist's career.

Torsten stares up the street to the U-Bahn. That's where Pankowitcz will come from – if he comes. And so he doesn't see the other guest he's detailed to look out for until the last minute, because he comes from the other direction.

The man is crossing the road now, looking the wrong way in the traffic. He's changed, but Torsten still recognises him from the night he first met him at *The Sharp Corner* all those years ago. He looks round uncertainly, checking his map. Torsten waves to him, and the westerner nods, smiles and waves back.

In the doorway, the two men shake hands. Torsten claps the westerner on the shoulder and turns to ask his wife to find the artist. But Magda is already weaving her way through the crowds towards them in her green dress.

For more great reading go to:

www.aurorametro.com

Select historical fiction to enjoy:

The Physician of Sanlúcar by Jonathan Falla
978-1-906582-38-8

Kipling and Trix by Mary Hamer
978-1-906582-34-0

Pomegranate Sky by Louise Soraya Black
978-1-906582-10-4

The River's Song by Suchen Christine Lim
978-1-906582-98-2

The Evolutionist by Avi Sirlin
978-1-906582-53-1

Liberty Bazaar by David Chadwick
978-1-906582-92-0

Tracks, Racing the Sun by Sandro Martini
978-1-906582-43-2